"Once again .... l tale."
—*Jim, Amazon reviewer.*

"This was the best Alastair Stone book yet!"
—*J. Michael Droke, Amazon reviewer*

"R. L. King does it again! Simply one of the best books I've read this year—and one of the best in an amazing series."
—*Greenlite350, Amazon reviewer*

"Warning—don't start reading this book if you have other things to do."
—*ARobertson, Amazon reviewer*

"What a ride!"
—*Wendy S, Amazon reviewer*

Praise for *The Infernal Heart*

"Another 'can't put it down' adventure in this series."
—*LC, Amazon reviewer*

"…The best book in the whole Alastair Stone Chronicles… this one really knocked it out of the park."
—*Christopher T, Amazon reviewer*

"Once you start, you need to get comfortable because you will stop reading all of a sudden and discover many hours have gone by."
—*John Scott, Amazon reviewer*

"…the best one yet! I couldn't put it down."
—*Kenneth B, Amazon reviewer*

Praise for *Flesh and Stone*

"A superbly constructed magical crime novel, sparkling with mordant wit."
—*Helena Echlin, author of* Gone *and* Sparked

"R. L. King has my purchasing dollars with fun-to-read, suspenseful, character-driven stories…Damn fun reads."
—*Amazon reviewer*

"I have been hooked on this series from the first book."
—*Jim P. Ziller, Amazon reviewer*

"Awesome and exciting. Love this series."
—*Cynthia Morrison, Amazon reviewer*

Praise for *Heart of Stone*

"Amazing series. The characters are deep and identifiable. The magic is only a small part of what makes these books great. I can't wait for the next one!!"
—*Amazon reviewer*

"This is my favorite book so far of the Alastair Stone Chronicles, and that's saying something, since I adore the series and its protagonist."
—*Shawna Reppert, award-winning author of the* Ravensblood *series*

"There are few books that strike a chord. This is one of them."
—*Jim, Amazon reviewer*

"Great series, awesome characters and can't wait to see where the story will go from here."
—*Amazon reviewer*

Praise for *Blood and Stone*

"I have read every book in this series and loved them all...this one is no exception."
—*Soozers, Amazon reviewer*

"The writing is extremely good, and the plot and characters engaging. Closest author comparison probably Benedict Jacka and the Alex Verus series."
—*MB, Amazon reviewer*

"The books keep getting better and better."
—*Jim P. Ziller, Amazon reviewer*

"Have followed our expat mage from the beginning and this time around, it's a home run."
—*Amazon reviewer*

Praise for *Core of Stone*

"Once again R. L. King has come up with another great story for Alastair Stone. I enjoyed this as thoroughly as all the others and look forward to more."
—*Tahlia Newland, Amazon reviewer*

"I love it when a writer starts out strong in her career and just gets stronger. I have loved The Alastair Stone Chronicles from the beginning, but this one just blew me away."
—*Shawna Reppert, award-winning author of the Ravensblood series*

"I have loved the series as a whole but have to say this is a favorite just for the character growth."
—*Amazon reviewer*

"The Alastair Stone Chronicles is one of the best series I have read in years..."
—*Judith A. Slover, Amazon reviewer*

Praise for *The Source*

"Perhaps the best addition yet to an already amazing series."
—*Greenlite350, Amazon reviewer*

"A continued thrill to the urban fantasy reader..."
—*Dominic, Amazon reviewer*

"I consumed the four pack in less than a week. This a great series and one of the best ones I have had the pleasure to read in a long time."
—*Skywalker, Amazon reviewer*

"If you like Harry Dresden and The Dresden files, or Nate Garrett in the Hellequin series than this series is for you."
—*Amazon reviewer*

Praise for *The Threshold*

"Once you enter the world of Alastair Stone, you won't want to leave."
—*Awesome Indies*

"Excellent story as are all the others in this series."
—*Tahlia Newland, Amazon reviewer*

"I LOVE THIS BOOK!"
—*Claryn M. Heath, Amazon reviewer*

Praise for *The Forgotten*

"Alastair Stone is like Harry Potter meets Harry Dresden with a bit of Indiana Jones!"
—*Randler, Amazon reviewer*

"I loved the first book in the series, but this book is even better! ... I didn't think I could be any more in love with the protagonist than I was in the first book ...My only hesitation in giving it five stars is that, if the next one is even better (as I suspect it may be) I won't have anywhere to go with the rating."
—*Shawna Reppert, award-winning author of* The Stolen Luck, Ravensblood, *and* Raven's Wing

"This is actually an original idea - such a rare thing these days. Well written too."
—*Tahlia Newland, Amazon reviewer*

"From the first paragraph I knew I was in the hands of a competent writer, and from the second paragraph I was hooked to read on...a novel deserving of the full 5 star rating."
—*Awesome Indies*

Praise for *Stone and a Hard Place*

"The magic is believable, the characters could be people you know, and the twists, turns and mysteries to be solved glue your eyes to the page. You will never forget these characters or their world."
—*Jacqueline Lichtenberg, Hugo-nominated author of the* Sime~Gen *series and* Star Trek Lives!

"Somewhat reminiscent of the Dresden Files but with its own distinct style."
—*John W. Ranken, Amazon reviewer*

ALSO BY R. L. KING

The Alastair Stone Chronicles
Stone and a Hard Place
The Forgotten
The Threshold
The Source
Core of Stone
Blood and Stone
Heart of Stone
Flesh and Stone
The Infernal Heart
The Other Side
Shadows and Stone (novella)
Turn to Stone (novella, coming soon)

Shadowrun
Shadowrun: Borrowed Time
Shadowrun: Wolf and Buffalo (novella)
Shadowrun: Big Dreams (novella)
Shadowrun: Veiled Extraction (coming in 2019)
(published by Catalyst Game Labs)

PATH OF STONE

ALASTAIR STONE CHRONICLES: BOOK ELEVEN

R.L. KING

MAGESPACE PRESS

| CHAPTER ONE

"**A**RE YOU SERIOUSLY GONNA EAT THAT? I thought British people were supposed to like bland food."

Alastair Stone paused to take a big bite of *camarones a la diabla* and savor it before replying. "Stereotypes, apprentice. Good Mexican food is one of the best things about this state of yours. The hotter, the better."

Verity Thayer tilted her head. "Maybe." She picked up the water pitcher and waved it at him. "But if flames start shooting out of your mouth, I'm dumping this over your head before the fire sprinklers go off."

"Damn. Guess I'll have to wait for some other time to show you the new spell I've been working on."

She looked down at her plate, toying with her half-eaten enchiladas. "What do I do, Doc?" she asked in a softer voice.

Stone considered her words carefully before answering. He sat across from her in a tiny Mexican restaurant near downtown San Jose; it was busy tonight, so they'd had to wait a while before their food arrived. They had spent most of that time in silence, each lost in his or her own thoughts as loud, bouncy recorded Mariachi music played over two TV screens showing different soccer games.

He sighed. "I wish I could assure you everything will be all right," he said. "But I'd be lying, and I don't ever want to lie to you."

Verity's gaze came up. Her dark eyes glittered out of shadowed hollows that could only be half-explained by her heavy goth-style makeup. "I can't stop thinking about what I did. Not so much that I did it—I told you, I'd do it again—but...*how* I did it. I didn't even know I had that sort of thing in me, and...it scares me, Doc."

"As well it should." Stone leaned back and regarded her, sitting there in her hooded sweatshirt and black leather biker jacket, looking younger than her twenty-one years—except for her eyes. Those made her look as if she'd aged at least ten years since he'd seen her last, only a few days ago.

She'd come so far since he and her brother Jason had found her, disoriented and mentally broken from the Evil's extradimensional influence, in a homeless camp not far from where they now sat. She'd been just shy of eighteen then, confused and uncertain about her place in the world, or even if she had one. He'd been terrified to take her on as an apprentice—his last attempt at that had ended in a tragedy he still considered his fault—but she'd somehow managed to get under his skin and convince him to take a chance on her.

It had been one of the best decisions he'd made in his life.

This was her third year as his apprentice, and though she'd spent almost half of that time studying under a woman whose magical philosophy was more in line with what she thought she wanted, she'd recently re-evaluated her life and decided to return to him for her final year. She'd solidified that decision over just the last few days after a trip to Las Vegas to help her brother with a case that led them to unearth a horrific crime, and forced her to use her magic in a way that left her once again reeling with loathing and self-doubt.

That was why she was here now, and why Stone—despite dealing with his own raw grief over the gruesome loss of a longtime colleague only a few days ago—was sitting across from her eating Mexican food instead of holed up in his study drinking until he couldn't remember anything.

He supposed the two of them were good for each other, in a disturbing kind of way.

"It should," he said again. "That's a healthy response. But what you can't let it do is paralyze you."

"I can't stop thinking about it. I can't stop thinking that I might be tempted to do it again." She dipped a tortilla chip in salsa and munched it thoughtfully, looking at the brightly colored tablecloth. After a moment, her gaze came up again. "Doc, did you ever do anything like that? Something you wish you didn't have to do, but would again if you had it to do over?"

"Oh, yes."

"What was it? If you don't mind telling me," she added hastily.

Curiosity was winning out over despair for control of her expression, and he thought that was a healthy thing. "I nearly lost my apprenticeship over it, actually."

Her eyes widened. "You're kidding."

"I'm not. I never told you much about my master. He was…quite formidable, shall we say."

"A real hard-ass, in other words." Her smile was reluctant, but it lit up her face. "Kinda like you."

"That…was a good way to describe him, yes. Though I'm a teddy bear compared to William Desmond. Bloody good teacher—one of the best around. Wouldn't have traded the experience for anything. But our first few weeks together were…quite rocky."

Verity leaned forward, interested now. "You were only fifteen, weren't you? Even younger than you were in that picture with my mom."

"Fifteen, yes. And like every other fifteen-year-old who ever lived, I was full of myself and thought I had all the answers. Desmond disabused me of that notion rather quickly."

She leaned further forward, propping her elbows on the table and cradling her chin in her hands like a little girl waiting for a good story. "Will you tell me about it, Doc? Tell me what you did, and how it worked out?"

Stone glanced around the restaurant. It was still packed, but the crowd was slowly beginning to thin. "Let's get another basket of chips, then. This will take a while."

| CHAPTER TWO

A S SOON AS HE GOT THE MESSAGE that the headmaster wanted to see him, Alastair Stone knew he was in trouble.

The word came at the end of Calculus, his last class of the day. The instructor, a tall, cadaverous man named Benbow, looked up as Alastair gathered his papers and headed for the door. "Oh, Stone?"

"Yes, sir?"

"Professor Carrowby wants to see you in his office at four o'clock. Best head over there straight away."

Alastair froze. "Did he say why?"

"They don't tell me these things." Benbow waved airily toward the door. "Off you go, now."

"Yes, sir." Alastair gripped the strap of his bag, the back of his neck growing hot. Professor Carrowby didn't have to say why. Alastair would have staked quite a lot of money that he already knew.

And he'd been so careful, too.

He'd never been to Roger Carrowby's office in all the years he'd attended Barrow; visits to the headmaster were usually reserved for students who'd gotten in big trouble—most commonly with drugs, alcohol, or indiscretions with local girls (or occasionally local boys). Alastair Stone wasn't the type of student who got into that kind of trouble. Top of his class, on track to finish secondary school at least a year early, he generally kept to himself and so far had done a good job resisting any temptation to get involved in potentially problematic activities. Not that there was much temptation, though: drugs held no interest for him, his brief experiments with alcohol had been discreet, and since Barrow was an all-boys school, he didn't get that many opportunities to interact with girls.

If he were to get himself in trouble, it would be for...other reasons. Apparently, those reasons were about to catch up with him.

He sat in a worn wooden chair in Carrowby's outer office, picking at imaginary dust motes on his dark blue uniform jacket and trying to ignore the curious gaze of the secretary. He didn't know her name, but she was middle-aged and wore glasses with points on the sides and seemed to disapprove of him for some reason. Perhaps she disapproved of any boy who landed here, and he was just the latest in the series.

Something on her desk buzzed. She spoke for a moment under her breath, then looked back at Alastair. "You can go in now."

"Thank you." He stood and crossed the room, wondering if the odd tone in her voice was only in his imagination.

Roger Carrowby's office looked almost exactly as Alastair expected the office of the headmaster of an exclusive old tradition-steeped school to look: all wood and dusty books and antique school memorabilia. Behind his desk, flanked by two tall, packed bookshelves, stood a cabinet containing a series of sports trophies that were probably older than Carrowby himself—and the man was no youngster. Alastair passed their more contemporary counterparts every day on his way to the dining hall, though he'd had no hand in winning any of them. A faint aroma of furniture polish and old books hung in the air.

He stopped in front of Carrowby's desk. "You asked to see me, sir?"

"Yes, Mr. Stone. Please sit down."

Alastair did as he was told, taking a seat in one of the ancient, brocaded chairs in front of the massive wooden desk. He'd never been this close to Carrowby before; the man had to be at least seventy, with wispy white hair, a stooped frame that didn't quite fill out his suit jacket, and shrewd, squinting brown eyes. Rumor was that he used to be a military man in his youth. Alastair waited for him to speak first.

Carrowby pulled over a thick folder, opened it, and flipped through several sheets of paper. "I've never seen you in my office before, Mr. Stone. Exemplary student, from what I see here. Aside from a few minor detentions, no black marks on your record at all. Admirable. Do you know why you're here now?"

"No, sir." On the off chance that his suspicions were wrong, Alastair had no intention of admitting to anything the headmaster didn't already know about.

Carrowby closed the file and looked up. He wasn't squinting now: his eyes were fixed on Alastair, calm and cold and steady. "Mr. Stone—have you been performing Satanic rituals in the attic of your dormitory?"

Well. That was a new take on things. "Er…no, sir."

Carrowby's gaze sharpened. "Mr. Stone, you're in serious trouble if these allegations are true. Best if you don't add lying to them. Remember, we do have an honor code here at Barrow."

"I'm not lying, sir." Alastair sat up a little straighter. He knew this would probably come eventually; he'd given a bit of thought to how he'd handle it when it did, but Carrowby's accusations had caught him off guard. Of all the things the man could have thought, he went *there?* "I haven't been performing Satanic rituals in the attic, or anywhere else."

Carrowby sighed and shook his head, clearly disappointed. He withdrew a few photographs and laid them on the desk facing Alastair. They were the instant type, the kind you could develop without having to take them in for processing. "Do you deny that you're responsible for this?"

Alastair glanced at the photos. He didn't have to look closely at them: what they depicted was as familiar to him as his own dorm room. "No, sir."

"But yet you've already denied it." Carrowby plucked a fountain pen from a marble holder and used it as a pointer, indicating the elaborate ritual circle drawn with numerous colors of chalk, the candles placed at strategic points around it, and the chalice situated at its center.

Alastair shook his head. "No, sir. I denied that I was performing Satanic rituals, because I wasn't. How could I be, when I don't even believe in Satan?" In for a penny, in for a pound, he figured. If he were to be expelled for what he'd done, at least he'd make sure not to hold anything back.

Carrowby's wild gray eyebrows crept up, and a brief expression of shock appeared on his lined face. "Indeed?" He paused, replacing the pen in its holder. "Well, that's a matter for another discussion. But tell me, Mr. Stone—if this isn't a Satanic ritual you've got set up here, then what is this?" He opened one of his drawers and removed something, which he placed on the desk.

Alastair realized only then what had been missing from the photos.

The book was old, bound in cracked red-brown leather. A depiction of an elaborate hermetic circle, debossed into the leather and emphasized with darker ink, dominated the cover. Two leather straps that normally held the book closed were open now. Carrowby opened the book to a page he'd marked. "I've no familiarity with such abominations, but whatever this is, it's an affront to God, no question about it."

Alastair pondered his response. He supposed this wasn't the time to admit to the assistant headmaster that he didn't believe in God, either. He recognized the spread the book was open to immediately: it was the one he'd been working with for the past few weeks, trying to get a simple ritual for locating a lost object to work. He'd finally succeeded just the previous night; he'd also nearly gotten caught out after curfew as he sneaked across campus to the boathouse at 3 a.m. to retrieve the old wallet he'd paid a younger boy to hide when he'd begun the whole process.

"Well?" Carrowby asked when Alastair didn't answer. "Would you like to tell me what this is?"

"It's…a magic book, sir."

"A magic book."

"Yes, sir."

"So you mean to tell me that you were performing *magic* in the attic?"

"Trying to, sir."

Carrowby examined the diagrams printed on the open pages. "And what sort of *magic* is this, then?" His thin lips curled around the word, coating it with contempt.

Alastair shrugged. "It's a tracking ritual. Designed to locate a missing object." There was no reason not to tell the truth—or at least part of it. As it happened, he did respect the school's honor code, so as much as he could, he intended not to lie as to the nature of his activities. Of course, knowing full well that Carrowby and anyone else he might pull in to this little investigation wouldn't believe a word he said figured prominently into that decision.

"What sort of missing object?"

"Nothing important. I asked someone to hide something of mine so I could try to find it. He had no idea what I was doing," he added.

Carrowby sighed again, and flipped through more pages in the book. "Where did you get this book, Mr. Stone?"

"I found it in a shop." Now the lies began. He'd hoped it would take a bit longer, but he couldn't reveal where he'd really obtained the tome. As long as it only affected him, he'd tell the truth, but implicating anyone else wasn't something he was willing to do.

"A shop. I didn't know there were magic book shops."

"Are you going to expel me, sir?" Best to get it out on the table sooner rather than later, since they both knew it was coming.

Carrowby's gaze snapped back up. "That's not something we're ready to decide yet, Mr. Stone. I've rung your father, though. He'll be here tomorrow to discuss our next steps."

Alastair stiffened. That wasn't good. He hadn't expected them to go to the nuclear option this early in the process. He'd thought perhaps he might have a chance of talking Carrowby into a couple of weeks of detention and perhaps a stint picking up rubbish around the campus first, but apparently the man had other ideas.

"Is magic against school rules, then?" He knew it wasn't—each student was expected to memorize the various rules they were to follow by the end of his first couple of months at Barrow. The list was more focused on things like keeping one's room clean, one's uniform properly laundered, one's academic experience honorable, and one's sexual experimentations nonexistent than in anything more esoteric.

"No, Mr. Stone. Magic is not against school rules. But sneaking out after curfew to perform unholy rites in restricted areas most certainly is."

Alastair didn't bother to reiterate that it hadn't been an unholy rite. Aside from being an ex-military man, Carrowby was clearly more religious than the average faculty member at Barrow. And to be fair, to the uninitiated, the diagrams in the book did look fairly unwholesome. "So...what now, sir?"

Carrowby's impressive eyebrows met as his brow furrowed. He seemed miffed that Alastair wasn't more cowed by the process, but all he did was close the tome and the file. "Now," he said, "you can go. We'll take this up again tomorrow when your father arrives." He stood. "And in case you were entertaining any ideas of finishing your...magical ritual,

I've already had your handiwork discreetly removed from the attic."

"Yes, sir." That much he'd expected. He, too, stood, and gestured toward the tome. "May I have my book back, sir?"

Brief anger flashed across Carrowby's face. "No, you may not. It will be given to your father tomorrow, and I am sure he will dispose of it properly."

"Yes, sir." Stone turned away so Carrowby couldn't see the combination of apprehension and amusement on his face.

He very much doubted his father would dispose of the book—given that it had been removed from his own magical library.

| CHAPTER THREE

THE MEETING THE NEXT DAY occurred not in Carrowby's office, but in a pleasant little sitting room off the main hall. Alastair made sure to arrive just on time: getting there late would have been unforgivably disrespectful, but showing up too early would make him look nervous. He *was* nervous, but they didn't need to see that. He had no idea how his father would react to these events, but his mind could conjure up several unpleasant scenarios without much effort.

He hesitated outside the door for just a moment, then knocked.

"Come in," Carrowby's voice called.

Alastair squared his shoulders, pushed open the door, and walked in with his head high. He'd taken a big chance, and he'd been caught. Whatever they chose to do to him, he'd deal with it.

"Ah. Mr. Stone. Right on time. Please sit down."

There were three men in the room, two on one side of a low table, and the third alone on the other side. They were all looking at Alastair, their faces unreadable. Spread out on the table were the photographs Carrowby had shown him yesterday, along with the leatherbound tome, its straps fastened now.

Next to Carrowby was Mr. Timms, the housemaster of Alastair's dormitory. The only open spot was on the small sofa. Alastair took a seat next to his father.

Tall and slim, with sharp, imperious features, dark hair, and an expression of controlled intensity, Orion Stone was a good indicator of what his son would look like in another twenty-five years. They differed only in the color of their eyes (the elder Stone's were gray, while Alastair's were bright blue) and in the fact that Alastair's father had apparently discovered the secret to keeping the unruly front part of his hair under control, a skill his son had not yet mastered.

Alastair glanced at him, trying to gauge his mood. Had Professor Carrowby told him about what had happened? It didn't matter—the presence of the photos and the tome would tell him everything he needed to know.

Carrowby cleared his throat. "All right, then. We're all here." He addressed Alastair's father. "Mr. Stone, we're terribly sorry to have to call you here, but as we've explained, young Alastair has committed some serious breaches of school rules."

Orion Stone nodded, still expressionless. He wasn't looking at his son now. "I understand."

"Normally," Carrowby continued, "this would be dealt with in the usual way: detention, perhaps a bit of service to the school, demerits—but this isn't the standard sort of transgression. Mr. Stone, please tell your father what you were doing when you broke curfew."

Here it was. Alastair turned a little on the sofa to face his father, meeting his gaze solidly. "I was performing a magical tracking ritual, sir."

A flicker of something—Alastair couldn't identify quite what—flashed across his father's features. "I see," was all he said.

Alastair took a slow deep breath and held it for several seconds. Since he'd been a small child, his father had been rather more like a force of nature than a parent—something that blew in and out of his life at brief intervals between his extended periods of world travel. That was part of the reason why Alastair was at Barrow, and had been since he was seven years old. Though he was well aware that Orion Stone was one of the most powerful mages of his generation, his father wasn't the sort of man one could sit down and have heart-to-heart talks with. Mostly, you stayed out of his way and didn't interfere with whatever he was doing. Thus, Alastair had essentially no idea how his father would respond to this latest news.

Carrowby picked up one of the photos and offered it to the elder Stone. "It's all preposterous, of course, but look at this. He must have spent days—weeks—setting all of this up. And this book." He undid the straps on the tome and opened it to the same page he'd shown Alastair. "He claims he found it in a shop. I can hardly bear to look at it. Clearly an unwholesome pursuit. Wouldn't you agree, sir?"

Stone made a noncommittal noise. He examined the photo, first with polite interest, but then his gaze sharpened. "May I?"

Carrowby surrendered the photo. "Of course."

So far, Mr. Timms hadn't said a word, and Alastair thought he knew why: the housemaster had been caught in an uncomfortable situation, unable to either defend Alastair or support Carrowby without alienating one or the other of them. Timms had been responsible for riding herd on twenty boys, ranging in age from ten to sixteen, since long before Alastair had arrived at Barrow. He was a kind man, attentive to the boys' needs and always willing to provide a sympathetic ear to romantic troubles, academic difficulties, and general emotional turmoil. Alastair had never approached him for such assistance, and had in fact felt that Timms considered him a bit of a ticking time bomb, but the man had never been anything but fair to him. He suspected Timms would miss him if he were expelled, and felt bad for putting him in such an position now.

Stone looked up from examining the photo, fixing a level gaze on Carrowby. "What's the next step, then? Is the boy to be expelled? I hardly think breaking curfew is grounds for expulsion."

"No, no." Carrowby waved his hands as if trying to clear the air of Stone's words. "Not for the curfew violation, nor for his obvious trespass into areas where he's not permitted to be. But this…ritual—"

Stone briefly closed his eyes. "Professor Carrowby, are you telling me—honestly—that you're considering expelling my son because he was attempting to perform *magic*?"

Carrowby's expression grew harder, more indignant. He picked up the book and held it out to Stone. "Look at this, Mr. Stone. Look at the diagrams. The drawings. It's sacrilege, I'm telling you. It's *unholy*."

Stone didn't take the book. "Professor," he said in the same even, steady tone, "I'm aware that the boys here are required to attend chapel periodically. However, I don't recall anything in the school rules that require actual belief. Merely attendance. Am I correct?"

Carrowby gripped his chair arms. A muscle in his jaw twitched. "You are correct, sir. It is not within our rights to compel any sort of belief in the Almighty. But—"

"So even if my son had been doing what you claimed—however unwise he might have been to do it—his only true transgressions are curfew violation and presence in an unauthorized area?"

Carrowby was almost sputtering now. "Yes—no! There's also the matter of vandalism of the attic, and, assuming he lit any of those candles, starting fires inappropriately."

"I see." Stone stood. "Well, then, Professor, I shall leave it to you to make your decision. When shall I expect to be informed?"

"Mr. Stone—" Timms began, rising a bit in his seat and glancing at Alastair.

Carrowby waved him back down. "It's too late to do anything over the weekend. We will discuss the matter next week and you will both hear the results of our decision by midweek."

Stone nodded once. "Thank you."

"Shall we—dispose of this?" He held out the book as if handling a basket of sunbaked roadkill.

Stone took it from him and tucked it under his arm. "Alastair?"

Alastair, more confused than ever, got up and followed his father out of the room. He didn't look back at Carrowby or Timms as he left.

| CHAPTER FOUR

H IS FATHER WAITED UNTIL THEY WERE OUTSIDE before speaking. When he finally did, his tone was even, unemotional, and unrevealing. "Pack a bag. You'll be returning home for the weekend."

That was unexpected. His father was rarely home himself for more than a day at a time. "Sir?"

"I'll wait for you in the common room. Be quick—I have appointments tonight that I cannot miss."

Stone didn't sound like he was in the mood for arguments or questions, so as soon as they arrived back at his dormitory, Alastair hurried upstairs and threw together a few things he'd need.

Since he didn't have a roommate, he thought he might make it out without having to answer any uncomfortable questions, but no such luck. As he emerged from his room carrying his overnight bag, Lucas MacNair and Ravi Patel were coming down the hallway, their sweaty T-shirts indicating they were returning from afternoon football practice.

"All right, Stone?" Lucas asked, eyeing Alastair's bag with curiosity.

"Yeah. Fine." Lucas and Ravi weren't his best mates or anything, but they were all right. "Just going home for the weekend."

"I heard you got in trouble for something," Ravi said. "Heard you might even get expelled." His tone warred between morbid curiosity and actual concern.

"What'd you do?" Lucas asked, definitely tilting more toward the morbid-curiosity end of the spectrum. "Get caught with a bird in your room?" He punched Alastair on the arm and waggled his eyebrows. "Or a bloke?"

Alastair sighed. Discretion, unfortunately, was something boarding schools were terrible at. Day-to-day life at Barrow was generally so predictable and regimented that any deviations from the norm were fallen upon with a level of enthusiasm that would embarrass of a pack of starving dogs. No matter how hard you tried to keep something secret—and often *because* you tried to keep it secret—somebody would overhear something and the story would spread like wildfire. It would be all over school by Monday, if it wasn't already.

"Got caught out after curfew, someplace I wasn't supposed to be, that's all. It's fine." Maybe it was and maybe it wasn't. Could they chuck him out for doing magic in the attic? Most likely his father would smooth things over, he'd get hit with some nasty detention time, and the whole thing would be forgotten by next week.

He hoped.

Ravi and Lucas looked disappointed that the truth wasn't juicier. "That all?" Lucas asked as he opened the door to his room. "Good one, Stone. If you're gonna get into enough trouble to get called in front of old Carrowby, at least you could do something worthwhile."

If you only knew. Alastair grunted noncommittally, shrugged, and waited for Lucas to disappear into his room and Ravi to pass by before setting off at a jog back downstairs. It wouldn't do to keep his father waiting.

Orion Stone summoned Alastair to his study the following Sunday morning. "You won't be going back to Barrow," he said without preamble. "I'll be arranging to have the rest of your things sent home."

Alastair gaped at him, unable to hide his shock. This was sudden, and unexpected. He hadn't seen his father since they'd arrived back at the house on Friday evening; the elder Stone had departed for his appointments, and left word with Aubrey that he would be away all day Saturday as well. Until the Sunday-morning call came, Alastair wondered why his father had bothered bringing him home at all. "They've rung you, then? I've been expelled?"

"They haven't called. I'll be withdrawing you on Monday."

"I—" Alastair's brain reeled as he struggled to come up with some appropriate way to respond. He swallowed. "But why? If they haven't—"

Stone pulled the tome he'd gotten from Carrowby from his desk drawer. "You stole this from my library."

"Borrowed. I intended to return it."

It was impossible to read his father's expression. "How many of my other books have you…borrowed?"

"Just that one."

"That was a tracking ritual you were attempting, correct?" He opened the book to the page containing the circle diagram.

"Yes, sir."

"And you were successful at it?"

Alastair nodded, wondering where this was going. Was he digging himself deeper into a hole? Even if he was, though, nothing his father could do to him could take away his pride in what he'd done.

"Why did you choose that particular ritual?"

Alastair shrugged. "It didn't look too difficult, and I figured there wouldn't be any chance of hurting anyone if I failed at it."

"How did you work out how to do it? Did anyone help you?"

"No, sir. I've been reading through some of your other books when I was home for holidays. I took that one with me because I knew I wouldn't have time to construct a circle during the time I was here."

"I see." He closed the book. "You know, I'm sure, that you were to finish your secondary schooling before you began your apprenticeship."

"Yes, sir."

"Yet you grew impatient and took it upon yourself to attempt magical techniques on your own."

Alastair ducked his gaze for a moment, then met his father's eyes. "Not attempt. Succeed."

Something flashed across his father's face and was gone. "Have you succeeded at any other techniques?"

Alastair paused. At this point, he couldn't make things any worse, he supposed. "I...can get magical sight to work, sometimes. Not consistently yet."

"Indeed." This time, Alastair didn't miss the surprise in his eyes. "Describe my aura, then."

Alastair concentrated, but didn't hold much hope that he'd get anywhere. *Sometimes* was actually optimistic: ever since he'd been working at it, he'd only been successful in using the odd form of perception mages employed to see auras and other supernatural phenomena a handful of times, and it didn't seem to get any easier with practice. In fact, it usually gave him a headache. The technique was similar to shifting one's perceptions to view an optical illusion—you had to look past the mundane world to see what lurked tantalizingly beyond it. The books he'd consulted, though, had been worded confusingly enough that he didn't quite grasp what he was supposed to do, and thus when he got it right, it was by sheer luck.

Now, after nearly a full minute of trying, he let his breath out in a frustrated sigh. "I'm sorry," he said. "I'm not getting it right now."

His father didn't seem disturbed by this. "Describe your own aura, then," he said. "Surely you examined it during one of the times when you did get it right."

"It's sort of...purple and gold," he said. "The gold glows around the edges of the purple."

Stone raised an eyebrow. "And no one's told you that?"

"Who would tell me?" It was true: he didn't even know any other mages, except his father's old friend Walter Yarborough, a stout, stodgy man a little older than Orion, whom he'd met a couple of times during dinner parties. From what he understood, Yarborough was to be responsible for his apprenticeship when he turned eighteen, but he hadn't seen the man for close to three years.

Alastair waited a moment, and when his father didn't reply, he ventured, "So...er...if you're withdrawing me from Barrow, where will I be continuing my schooling?"

Stone regarded him silently for several moments. "I've arranged for a private tutor for you," he said. "The details will be confirmed shortly."

A tutor? What was going on? "All this because I was trying to do a bit of magic?" He tried to keep the indignation from his voice, but didn't succeed very well. "You're telling me that you didn't ever—" He stopped when his father's expression hardened. Had he gone too far?

"You'll have a tutor," Stone said, "to work with you so you can finish your secondary education in conjunction with your apprenticeship."

Alastair froze.

Surely he couldn't have heard that correctly. "My—apprenticeship?"

"That's what you were working toward, isn't it?" Stone asked. "To learn magic?"

He was dreaming. He had to be. He was only fifteen. Nobody started their apprenticeship at fifteen. Most teachers wouldn't even look at a potential student younger than eighteen. "Well—yes. Of course. But—" He swallowed and took a deep breath. "How did you convince Mr. Yarborough to—"

"You won't be apprenticing with Walter."

"I...won't?" As far as he knew, that had been the plan ever since he was a small child. Whenever his father mentioned his eventual apprenticeship, it was always in connection with Yarborough.

Stone leaned back in his chair. "No. I know that's what I've always told you, but...recent events have changed my mind."

Alastair took that in silently. He had no idea what it meant. Had Yarborough refused to work with him because of his insubordination and willfulness? Perhaps his father had been forced to seek someone less desirable, who'd be willing to take on a rebellious, impatient boy. But if that were true, why let him start so young at all? Why not simply forbid him to try out any more unsanctioned magic and send him packing back to Barrow, or to some other school where they hadn't heard of his transgressions?

"I've managed to convince William Desmond to give you a trial," Stone said.

"I...don't know who that is, sir."

"You wouldn't. I'm quite surprised I was able to convince him at all. He hasn't taken an apprentice in years, and certainly never one of your age."

Alastair dropped his gaze, struggling not to let his father see the dismay he was sure showed in his eyes. That was it, then. Instead of his father's colleague as originally planned, he'd have to make due with some retired old man who didn't even want him around. He supposed it was his own fault, though, so there was no complaining about it. He'd just have to study harder on his own if he wanted to get anywhere.

He nodded as he tried to hide his growing mixed emotions: elation that he would be allowed to start his apprenticeship so early, and disappointment that he'd apparently given up his chance at a top-tier teacher.

"Is something wrong?" his father asked. "You look troubled. I thought you would be pleased at this opportunity."

"I am," he said quickly. "It's just that—" he spread his hands. "No, it's fine. I understand I've caused my own problems, and if that means I won't have the best teacher—"

Stone's eyes widened. "What do you mean, not the best teacher? I don't think you understand: William Desmond is one of the most powerful and influential mages in Britain. Quite likely among the top ten in the western world."

Alastair stared at him, not even trying to hide his shock.

"I never thought you had a chance that he'd take you on," Stone continued. "But after what happened on Friday, I arranged to meet with him in London yesterday. I told him about your initiative, and how you'd managed to work out a difficult magical technique on your own, with no assistance. He was impressed. He agreed to give you a trial." His eyes narrowed. "It's just a trial, though. If you want him to apprentice you, you'll have to impress him a lot more, and that won't be easy. I don't know if what you've done already will be enough."

Alastair kept staring. He felt numb. His hands shook. A tingle crept around the back of his neck and down his spine. Any minute now, he would wake up back in his dormitory at Barrow, and none of this would be real. "I—"

"Don't get too full of yourself," Stone said. His eyes were still cold. "Desmond's an old-school traditionalist, and hard as nails. If you impress him enough to take you on, you'll work harder than you ever have in your life—especially since I expect you to keep getting top marks in your mundane schooling as well. You won't have time for any sort of social life. Desmond won't coddle you. He'll try his best to break you, in fact—and if he succeeds, don't expect me to rescue you. Magic isn't for children, Alastair. It's difficult, dangerous, and most apprentices—even those of a more traditional age—don't make it through their training." He paused. "So I'll give you one last chance: You can end this now. You can give me your word you won't attempt any more magic until you're eighteen and properly apprenticed with Walter. If you do that, you can go back to Barrow on Monday and we'll say no more about this. But if you decide to pursue it, I'll expect you to give it the proper respect. And I'll expect you not to fail." He stood. "Think about it today, and give me your answer by this evening."

Alastair stood as well, as he came around the desk. "I don't have to do that, sir."

Stone stopped. "Oh?"

He felt a little bit like someone else was using his voice; as if he were hovering somewhere above himself, watching the next few seconds play out on a screen. He didn't know who William Desmond was, but if his father, an adherent of the old techniques in his own right, called him an old-school traditionalist and one of the best around, he must be formidable indeed. He had no doubt everything his father said was true: he'd work so hard that everything he'd done at Barrow would seem like play by comparison. He'd probably spend most of his time exhausted, and would never have a chance to do the sorts of things normal teenagers did. Somewhere in the back of his mind, he thought he could be seriously injured, or even die. It wasn't common these days, but apprentices sometimes did get hurt when they tried magic they weren't ready for, or when rituals, as they sometimes did, simply went wrong for no discernable reason. Studying under this Desmond might even increase that possibility, since it sounded like the man was set to drive him even harder than a normal master would push an apprentice. The decision he made now would affect the rest of his life.

He didn't hesitate. It didn't even occur to him to hesitate.

"I want to do it," he said. "Please thank Mr. Desmond for his offer, and tell him that I won't fail him. Or you."

A brief expression Alastair couldn't identify crossed Stone's face and was gone. He nodded once. "All right, then. I'll let him know. In the meantime, there's the matter of your punishment."

Alastair supposed there was no getting around that—he *had* broken school rules, after all. He waited.

"You won't be leaving for London until next Sunday. Until then, you'll spend at least five hours per day assisting Aubrey with whatever tasks he sets you around the grounds. I've instructed him not to go easy on you, so expect the tasks won't be pleasant."

Alastair nodded. "Yes, sir."

"In your remaining free hours, I'd advise you to spend as much time in study as you can manage. I'll open part of my library to you, and you can use the circle if you wish. I don't expect you'll come up with much more in a week's time, but anything you can work out will be to your advantage. I'd say it would help you to get on Desmond's good side, but I'm not sure he has one."

That sounds promising… "Yes, sir," he said again.

Stone waved him out. "Off you go. Go find Aubrey and tell him you're ready to work."

Still feeling numb, still half-convinced that none of this was real, Alastair nodded and turned to go.

"Alastair?"

He stopped and turned back. "Yes, sir?"

His father's stern visage held an odd expression, one Alastair couldn't remember seeing in a long time. It was a moment before it dawned on him that what he was seeing was pride.

"Well done," his father said.

Alastair smiled, just a little. "Thank you, sir."

| CHAPTER FIVE

A HARD, GRAY RAIN WAS FALLING when Alastair emerged from the train station in London and looked around for a cab. The rain fell so heavily it was difficult to differentiate the packed line of vehicles creeping along, and pedestrians hurried this way and that, intent on their errands. The only time they noticed Alastair was when he was in their way and they pushed past him with a coldly polite "pardon me."

For just a moment, he allowed himself to resent the fact that his father not only hadn't accompanied him on his journey to William Desmond's London house, but had in fact refused to do so. "You wanted to begin your apprenticeship early," he'd said when Alastair had asked. "That means I plan to treat you as a proper apprentice. I expect you to handle your affairs as an adult would."

The thought of being treated as an adult had been heady stuff for a while, until he'd reached London. He'd taken the train from his small village in Surrey to Victoria Station, where he transferred to another train to Kensington High Street. That was where he was now, struggling to keep his umbrella upright in the driving rain with one hand while he bobbled a suitcase and soft leather briefcase in the other. The rest of his things—what few he'd been permitted to bring—had been sent ahead and would be waiting for him when he arrived.

Despite his sturdy umbrella, he was already soaked due to the whipping, unpredictable winds. It was a lousy day to be out in the weather. He thought about Barrow, with its warm, panel-walled dormitory common room—Mr. Timms would no doubt have a roaring fire burning to await the return of the boys from their afternoon classes.

This is what you wanted, he told himself, tightening his fist around the umbrella's handle. A three-year head start on his magical training was worth enduring a lot more arduous hardships than a rain-soaking. He shifted his suitcase and briefcase and tried to pull his overcoat closed, but his hand was so cold he couldn't manage the buttons.

He spotted a cab and stepped out to wave it down. As he tossed his suitcase in the back, he wondered why Desmond hadn't sent someone to pick him up—a servant, perhaps, since his father had told him his new master was quite wealthy. It was probably more of the "self-reliance" thing, he decided. If he couldn't manage to find his way to his new home, he could hardly be expected to learn magic properly.

"Where to?" the driver asked.

Alastair dug the paper containing address out of his inner pocket and told him, then concentrated on getting his things in order while they drove.

Several minutes later, the cab pulled up in front of a large, ornate building on an old, tree-lined street. Alastair got out, retrieved his bags, and was about to dig out some of the cash his father had given him to pay for the ride when suddenly another man was there. "I'll take care of that, sir," he said.

Alastair blinked. The man was tall, dark-haired, and about the same age as his father. He wore an elegant uniform of black and gold, complete with cap. He gave Alastair a smile. "You go on in, sir. You're expected. Fourth floor. You can leave your bags—I'll take care of everything."

"Er—thank you," Alastair said. He nodded to the cabdriver and hurried up the walk and inside.

Past the doors was a different world. As soon as they closed behind him, the sounds of the street outside melted away, replaced by soft classical music—Mozart, if Alastair remembered his music-appreciation classes. Everything about the space spoke of the kind of wealth that had no need to boast or advertise itself—the kind that had been in a family so long that its members simply took it for granted.

He was certainly no stranger to wealth himself, though despite the vast house and grounds of his family's own place in Surrey, and his attendance (*former* attendance, he reminded himself) at one of southern England's elite public boarding schools, this was a level of opulence he was not used to. Frankly, that sort of thing didn't impress him that much—he found an over-infatuation with one's personal finances often went hand in hand with the sort of people he didn't like being around. But this place was different. It wasn't as if it were trying to impress anyone. This was the kind of wealth that just *was*, irrespective of anyone who might have opinions about it.

He walked slowly through the large lobby, his feet making no sound on the plush carpeting, until he reached the marble staircase. As he mounted it and began trudging upward, he wondered if Desmond owned this entire building, and if he had other holdings elsewhere. Would he be doing his apprenticeship here, or was this simply the place where he would meet his new master?

The fourth-floor landing was a large anteroom carpeted in thick, deep red. A crystal chandelier hung overhead, and on either side were two tables with elaborately carved legs. The left one sported a large vase, and the right held a sculpture of a man mounted on a horse. Above each hung framed oil paintings that Alastair would have bet the remainder of his cash would be at home in the British Museum.

Directly in front of him, pair of double doors loomed, carved of dark wood and somehow ominous. He paused a moment, looking down at himself to see if he was presentable before knocking. He'd worn a suit at his father's suggestion— Desmond was old-fashioned, and wouldn't approve of jeans and a T-shirt with some band logo on it. Still, given how soaked he was at the moment, he thought Desmond might not consider it much of a difference.

Enough stalling. Desmond had agreed to take him on— that meant the man had to have seen something in him that he thought was worthwhile. Now, all Alastair had to do was prove to him he hadn't been wrong. He marched up to the door and knocked three times with what he hoped was sufficient confidence.

A brief time passed. Alastair was wondering if he should knock again when the left-side door opened, revealing a tall man in an old-fashioned suit. "Good afternoon," he said, his voice severe but politely pleasant. "You must be young Alastair Stone."

"Yes, sir." Alastair realized that he had no idea what Desmond looked like, but was reasonably sure someone who owned a place like this didn't open his own doors.

"My name is Kerrick, sir," he said, and stood aside. "Please come in. Mr. Desmond is expecting you, of course."

Alastair followed him into an interior entry hall with a soaring ceiling and doors leading off from all three sides. The ones in the back, another wide set of double doors, stood open to reveal a hallway. Alastair hoped he wasn't dripping too badly on the Oriental rug underfoot.

"May I take your coat and umbrella, sir?" Kerrick asked.

"Er—thank you." He handed over the umbrella and shrugged out of his overcoat, handing them both over.

Kerrick put the umbrella in a stand near the door, and draped the coat over his arm. He said nothing about the fact that it was soaked. "This way," he said, and headed off down the hallway.

Alastair got a brief impression of more no-doubt priceless paintings as he hurried after the man (was he a butler? They didn't have a butler at his place—since his father was almost never home and Alastair spent most of his time away at school, they didn't even have servants. He supposed Aubrey was technically a servant, but he was more like family).

Kerrick led him into an enormous sitting room that could have stepped bodily out of one of those television period dramas. Everywhere he looked was fine old furniture, artwork, heavy drapes, and soaring windows looking out over the gray, stormy day. "Please, sit down," Kerrick said. "Mr. Desmond will be along in just a moment. Would you like something to drink?"

"No…thank you," Alastair said. "I'm fine."

He wasn't sure that was true—he wasn't sure he hadn't made a big mistake by agreeing to this. *Magic,* he reminded himself. *That's all that matters. You can do whatever it takes.* He didn't want to get one of the antique couches or upholstered chairs wet, so he perched on the edge of a wooden chair and stared out the window.

As he waited, he wondered what William Desmond would be like. Would he be similar to Walter Yarborough: old-fashioned, a bit stuffy, but cheerful? His father had said he didn't think Desmond "had a good side," so cheerful was probably optimistic. Perhaps he'd be more like his father, severe and focused and utterly dedicated to the Art. He could deal with that. He didn't spend a lot of time with his father, though—he wondered what it would be like to be around that kind of intensity all the time.

He also wondered how long Desmond would make him wait. Perhaps this was some kind of test, to make sure he wasn't one of those fidgety boys who couldn't sit still. Well, if it were, he could pass it. Meditation was something he'd taught himself long ago—one of the few bits of the apprenticeship process he could start working on long before he actually needed it.

"Good day, Mr. Stone," a firm voice said from behind him.

He almost jumped, startled, but managed to confine it to a twitch. Instead, he stood quickly and turned around, pulling himself up straighter. "Mr. Desmond."

It wasn't a question. There was no doubt in his mind that this man had to be William Desmond.

He seemed to fill the room. Tall, broad-shouldered, with steel-colored hair swept back from a high forehead, he regarded Alastair with no expression. His glittering, pale-blue eyes took him in as if examining a prize racehorse. Even inside his home he wore a fine, old-fashioned suit that made him look like he'd just stepped out of a historical novel.

He definitely went with the house, Alastair observed. He had no idea how old the man was. As a mage, he could be an old fifty, or he could be over a hundred. His father had told him that mages lived considerably longer than their mundane counterparts, and tended to age much more slowly.

Desmond studied him for a while longer, now more like a bug under a microscope than a racehorse. "Your trip went well, I trust."

"Yes, sir." He indicated his soggy suit. "Bit wet, but fine."

Desmond's expression didn't change. "If you'll follow Kerrick, he'll show you where you'll be staying tonight."

"Tonight, sir?"

"Yes. We won't be remaining here. For now, your apprenticeship will take place at my country house—it is better suited for the sorts of things you'll be studying, and more removed from…distractions. Broadsby has brought up your bag. The rest of your things will be sent on tomorrow. You can change into something dry, and then we'll meet."

Kerrick showed up behind him as if on cue. Without waiting for a response, Desmond turned and headed off down another hallway.

Alastair watched him go. His father was right: it *didn't* appear the man had a good side. Or possibly that he was even human.

"Ready to go?" Kerrick asked. At least he had a smile.

"Er—yes. Thanks." He wondered what his temporary accommodations would look like. His father hadn't said anything about a country house—he thought he'd be studying here in London. It didn't matter, though—he didn't care if Desmond took him to Mars, as long as he could learn magic there.

Kerrick led him down another hallway and stopped at the end, where he pushed open the last door on the right. "Here we are." He stood aside to allow Alastair to enter first.

The room was unremarkable, furnished in the impersonal style of the sort of guest room one used for guests who weren't altogether welcome. Alastair walked in, dropped his bag on the bed, and turned back to face Kerrick, unsure of what was expected of him.

"Lav's just down the hall," the man said, pointing. "As Mr. Desmond said, this is only for the night. If you want to clean up a bit, I'll return to take you back to Mr. Desmond. Fifteen minutes?"

"That's fine. Thank you, Mr. Kerrick."

"Just Kerrick," he said cheerfully. "I'll be back, then." He closed the door behind him, leaving Alastair alone.

It was only then that he realized his heart was pounding. What had he gotten himself into? *He's just another teacher,* he told himself. He'd dealt with many hard-case instructors over his years at Barrow. Desmond couldn't be any worse...right?

He picked up his suitcase, opened it on the bed, and quickly searched for something presentable to wear. He suspected showing up looking like a half-drowned cat had probably added another red mark in a ledger that no doubt already contained at least a couple, so he didn't need to add yet another one by being late.

He pulled on a fresh button-down shirt and black dress trousers, wishing he'd had another jacket to put over them. But his suits were in his other bags, which were apparently in some sort of holding pattern between here and wherever they'd ultimately end up.

The whole process struck him as odd—why have him show up at the London house if he wasn't going to be staying for more than a single night? Why not just have him arrive at this mysterious country house straight away? And why would his bags be sent here and then on to the other house tomorrow? Wouldn't it make more sense to just send them directly there to start with?

It wasn't until he'd ducked down the hall into the lavatory (it was as impersonally posh as the room had been) to attempt to put his hair into something approximating order that it came to him, sending a chill running down his back.

He was already being evaluated.

He was here because Desmond didn't want to expend the time and effort to send him to the country house if he couldn't even pass the first interview. Everything he did here would be inspected, scrutinized, and tallied, and if he put a single toe out of line or didn't live up to Desmond's expectations, he was suddenly certain he'd be in a cab and headed back to Surrey before it got dark tonight.

No pressure, then. None at all.

He stared at his reflection in the mirror, made one final effort to put his hair in order (*if he turfs me out because he doesn't think my hair's neat enough, maybe it's best I learn that early,* he decided), and headed back to his room. By the time he got back inside, a bit breathless, he had a minute to spare.

Kerrick arrived a few moments later, knocking softly on the door. "Ah," he said in approval. "You're looking much more comfortable. If you'll come with me, Mr. Desmond will see you now."

Alastair followed him down another painting-lined hallway to a closed door at the end.

He knocked on the door and called, "Mr. Desmond? Mr. Stone is here."

The door opened on silent hinges. No one stood behind it. "Thank you, Kerrick," came a voice from inside. "Come in, Mr. Stone."

Alastair stepped inside, and the door closed behind him.

This room was clearly some sort of study. Three of the four walls were lined with bookshelves, and each bookshelf was filled, floor to two-story ceiling, with volumes. A massive, carved wooden desk dominated the center of the room, in front of a large window currently covered by more heavy drapes. Desmond sat behind the desk. He indicated the chairs in front of it. "Sit down, please."

Alastair did as he was told. He wanted to look everywhere in this fascinating room—there was a lot to see—but he didn't. Instead, he sat up straight, kept his hands in his lap, and waited for Desmond to speak.

For a time, he didn't. He merely sat there and fixed his gaze on Alastair as if he, too, were waiting.

Alastair wasn't sure whether he was supposed to speak or prove he could stand up under a stare-down without looking away, so he chose the latter. He kept his expression neutral and respectful, but he neither fidgeted nor dropped his gaze.

After several more uncomfortable seconds passed, Desmond steepled his fingers. "I didn't want to take you on," he said. "When your father came to me with his request, I almost turned him down."

Alastair remained silent; that didn't seem like a statement that invited a reply.

"I understand you were nearly expelled from your school for constructing a ritual circle in your dormitory building."

"Yes, sir. Well, mostly."

"Mostly?"

"Yes, sir. I was nearly expelled for practicing unholy rites in the attic."

Desmond nodded. "Do you believe magic to be unholy, Mr. Stone?"

"No, sir."

"Tell me," he said, rising from his chair and beginning to pace, prowling the large room like a predatory cat, "what was it that prompted you to do such a thing?"

"I...wanted to learn magic, sir."

"But you knew that you would be learning magic—when you finished your secondary education."

"Yes, sir."

"Your father had plans for you to study with Walter Yarborough, and you were aware of these plans."

"Yes, sir."

"And yet you took it upon yourself to change them. To go against your father's wishes."

"Not...exactly, sir." When Desmond arched an eyebrow, he added, "My father never told me not to try to learn magic on my own."

"He approved of your experimentations, then?"

Alastair paused. "No, sir," he said at last. "It was more...that I never asked him."

"Better to ask forgiveness than permission, is that it?"

"I—suppose so, sir."

Desmond magically summoned a book to his hand from one of the far shelves and paged through it. "Tell me about this ritual you performed in your attic."

"It was a tracking ritual, sir. I used it to find an object I asked someone to hide."

"This ritual?" He brought the book over and put it down on the desk, open to a page.

Alastair examined the book, and instantly recognized it as a copy of the same one he'd "borrowed" from his father's library. "Yes, sir."

"You had no help with this? You obtained the components, cast the circle, and performed the ritual entirely on your own?"

"Yes, sir."

"Were you successful on your first attempt?"

He shook his head. "No, sir. Not even close. I was almost ready to give up on it the night I finally got it to work."

"Were you able to perform any other magic?"

"I...can use magical sight," he said. "Not consistently, though. I'm still working on that. And this week I produced a minor ward around a small area."

"Indeed," he said. "Did your father assist you with any of these endeavors?"

"No, sir, except for giving me access to his library and the permanent circle at our house last week."

"I see." Desmond walked over until he was standing next to Alastair. Or perhaps "looming" was a better description. He paused there a moment, his intense gaze fixed on him, and then turned the second guest chair so it faced Alastair's and sat down in it. "Face me, please."

Alastair, wondering what he was doing now, nonetheless got up and turned his chair toward Desmond. Was the man going to ask him for some demonstration of magical skill?

Desmond regarded him in silence for a moment longer, then leaned forward. "Remain still, please. With your permission, I am going to touch your forehead."

"Er—of course, sir." Alastair did as he was told, sitting up straight and staring at a point past Desmond's shoulder as the older man extended a hand and pressed two fingers against the center of Alastair's forehead.

Alastair didn't shiver as he caught on to what Desmond was doing, but it wasn't easy. His father had done this to him once, a couple of years ago. When he'd finished, he explained the reason for it, though he'd never revealed anything about what he'd discovered.

A mage couldn't normally identify another mage simply by examining his or her aura. While it was true that powerful mages often had auras that were interesting in some way—two or even three colors instead of one, extension farther out from the body than a mundane's, or unusual hues were three of the more common variations—the mere existence of one or more of these nonstandard aura types didn't confirm magical talent.

There were only three ways to identify a mage. The first and most immediately obvious was to catch them in the act of performing magic. The second was to examine their aura shortly after they had used magic, since the traces of power lingered around their body for some time—the stronger the magic, the longer its traces stuck around if the mage didn't do something about them.

The third and most definitive, as Alastair's father had explained to him, was to do an astral examination on the prospective mage. Not every mage could conduct such an examination; it required a certain degree of power and control to get it right. But for those who could, a few moments' contact with the subject was enough both to confirm the necessary genetics for magical talent and to discern an approximate potential power level.

Desmond was taking a long time. His fingers, dry and a little cool, shifted minutely, giving Alastair a sudden absurd image of Mr. Spock doing a mind meld on *Star Trek*. *My mind to your mind...my thoughts to your thoughts...*

A moment later, the image fled in favor of more irrational notion: *What if he doesn't find anything? What if I'm not a mage after all?*

Of course *you're a mage, you prat. You couldn't have made that ritual work if you weren't.*

Desmond broke the contact and stood. "Thank you, Mr. Stone."

Alastair couldn't help asking: "What did you find, sir?"

"What I needed to know." Without offering any further explanation or report, he returned to his own chair behind his desk. "As I told you, I didn't want to take you on. You're far too young for apprenticeship—normally I won't even consider anyone under seventeen. So I want you to understand: this is a probationary apprenticeship. Do you understand what I mean by that, Mr. Stone?"

Alastair had been ready for this, but he had to struggle not to shift in his chair. "A temporary period," he said. "So you can determine if I'm worth your time."

What if he failed? The thought of riding the train back home, of facing his father after washing out as an apprentice, filled him with apprehension. If he failed with Desmond, would he even be allowed to study with Yarborough when he was eighteen? *Don't do this,* he told himself firmly. *You aren't going to fail. Don't let him get into your head. That's what he's trying to do.*

"Precisely. Because I'll be honest with you, Mr. Stone: I don't think you are. Don't take that personally—I'm sure you're a fine young man, and your magical potential meets acceptable parameters for my instruction. But magical apprenticeship is a serious thing. It's difficult, it's arduous, and it can be dangerous. Do you know what percentage of apprentices pass their training and are considered fully qualified?"

"No, sir."

"I don't have exact numbers, but it's quite low. I would estimate no more than fifteen to twenty percent, as a whole. And those are adults, Mr. Stone. They begin their training at eighteen. I have taken five apprentices so far, and of those five, only one has successfully completed the training to my satisfaction. Three dropped out and either finished their apprenticeships with other, less demanding masters, or gave up entirely. One died. Do you still want to study with me, Mr. Stone?"

One *died?* He wanted to ask about that, but it didn't change his answer. "Yes, sir. More than ever."

"What makes you think you'll succeed when those others failed?"

"I don't think I will, sir. I *know* I will. Being a mage is all I've ever wanted, since I knew what magic was. It's what I'm meant to be. Failing isn't an option." Strong words, and he hoped he didn't come off sounding cocky—he certainly didn't *feel* cocky—but he suspected William Desmond was not a man who valued false modesty. "I appreciate this opportunity, and I'm not afraid of hard work."

Desmond studied him, his expression still unreadable. "All right then, Mr. Stone. We shall see. That will be all for now. As I'm sure Kerrick has told you, your things will be sent on to my country house tomorrow, and he will see to your transportation. You leave promptly at eight a.m.—meet him downstairs with your bags, and do not be late. We will meet again tomorrow after you have arrived and settled in."

He waved his hand at the bookshelf, and two other volumes flew off and landed on the desk in front of him. He picked them up and offered them to Alastair. "For tonight, take these. You won't have time to read through them before tomorrow, but spend the rest of the day familiarizing yourself with them as much as you can. Bring them along with you—I reserve the right to ask you about your understanding of them tomorrow."

He stood. "Good day, Mr. Stone."

"Yes, sir. Thank you, sir." Alastair picked up the books, nodded farewell, and followed Desmond out.

Apparently, he'd passed the first hurdle.

He maintained his confident demeanor until he got back to his room and closed the door, at which point he collapsed on the bed and let his breath out in a loud *whoosh*. What had he been *thinking?* What made him think he'd be able to train as a mage at least two years earlier than anybody he—and apparently even Desmond himself—had ever heard of? Okay, so he did very well in school with little effort. He had an innate understanding of some of the things he knew were important to magic, like maths, and he had a strong will. You had to have a strong will to live with his father, and he guessed Desmond would be even worse.

He had the genetics for it, too, if that even mattered: his father had once told him that he was the sixth in an unbroken male line of mages (since magic tended to almost always pass along gender lines, though nobody knew why), and that was unusual almost to the point of being unique. Magic often skipped one or even several generations, either because of the gender thing or because the Talent, more often than not, simply didn't get inherited. Sometimes even when it didn't skip a generation it fluctuated wildly in power, to the point where the child of a potent mage might exhibit only minimal talent, or vice versa. But in Alastair's case, it had managed to stay strong enough to produce six powerful mages in a row.

Well, five, anyway. Whether he was the sixth remained to be seen. At least Desmond didn't seem to think he was completely hopeless, although that didn't make him feel much better in the short term. He'd have to stay confident, but he'd also have to put aside everything he'd learned about magic from his scattershot studies. This was the kind of opportunity he'd never have dreamed possible, and he wasn't going to blow it by taking anything for granted.

He raised his head from the pillow and looked around the room. It looked so bare without any of his clothes or personal items.

Not that he'd been permitted to bring much: the instructions he'd received had specified only clothing (for everyday wear, business and formal occasions, and exercise), toiletries, and anything he'd require for study. No posters, frivolous or decorative items, music, or books not related to his mundane schoolwork or the study of magic. Alastair had been taken a bit aback by the harshness of the directive, but he'd followed it nonetheless. "Best get used to it," his father had told him before leaving on yet another business trip. "Desmond's got a reputation as quite the drill sergeant. You might be best off thinking of it as joining the military." Alastair had wondered if there *was* such a thing—a sort of Queen's Secret Magical Service—but he didn't ask. He just hoped Desmond wouldn't make him shave his head or anything.

Since he had nothing to unpack, he instead sat down at the desk with the two books Desmond had given him. Both were thick and looked quite old. The first seemed to be a sort of history book, with sections describing magic throughout the ages and around the world. The second was a primer on magical symbols, sigils, and languages. Both were densely packed with text. Desmond wanted him to learn *this* well enough for a quiz by tomorrow?

Well, best get started, then. He opened the history book and began skimming.

There was a soft knock on his door. "Sir?" It sounded like Kerrick.

Alastair jerked his head up. He had no idea how long he'd been reading, but his whole body felt stiff. He jumped up and opened the door.

It was indeed Kerrick. "Sorry to disturb you, sir, but dinner's served."

"Oh!" He looked down at his watch: it was five after seven. He'd lost track of time, and had been studying for over two hours without a break. "I'm sorry," he said. "Got a bit— caught up in what I was doing."

Kerrick chuckled. "It's fine, sir. It happens a lot around here. Mr. Desmond has already left for Caventhorne, so you'll be dining alone."

Alastair nodded. "Thank you," he said. He liked Kerrick already—the man reminded him of a younger version of Aubrey, the caretaker at his home, and certainly seemed a lot less intense than Desmond. He wondered if he went with the London house, or if he'd be accompanying them to this Caventhorne place.

As he followed Kerrick to the dining room, he said, "You're not alone here, are you?"

"Oh, no," Kerrick said. "Not at all. There are quite a number of others: maids, the chef and his assistants, a driver...we bring in others on a temporary basis as needed when Mr. Desmond is in residence."

"Do you...know about...?" Alastair trailed off, unsure of how to ask the question. If Kerrick *wasn't* familiar with Desmond's activities, he certainly didn't want to give anything away.

"Mr. Desmond's magic?" He chuckled. "Oh, yes sir. It would be difficult not to."

"Everyone here does, then?" That surprised him. The magical community was generally fairly secretive about its existence.

"Not everyone," he said. "Just the full-time staff. More at Caventhorne." He stood aside and waved Alastair to a chair at a long wooden table. Only one place had been set.

Alastair sat down. The room was huge and gloomy; the table was big enough to accommodate ten people at least. He wondered if he'd be eating his meals alone every day once he arrived at the country house, or if Desmond would join him. He didn't mind being alone—in fact, he often preferred his own company to that of others his own age—but this might be taking things a bit far.

"How does that work?" he asked. "You can't exactly advertise in the newspaper, can you? *Seeking staff for home in Kensington. Must approve of magic.*"

Kerrick chuckled again. "Not exactly, sir. Most of the staff come from families already familiar with the Art. If you'll excuse me—I'll bring your dinner and then I must attend to some last-minute duties."

Alastair pondered that as he waited. So Desmond hired his servants from among failed mages, or those from magical families who didn't inherit the Talent? He supposed it made sense in one way, but in another it seemed a bit cruel to keep anyone who might have had magic but didn't in a situation where they were surrounded by it. Desmond must pay very well, was all he could think of.

Kerrick returned with a covered tray and a goblet. He set both in front of Alastair and removed the cover. "I hope everything's to your liking, sir."

Alastair eyed the roast beef and vegetables. They looked and smelled delicious, especially given that he'd missed lunch. "Thank you. It's great. And—"

"Yes, sir?"

"Well…do you have to call me 'sir'?"

"You're Mr. Desmond's apprentice. It's generally considered proper."

"Not yet I'm not," he said wryly. "Not until I pass my probation." He twisted in his chair a bit. "Could I ask you a question? I don't want to ask anything I'm not supposed to, but I'm curious."

"I'll certainly do my best to answer, if I'm permitted to."

"Mr. Desmond told me today that one of his apprentices died. Do you know anything about that?"

Kerrick's cheerful expression clouded. "It's been many years, sir. And no, I'm not permitted to discuss the details. I'm sorry."

"It's all right. Sorry. I'm fine here, thanks. Don't let me keep you from anything."

Kerrick nodded. "Just remember, Mr. Stone—he wouldn't have agreed to give you a trial if he didn't think you could succeed. Mr. Desmond doesn't waste his time on anyone he doesn't think has potential."

Alastair nodded. Given that Desmond hadn't met him before today, he wondered how true that was—or if the man was just doing his father a favor. "Thanks. I'll keep that in mind."

"Best if you do. There will be times when you'll find it difficult to believe, but as long as you do what's expected of you and Mr. Desmond determines that you're performing at the levels he requires, you'll be fine. I must go now, but I'll meet you downstairs tomorrow morning at eight. You can come to the kitchen at seven for breakfast if you wish."

"Thank you."

Kerrick left to continue with his duties, and Alastair ate quickly—not just because he was hungry, but because the cavernous dining room made him uncomfortable, like someone was watching him.

He wondered if anyone was.

| CHAPTER SIX

A LASTAIR DIDN'T HAVE TO WORRY about oversleeping and missing his ride at eight o'clock the following morning, because he barely slept at all. He'd stayed up until well after midnight studying the two books Desmond had given him, trying to memorize as much of them as he could. Then, when he finally fell into bed at a bit after three a.m., he tossed and turned and woke up every half-hour or so to check the clock and make sure he hadn't missed the time, even though he'd set an alarm.

He wasn't hungry in the slightest, but decided he'd best eat something or at least get a cup of coffee, since he had no idea how long the trip would take or when he'd get a chance to eat again. He bolted down a couple pieces of toast and coffee, then hurried downstairs with his bags at seven forty-five.

Kerrick was waiting for him. "Good morning, sir. I hope you slept well."

"Well enough, I suppose."

"Which is to say very little, yes?" Kerrick smiled knowingly. "Well, that's fairly common, so I suppose you'd best get used to it. Let me take those bags for you."

"It's all right. I've got them."

"Good enough. The car's waiting for you out front."

Alastair wondered again if Kerrick would be joining them at the country house, but didn't ask. He followed him outside, where a staid, shining black Mercedes sedan waited. It was a lovely car, many years old but immaculately maintained. A man Alastair couldn't see clearly sat behind the wheel.

"Right, then," Kerrick said after they'd stowed Alastair's bags in the trunk and he'd settled into the back seat. "You're off. I'll see you again this evening, after I've seen to things here." He patted the car's fender and the driver pulled smoothly out into traffic.

Alastair sat back and watched the drizzly London scenery crawl by as the driver picked his way through the heavy traffic. From his position, Alastair couldn't get a good look at the man, other than to tell he was probably in his forties, pale and dark-haired, and dressed in a severe black suit. He'd half expected a formal chauffeur's uniform, but perhaps even the lofty and ultra-traditional Desmond didn't go *that* far.

The man didn't seem inclined to talk, so Alastair took the opportunity to think over the events of the previous day. His father hadn't done much to prepare him for his eventual apprenticeship (probably thinking he still had three more years to do so), but he doubted it would have been anything like this if he'd ended up studying with Walter Yarborough. He thought about Barrow—what had the other boys been told about why he'd suddenly disappeared? Did they think he'd been expelled? *Had* he been expelled? His father hadn't shared the details of the inquiry with him, but he supposed it didn't matter. If he failed with Desmond, his father would no doubt send him somewhere else, or arrange for a private tutor until he was old enough to either start with Yarborough or enter University.

He pulled one of the books Desmond had given him from his briefcase and opened it to where he'd left off last night. He was *not* going to fail! That wasn't an option. He'd never be able to face his father again if he did—not after he himself had taken such a big risk by trying to learn magic on his own, and after his father had convinced Desmond to take him on.

He only looked up occasionally from his books during the hour-long trip once they'd gotten out of London proper. The weather didn't improve; in fact, the rain fell harder as the driver maintained a steady pace on the motorway. Eventually they left the main road and wound their way through a series of increasingly narrower lanes bordered by rolling hills, forest, and hedgerows.

The Mercedes pulled up in front of a set of high, wrought-iron gates set into a stone wall. Though the driver did not appear to call or otherwise announce their presence, after a few seconds the gates swung inward to admit them. The driver didn't seem at all fazed by this, but merely drove in and continued up a meandering lane through a thicket of trees.

Alastair put the book away, finally taking an interest in his surroundings. It took nearly five minutes once they'd passed the gates before they rounded a last bend and the house rose into view.

Alastair couldn't help gaping a little, gripping the back of the seat in front of him to take the place in. He was no stranger to large houses—his own ancestral home in Surrey was a vast, rambling thing on a wooded estate not entirely unlike this one—but the sheer size and grandness of this place made the Stone home look like a two-bedroom council flat in Hackney.

For one thing, it was in a lot better repair than his own home. Rising three stories and stretching out on both sides of a central main hall, it was at least twice the size of the place in Surrey. Alastair wondered how long it would take to get from one side of it to the other. It must cost a fortune to heat.

The driver pulled up in front of a set of marble steps leading to the front door. "Here we are, sir. May I help you with your bags?"

"Er—no. Thank you. I'll be fine." Alastair scrambled out with his briefcase and smaller bag. While he waited for the driver to open the trunk and retrieve his larger one, he wondered if anyone was waiting for his arrival, or if he'd have to knock on the door as if he were selling encyclopedias or something.

He needn't have worried. A moment later, one of the elaborately carved front doors opened and a man in a formal suit similar to the one Kerrick had worn emerged. "Good morning, Mr. Stone. Welcome to Caventhorne Hall."

The man didn't look as cheerful as Kerrick, but at least he didn't look like he'd swallowed a lemon. He was perhaps forty-five, with sandy, short-cut hair, a neat moustache, and a profile that had probably been sharp at some point but was now softened by extra weight. "Thank you," Alastair said.

"I'm Samuels, the estate steward. Let me get your bags, and I'll show you to your room so you can get yourself settled in."

Alastair kept hold of his briefcase, but let the man take the other bags. "Is Mr. Desmond here?"

"He'll arrive later this afternoon, sir. Please follow me."

Samuels led the way through a formal entry hall into a massive great room, and then up a flight of stairs to the top floor. Alastair did his best to take the place in, but he had had hurry to keep up with the steward's quick steps. His overall impression was that William Desmond wasn't simply well-off—he was wealthy on a scale Alastair had never seen before. Once again, he wondered how old his prospective master was, and how many holdings and business dealings he must be involved with.

Samuels hurried down a hallway lined with paintings and pushed open a door at the end. "Here we are, sir. Your things have arrived already. You'll have until three o'clock to un-pack and settle in before Mr. Desmond wishes to see you. Your lavatory is across the hall. Will you be needing any fur-ther assistance?"

Alastair didn't know what he'd been expecting, but he supposed somewhere in the back of his mind, he'd thought his room would be decorated similarly to what he'd seen so far in the rest of the place: perhaps an ornate wooden bed, heavy curtains, antique furniture. Maybe even some priceless work of art hanging on the wall.

As soon as he saw it, he realized he should have known better.

The room wasn't exactly bare. In fact, it was quite ser-viceable, and included all the things one might expect a bedroom to have: a bed, a nightstand, a chest of drawers, an armoire, a desk, a lamp, and a bookshelf. It even had a rug, though it was a simple brown one rather than any kind of priceless Persian.

Alastair took the place in quickly: the bare walls, the simple bedspread, the sturdy but unremarkable furniture, all of it of fine construction and possibly antique, but simple and functional. It looked a bit like the cell of a well-to-do monk.

Or his dorm room back at Barrow, before he'd done anything to decorate it.

I'm not here for luxury, he reminded himself. *I'm here to learn magic.*

He realized Samuels was still standing in the doorway, waiting for an answer. "Er—no. Thank you. I'll be fine. Where will I find Mr. Desmond?"

"I'll come back for you at two forty-five to show you to his study. Will that be all, sir?"

Already, Alastair was growing uncomfortable with the level of formality around here. Despite the fact that almost all the boys at Barrow came from wealthy families, nobody was coddled or called "sir" there—and Aubrey, while he did refer to both Alastair and his father that way, was more like a sarcastic but kindly uncle than a servant. Right now, all Alastair wanted was to have a little time to himself to decompress and come to terms with the circumstances of his new life. "I'm fine, thanks."

I am fine. Once I talk to Desmond and we get started with magic training, none of the rest of this will matter.

"Very good, sir. Later on, after you've settled in and spoken with Mr. Desmond, I'll arrange for a more formal tour. If you need anything, there's an intercom by your desk."

Alastair hadn't noticed that. Given the rest of the place, he'd have expected one of those old-fashioned bell pulls. "Got it. Thanks."

Samuels departed, closing the door behind him and leaving Alastair standing in the middle of his new home. *At least for the next month,* his cynical mind supplied helpfully. *Unless I wash out before then.*

Angrily, he shoved the thought aside and attacked the task of getting unpacked. As Samuels had said, his things had arrived: a neat stack of three boxes stood in one corner of the room; another small one, labeled *BOOKS,* sat on the desk, and when he opened the armoire door he found his jackets, shirts, and trousers already hung neatly inside.

By the time he'd put the rest of his clothes in the armoire and dresser drawers, installed his toiletries in the lavatory (which was as spartan as the bedroom), and put his notebooks, pens, and other school supplies in the desk, it was barely one o'clock.

Last, he opened the box of books and began arranging them on the shelf. There weren't many—he shelved a few textbooks he'd brought from his Barrow stash in case his tutor wanted to see how far along he was in his studies, then paused a moment, staring down into the box as memories returned.

Before he'd headed off on another trip two days before Alastair was set to meet Desmond, Orion Stone had called his son once more into his study. "I've got something for you," he said.

Alastair had no idea what it might be—though his father always made sure he had everything he needed, he was rarely the spontaneous gift-giving type. "Sir?"

Stone levitated a box from behind his desk and settled it on the top. "I was going to give you these when you started your apprenticeship—I never thought it might be this soon."

Holding his breath, Alastair opened the box to discover a series of large tomes bound in fine brown leather, each one with a title in either Latin or some language that looked like Latin, but wasn't quite. They were clearly very old, but had been immaculately maintained.

He glanced up at his father in surprise, then carefully removed one of the volumes and opened it to a random page. On it was an elaborate diagram, along with what looked like a spell formula and list of reagents.

Stone favored Alastair with one of his rare small smiles. "It's quite basic as magical libraries go—someday you'll have all of mine, of course, but you'll want to add your own touches as your experience grows. These are some introductory reference books that got me started during my own apprenticeship. You should find the formulae useful through at least your second year, and some of the reference material longer than that."

Alastair's grip had tightened on the book he held, and he struggled not to let his reaction reach his face. His father wasn't a fan of emotional displays, but more than anything else, the gift of these books—books his own father had used during *his* apprenticeship, and possibly his grandfather before that—had made the whole thing real to him in a way nothing else had so far.

"Thank you, sir," he said softly, closing the book and putting it back in the box. "I'll take good care of them."

"I know you will." And then the moment had passed and he was off again, clapping his son on the shoulder as he swept by on his way out, leaving Alastair to gaze down at the box, his mind whirling with possibilities.

Now, he carefully gave the volumes pride of place on the top shelf, along with one of the two Desmond had lent him yesterday. He still had nearly two hours before Samuels would return, and as much as he might enjoy doing a bit of exploration on his own, he thought that might be best saved for after he'd spoken with Desmond. *Just hold it together for a month,* he told himself as he sat down at the desk and opened the other book. Once Desmond had accepted him as a formal apprentice, he was sure things had to loosen up at least somewhat.

Nobody could be that stiff and formal constantly.

He hoped.

| CHAPTER SEVEN

S AMUELS KNOCKED ON ALASTAIR'S DOOR promptly at two forty-five.

"Mr. Desmond is waiting for you, sir. You'll be dining later this evening, after your session."

Alastair put the book aside and followed the steward down the hall toward the stairway. They descended to the ground floor, crossed the great room, and headed down another hall.

Alastair was surprised when Samuels stopped in front of a lift with the same carved wooden doors as he'd seen around the rest of the place. "Where are we going?"

"To Mr. Desmond's workroom," he said. He hit a button; when the door slid smoothly open, he stood aside and motioned Alastair in. "Just down the hall when the doors open, sir. You can't miss it."

Alastair stepped slowly inside and the doors closed behind him. After a moment, the lift headed downward, opening a moment later on another hallway. Alastair took in the richly paneled walls; instead of being lined with fine paintings, they featured elaborately framed scrolls with magical sigils, ritual diagrams, and artwork depicting ancient people performing what was obviously magic. He slowed to take each of them in as he walked down the carpeted hallway toward the only door, but didn't take long. He could look at them in more detail later, and it wouldn't pay to keep Desmond waiting for their first session.

He paused a moment a few feet from the door, suddenly convinced he'd buttoned his shirt wrong, forgotten to zip up his trousers, or put on two mismatched shoes. A quick check assured him he hadn't done any of those things. *Stop it,* he told himself angrily. *He's just a man. Just like Dad. You're never going to succeed at this if you let him get to you this early.* He strode forward with fresh determination.

The doors didn't wait for him to knock, but swung open as he approached. He stepped inside and they closed behind him.

"Good afternoon, Mr. Stone," Desmond called. "I'm pleased to see you are prompt." He stood on the other side of the room, dressed in an immaculate dark blue suit in a classic style.

Alastair crossed the room, looking it over as he went. It was huge, probably covering at least the entire area of the great room above, with elegant support columns spaced at regular intervals. The walls were covered with the same dark paneling as the hallway had been, and some of them were lined with more shelves full of books. Off to one side was a work area with a table and a series of cubbies containing objects Alastair couldn't identify from this distance. Directly in front of him, between him and Desmond, the shining marble floor included an inlaid ritual circle nearly fifteen feet in diameter, its edges defined by a gold-colored metal. For all Alastair knew, it probably *was* gold.

He stopped a few feet in front of Desmond and clasped his hands behind his back. "Good afternoon, sir."

"Did Samuels get you settled in to your room?"

"Yes, sir."

"I trust you find it acceptable."

Alastair didn't miss the test in his tone. "Of course, sir."

The mage fixed him with a piercing stare. "Before we begin, Mr. Stone, I have a few things to tell you. I want you to listen carefully. Do you understand?"

"Yes, sir."

"I already told you that I didn't want to take you on, and that I still think you're too young for this. But I've nonetheless agreed to give you a probationary period. That means that from now on, I will treat you as I would treat any of my apprentices, and I expect you will behave accordingly."

He seemed to be waiting for a response, so Alastair nodded. "Yes, sir. Of course."

"My apprentices are adults, or very nearly so. You may only be fifteen years old, but I warn you: I have no tolerance whatsoever for immaturity. That includes many things that might be considered normal teenage behavior. I trust your father informed you that becoming an apprentice would mean giving up certain freedoms you might otherwise enjoy?"

"Yes, sir."

"And you're prepared to accept that?"

"Yes, sir." Alastair didn't add that most of the 'freedoms' Desmond no doubt referred to were things he wouldn't have done even if he'd remained at Barrow.

"Your magical training will occur in the morning from eight until eleven a.m., and then again in the afternoon from three until six p.m. During the time when you are not attending training, you'll be free to pursue your own interests—but most of that time will likely be spent doing outside work for your magical and mundane studies. Weekends will be free, as will most weeknights, though there will be occasional additional sessions you will be expected to attend. As you progress in your apprenticeship, I will expect you to design your own independent study projects in your areas of particular interest, which you will pursue *only* after I've approved them. Do you understand?"

"Yes, sir." His father had not been exaggerating: this sounded like it would be orders of magnitude more work than he'd had at Barrow—but that wasn't necessarily a bad thing. He'd found Barrow's classes to be, for the most part, stiflingly dull.

Desmond's expression grew, if possible, even more grim. "You might have noticed my emphasis on the word *only*. Let me make it absolutely clear: you are *not* to pursue any magical activity outside the scope of what I've assigned you. That includes any additions or augmentations to the assignments I've given you. Do you understand?"

Alastair nodded. "Yes, sir. No experimentation. No outside projects." He wondered if Desmond had included that part because of his illicit activities at Barrow. That seemed odd, given that those activities were the very things that had brought him to Desmond's attention in the first place, but if the man had issues with improvisation, that was fine with him. At least at first, he'd probably be spending so much time trying to master the techniques he was supposed to be learning that he wouldn't have much for independent experimentation.

"Excellent. I want you to keep that in mind, because failing to heed my requirements in that regard—during the entire course of your apprenticeship, I might add—will be one of the swiftest and surest ways to end it. Do you understand?"

Alastair swallowed. This was apparently a bigger deal with Desmond than he'd thought. "Yes, sir. I understand. I'll do as you say."

"See that you do, Mr. Stone. Of course, aside from the prohibition on unauthorized study, much of this will not be a factor until after you've passed your probationary period. That period will be one month. During that time, if at any point I don't consider that you are making satisfactory progress, your talent fails to meet my expectations, or if your actions or behavior convince me that you don't have the maturity to pursue serious magical study, I will terminate your apprenticeship immediately."

"I won't disappoint you, sir."

"That remains to be seen, Mr. Stone. One more thing: As I said, you are taking on an adult's responsibility, and I will treat you as such. Therefore, you will have no curfews, nor will you be required to go to bed at any specific time or to participate in meals if you don't choose to. You are welcome to leave the house as you see fit, go where you like, and do what you like, within the limits of the law. But before you start to revel in your newfound freedoms, keep in mind that I reserve the right to end your apprenticeship early for any immature or irresponsible behavior. If you fail me, Mr. Stone, you won't last the month. Do I make myself clear?"

"You do, sir." Alastair hoped Desmond didn't notice the pounding of his heart. One chance—that was all he'd have. One chance to prove himself.

No pressure.

"Because of the accelerated nature of this probation period, your mundane studies will be put on hold for the month. I will expect you to keep up as best you can on your own. If you successfully pass your probation and I accept you as my apprentice, you will be provided with a tutor who will be responsible for your non-magical education. I trust you are both bright enough and responsible enough to keep up on your own until I make my decision."

"Yes, sir. Of course." It would be dead boring, having to pay attention to things like history and maths when all he wanted to do was learn magic, but it wouldn't be difficult. He'd read ahead in most of his textbooks already anyway.

"All right, then. Did you have a chance to peruse the books I gave you?"

"Yes, sir."

"How far were you able to progress?"

Alastair wondered if he should have brought them with him. "I've finished an initial read through the one with the sigils and ritual diagrams, sir. I'm still working on the history book."

Desmond made no sign that he approved or disapproved of Alastair's progress, nor did he ask any questions. "Finish reading those books, and then I will give you others. I expect my apprentices to have a strong grounding in theory—there's no point in knowing how to do something if you don't know *why* it works the way it does. If you are familiar with the underlying principles of magic, you will then be able to design your own techniques—either basing them on existing work or creating something entirely new. That will be one of your independent study projects, if you pass your probation. Now, then." He stopped pacing and faced Alastair. "You've mentioned that you can use magical sight."

"Intermittently, sir."

"Describe my aura."

Alastair's heart pounded harder. In the past, the only time he'd been able to get the sight to work was when he was alone, looking at his own aura. He'd managed that four times over the course of the last couple of months, but each time had been almost by accident, as he'd somehow slipped into the proper frame of mind without any idea of how he'd done it.

He swallowed, took several centering breaths, and closed his eyes for a moment, then looked at Desmond. The only reference material he'd been able to find in his father's library about the process had mentioned that you had to shift your perceptions in much the same way a mundane would look at an optical illusion—the type, for example, where if you looked at it one way it was an old woman, but another way showed a young one. He studied Desmond, noting the fine cut of his suit, the way his hair was almost preternaturally in place, the spotless shine of his shoes. He avoided looking into the man's icy blue eyes: he was nervous enough without watching Desmond stare at him.

As time ticked on and nothing changed, his heart beat even faster. He felt a thin sheen of sweat forming on his forehead. Would Desmond chuck him out already for his failure to master such a basic technique?

"Well, Mr. Stone?"

Alastair let his breath out in a rush when he realized he'd been holding it. "I'm…sorry, sir. I've only been able to get it to work a few times, and only on myself."

Desmond didn't look surprised; Alastair couldn't figure out whether that was because it confirmed his suspicions or because he didn't expect him to be able to do it yet. "How are you attempting to initiate the sight?" Desmond asked.

"My references said to…sort of treat it like an optical illusion," he said.

"That is a good start," Desmond said. "But not sufficient. You must concentrate on the essence of your subject. Don't look at the details—the moment you start looking at details, you'll never get it. A being's aura is associated with his inner essence, not his outward trappings. Do you understand?"

"I…think so, sir. Let me try it again."

"Remember—don't focus on the details. Clear your mind, and try to see your subject as more of a general concept than a collection of individual parts."

Alastair resisted the urge to tug at his collar. He took another breath, closed his eyes again to center himself, and then looked at Desmond once more. This time, he consciously avoided looking at things like his suit or his shoes. He shifted his gaze to focus a little past the man, so he could see his basic form but not any of the specifics about him. He let his mind drift over what he knew of Desmond's essence— intelligent, disciplined, unyielding—and tried not to let stressful thoughts of what might happen to him if he failed sneak in.

For several long moments, he was sure it wouldn't work. He saw nothing but Desmond's somewhat blurry form in front of him, standing still, facing him.

But then—

—was that just his eyes playing tricks on him, or was Desmond's body suddenly wreathed in a brilliant gold nimbus of energy?

Startled, he blinked, and the nimbus winked off. Or had he even seen it at all?

"Mr. Stone? Did you see something?" Desmond's voice was calm.

"I—think so, sir. I'm not certain."

"Don't keep me in suspense, then. What do you think you saw?"

"Just for a moment, I thought I saw gold."

Desmond nodded. "Good. A good start. But you're not finished yet. Try again. Try to keep your concentration focused more this time. By way of encouragement, I will tell you that this technique, once you get the trick of it, is not something you'll have trouble with in the future. To use a crude popular analogy, it is similar to learning to ride a bicycle."

Alastair quickly squelched a traitorous mental image of William Desmond tooling down the streets of London on a ten-speed, and focused his thoughts once more. For a moment he wasn't sure what Desmond had meant about his 'not being finished,' but then his mind went back to the times he'd seen his own aura. It hadn't been a single color, but a mix of two: purple closest to his body, and a thinner stripe of gold farther out. Maybe Desmond had more than one color too.

He went through his process again, looking past Desmond's body and using his meditation technique to clear the stray thoughts from his mind.

This time, the golden nimbus showed up faster. Bright and strong, it extended more than a foot from Desmond's body. Alastair focused on the edges, taking a moment to re-establish his calm, and after a moment, a second band of electric blue shimmered into being. It was harder to see, both because of the gold part's glare and because it didn't stand out as well against the dark paneling and the floor, but it was definitely there, pulsing like a living thing all its own. It was beautiful. The interplay of the two colors dazzled him, and he didn't want to look away—

"Mr. Stone!" Desmond's sharp voice broke into his concentration.

He jumped, startled, and the pulsating aura winked off as if he'd hit a light switch. "Er—yes, sir. Sorry, sir."

Desmond didn't look angry. He watched Alastair silently, arms crossed over his chest. "I trust your efforts were a bit more fruitful this time?"

He nodded. "Yes, sir. Your aura is bright gold closest to your body, and a sort of electric blue farther out."

"Well done, Mr. Stone. Now—look again."

Alastair did as he was told, sure he'd have no trouble re-producing the steps this time. Desmond was right—once you got the hang of it, you just had to—

Nothing happened. Desmond's aura did not reappear.

Alastair tried again. He did everything he'd done last time, but saw no sign of the gold or the blue. Frustrated, he clenched his fists and focused harder. A dull ache formed in the back of his head.

"What's the matter, Mr. Stone?"

"I—can't get it back, sir."

The brilliant aura sprang into being. Alastair took a step back, surprised. "What—?"

"An advanced technique," Desmond said. "When you are fully trained, you will be able to hide your aura—or even disguise it. I wanted to show you it was possible."

"Yes, sir." Alastair thought it was a bit unfair, when he was only just learning to see the things in the first place, to fool him like that, but he reminded himself never to form any expectations about Desmond. Just take things as they came— that was looking like the only way to survive with this man. He rubbed at his forehead.

"Does your head hurt?"

He nodded. "A little, sir. Nothing to worry about."

"No," Desmond agreed. "You'd best get used to headaches, especially when you're starting out. You're working muscles you've never worked before, so a certain strain is to be expected. I won't push you too hard today. And in any case, there is more to apprenticeship than practicing magical techniques. Come with me."

Alastair followed him over to a corner containing a series of crammed bookshelves. "This will be your library, Mr. Stone. Each of the books here includes information about topics and techniques we will be studying during the early part of your apprenticeship."

Alastair stared at them, his gaze skipping over their spines. There must have been at least a thousand volumes here, ranging from ancient leather-bound tomes to a few modern hardcovers in dust jackets and even some brightly colored paperbacks. Did Desmond expect him to read them all?

Before he could say anything, Desmond raised his hands and gestured. One by one, each floor-to-ceiling shelf's collection of books flew out, shifted themselves around in midair, and landed in untidy piles. As Alastair continued to stare, shocked, he did the same thing with the other shelves until all the books were jumbled in a massive mound on the marble floor.

Desmond offered him a challenging gaze, as if expecting him to say something.

He didn't. Instead, he merely continued looking at the pile of books. He had a sinking feeling he knew what was coming next.

"As I said, Mr. Stone, this library will be at your disposal for the duration of your apprenticeship," Desmond said, looking rather like a cat who'd just gotten hold of a particularly tasty canary. "No two mages agree on how one's library should be organized. Therefore, your next assignment is to organize yours. Examine each book, sort them in a way that makes sense to you, and reshelve them. I will not offer an opinion as to your organizational methods, but I will expect you to be able to put your hands on any book in your library in a few seconds' time. Understood?"

Alastair regarded the books with dismayed fascination. It would take him days to get all that sorted out...but how many interesting books and how much magical knowledge were likely to reside in that pile? "Yes, sir."

"I hope they've been teaching you Latin in that school of yours. Many of the books are written in that language. Some are written in other languages, including magical ones—anything you can't read yet, just shelve them together at the end until you can determine where to put them."

He turned away from the piles, toward a closed wooden armoire along the adjacent wall. "You will have another task as well. None of the staff are permitted to enter my workroom, which means that its upkeep is not their responsibility. It now becomes yours." He waved, and the closet opened to reveal a series of brooms, dusters, buckets, and other cleaning products. "I'll expect you to keep the shelves dusted, the floor clean, and of course to tidy up after any assignments that might go awry. You'll find a large sink in the lavatory through that door," he added, pointing. "It shouldn't take you long each day, but there will be periodic inspections. Understood?"

"Yes, sir." So his apprenticeship would involve some grunt work as well as learning magic. He supposed it was sort of classic. A vision of himself dressed as Mickey Mouse and directing ambulatory brooms around a sodden floor flashed to mind, but for now, at least, he'd have to do things the old-fashioned way.

"All right, then. You've four hours left until dinner is served. Your assignments for today are to begin sorting and shelving the books and clean the place up a bit. We don't typically serve formal breakfast or lunch here, but the kitchen staff take requests within reason, and the basics are always available. In general, however, I'd advise you not to linger long over meals. You won't have time."

"Yes, sir." That wouldn't be a problem. He often forgot to eat or bolted something down from the vending machines when busy on a project at Barrow.

"One more assignment you might find more interesting: you'll need to introduce yourself to the household staff and become acquainted with them, so by tomorrow morning I'll expect a report from you including the name of each person, his or her position, and the appearance of his or her aura. Kerrick will arrive shortly; you can ask him to give you a tour of the house and introduce you."

"Yes, sir." That one might prove a bit more challenging, and not because he didn't think he could view the auras. He was already fairly certain that Desmond's comment about riding a bicycle was correct. No, the challenging part would be interacting with the staff. Meeting new people wasn't his favorite thing to do. At least Kerrick was here now, so he didn't have to ask Samuels to introduce him. The steward was far too formal and stuffy for his tastes. "Are—they expecting me to be staring at them, sir?"

"Believe me, Mr. Stone, a bit of staring is one of the least odd things they'll be expecting from you."

Oh. Well, that was…encouraging. Maybe. "Understood, sir. Thank you."

Alastair barely got a quarter of the way through sorting and shelving the books before he glanced at his watch and discovered it was already six forty-five. That meant he'd only have half an hour to tidy up before he had to be upstairs for dinner.

Aside from the week before he'd headed to Desmond's, he'd never technically been allowed in his father's library; the book he'd borrowed to work on his ritual at Barrow had been taken surreptitiously, without knowledge or consent. Now, here were a thousand or more books, every one of them about some aspect of magic—its history, its study, or its applications. There were dictionaries, reference books, workbooks, books of formulae, biographies…each time he picked one up and riffled through it, his curiosity grew. At first he'd set a few aside, planning to take them back to his room with him for further study. But when his stack grew to twenty volumes and he'd barely worked his way through fifty, he changed his plan. He'd just leave them here for now—if he did what Desmond had ordered him to do, he should have the whole thing organized so he could find anything quickly.

Even so, he'd moved a lot slower than he'd planned to. This wasn't good. The books still littered the floor, though he'd managed to start several stacks alongside the heap. He hadn't done any of the cleaning yet. He wasn't sure what would happen if he skipped his first dinner at Caventhorne, despite Desmond's assurance that he wouldn't be required to attend meals if he chose not to. And, to top things off, he'd forgotten to ask Desmond where to meet Kerrick.

Brilliant, Stone, he thought. *You're off to a great start.*

Hastily, he gathered a couple of his stacks and returned them to two different bookshelves. He wasn't sure he'd keep that sorting method, but for now at least he was following the letter, if not the spirit, of Desmond's directive: begin sorting and shelving the books.

He took a quick glanced around the room, hoping Desmond wouldn't come back here to check on things until he'd had more time to make progress later this evening, then hurried toward the armoire full of cleaning supplies. He wouldn't have time to do much now, but at least he could manage a bit of dusting.

He needn't have worried about Kerrick—he found the man in the great room when he took the lift back up to the ground floor a half-hour later. "Ah, sir," Kerrick said, smiling. "I was beginning to wonder if you'd lost track of time."

"I almost did," he said. "Can you show me where the dining room is? Mr. Desmond said dinner was at seven-thirty."

"Of course, sir. Mr. Desmond will be out for the evening, so he asked me to dine with you a bit more informally, if that's all right. He thought I might be able to answer any questions you might have about the nonmagical aspects of life around here."

Alastair tried not to let his relief show—both that he wouldn't have to eat his first meal in this huge, formal place alone, and that he wouldn't have to eat it sitting across from the stern, judgmental scrutiny of William Desmond. "That's brilliant. I'd enjoy the company—and the answers."

Kerrick chuckled and indicated for Alastair to follow him. "This way, then. I'd imagine this is all quite an upheaval for you."

He wasn't quite sure how to answer that. "In a way," he said at last. "Bit more formal than I'm used to—and given who my father is, that's saying something."

"This place is likely a bit more formal than almost *anyone* is used to," Kerrick said wryly, leading the way down yet another hallway and into a long, narrow dining room featuring a table twice the size of the one at the London house. Two places had been set halfway down its length, one on each side. "If you'll excuse me a moment, I'll let the kitchen know you're here. Please, sit down. By the way," he added, "just a tip I might offer, if I may: It's quite all right tonight, of course, but on nights when you're to be dining with Mr.

Desmond, he prefers—well—" He gestured in Alastair's general direction and appeared to struggle for the right words.

Alastair looked down at himself and sighed. He'd been so focused on sorting through the massive stacks of books and doing as much tidying up as he could manage in the brief time he'd had left that he hadn't paid any attention to his appearance. His white shirt was streaked with dust, his shirttail was coming untucked, and he was sure his hair must be more of a rat's nest than usual. "I'm sorry," he said, forcing himself not to stuff his shirttail back in before Kerrick departed. "I'll make sure it won't happen again."

Kerrick's expression settled back to its normal pleasantness. "Don't worry about it, sir. Really. Believe me, I've seen older apprentices than you get even more unsettled during their first few encounters with Mr. Desmond. He's—quite a formidable person. You're doing fine. Just think of me as a sort of...buffer between the two of you, to help you adjust to life around here as easily as possible."

"I do appreciate that," Alastair said, and meant it.

"Right, then. Sit down, please, and let me see to dinner, and then you can ask your questions."

Alastair fixed his shirt, tried his best to brush off the worst of the dust, and ran his fingers through the front of his hair before choosing the spot on the far side of the table. Left alone, he took an interest in his surroundings.

Desmond definitely wasn't a fan of your typical posh-and-boring upper class decorating style. Alastair was sure all the items hanging in the dining room, from paintings to odd-looking items couldn't identify, were both very old and very valuable, but he didn't see any standard pastoral scenes or coats of arms. Instead, the paintings depicted stern-looking men and women dressed in clothes that didn't quite fit into a particular historical era, interior scenes that looked like the sanctums of rich old wizards, and scraps of scrolls written in languages he couldn't begin to identify. One object looked like a cross between a dagger and some kind of spear point made of an unusual, multicolored metal, and another appeared to be a round shield far too small to be useful to anyone larger than a toddler.

On a hunch, Alastair took a few deep breaths to calm himself, put his hands on the table, and tried to activate his magical sight. After a couple of failed attempts, the familiar purple-and gold aura sprang up around his hands. Without letting his gaze slip, he raised it to the walls.

None of the paintings glowed, but both the tiny shield and the odd weapon did—the former with a weak, pulsing blue nimbus, and the latter with a brighter red one that seemed to poke out in pointed shards around its outlines. A couple of the scroll fragments put off faint golden illumination.

"Sir?"

Alastair jumped, startled out of his focus as all the glows winked out. Kerrick had returned, followed by a white-clad woman pushing a cart. "Sorry—was just—" He waved vaguely toward the walls.

"Of course, sir. No need to explain."

The woman said nothing as she worked. She put covered plates down at Alastair's place and then at Kerrick's, followed by a crystal goblet and a wineglass at each setting. She finished up with a bottle of wine, a carafe of water, and a basket of bread, then bowed slightly and departed.

Alastair didn't remember his assignment until after she'd left, mentally kicking himself for not getting a look at her aura. He surreptitiously tried shifting back to magical sight again so he could look at Kerrick's, wondering if he could do it without the concentration ritual. To his surprise and delight, it worked immediately. He supposed Desmond must have been right about it being like riding a bike—it got easier each time he tried it. Kerrick's aura was a strong, clear medium blue, and extended about three inches from his body.

Kerrick must have noticed what he was doing, because he looked at him oddly. "Sir?"

"Sorry. Mr. Desmond gave me an assignment to look at everyone's auras."

"Ah. Of course. You must forgive me—it's been a while."

"After we're finished here, would you have time to introduce me to the rest of the staff? He wants a report by tomorrow morning."

"Certainly." He popped the cork on the wine bottle and indicated Alastair's glass.

Apparently Desmond wasn't kidding about treating him like an adult. On the one hand, a little wine might calm him down; on the other, it might be a test. And the last thing he needed was to have Desmond make a surprise appearance and find him at less than his sharpest. "I'll...just have water, thanks," he said, and poured himself a glass.

For a few minutes they said nothing as they ate. The fare was simple but exquisitely prepared, and Alastair, who hadn't had anything to eat since that morning, forced himself not to wolf it down. Instead, he thought about Kerrick's words until his curiosity finally got the better of him. "Kerrick..." he began tentatively.

"Yes, sir?"

"You said before that it had been a while since you've had apprentices around here looking at auras. It reminded me of something my father told me when I first found out I'd be coming here."

"What is that?"

Alastair took another sip of water to hide his apprehension. "He said that Mr. Desmond hadn't taken an apprentice in many years, and that he was quite surprised he even agreed to give me a trial."

For several seconds that stretched out longer than they should have, Kerrick didn't reply. "I must admit I was surprised as well," he said at last.

"Surprised that he decided to take an apprentice—well, a trial one, anyway—at all, or that he took one so young?"

"Both, actually." He set his wineglass down.

Alastair stared down at his now-cleared plate. He wanted to ask Kerrick another question—whether Desmond's long period without an apprentice had anything to do with the one who'd died—but Kerrick had already told him in his oh-so-polite way that that subject was off limits. Instead, he asked, "Why do you suppose he did it, then? Does he know my father?"

A sudden thought knifed at him: his father was, as far as he knew, powerful and influential in Britain's magical community. What if Desmond owed him a favor, and that was the only reason he'd agreed to give Alastair a shot? What if this whole thing was an elaborate ruse, with Desmond playing along long enough to make it seem as if he'd devoted sufficient attention to the trial before unceremoniously terminating it?

"I...don't think he does," Kerrick said. He seemed relieved, as if he'd worked out Alastair's other question and was glad he didn't have to tell him once again to keep his nose where it belonged. "I believe when your father came to speak with him, it was the first time they had formally met. Although I'm sure they've encountered each other at various functions over the years."

"I suppose it would be hard not to." Alastair's father had been adamant about not allowing him access to the practical aspects of magic too young, but he couldn't help picking up a working familiarity with the way British magical society operated. For the most part, the power was concentrated in a few old families, along with a smattering of unaffiliated but highly talented individuals. No formal structure or governing body, but definitely a meritocracy as far as prestige went. Orion Stone had to be somewhere near the top, and William Desmond was clearly even higher.

That still hadn't answered Alastair's question, though, and he was sure Kerrick knew it. He waited.

For a few beats, Kerrick tried to wait him out. Then, as if realizing it wouldn't work, he sighed and spread his hands. "Sir, I would never presume to speculate about Mr. Desmond's motives. As I mentioned before—if he agreed to give you a trial, he must have seen something in you that he found worthwhile. If you're worried that this is some sort of sham arrangement cooked up by Mr. Desmond and your father, I can give you reasonable assurance that it isn't the case."

Alastair couldn't help looking startled that Kerrick had zeroed in so quickly on his fear. Was the man withholding the truth about some magical talent he might possess, at least enough to let him view auras as well?

"I've been in Mr. Desmond's employ for many years," Kerrick continued. "And one thing I can tell you with absolute certainty is that he never does anything he doesn't wish to do. Certainly not regarding his apprentices, who are of utmost importance to him. He can't be coerced, bribed, begged, or otherwise compelled to accept anyone he doesn't deem worthy of his time. So you can rest assured, Mr. Stone—if you're here, you've got the potential."

Alastair nodded. It was a relief to know—at least as much as Kerrick *could* know, anyway, since he was sure Desmond didn't tell even his most loyal manservant everything—that he wasn't here under false pretenses. But he hadn't really believed that anyway. He knew he had the chops, or at least the potential for them. But… "I suppose you won't be answering my other question, then. The one about why it's been so long since Mr. Desmond's taken an apprentice."

"I'm afraid not, sir. Partly at least because I don't entirely know myself. And if you'll accept another bit of unsolicited advice: I suggest you don't ask him. At least not until after you've passed your trial."

Alastair chuckled. "I've worked that one out on my own, I think."

Kerrick's easy smile, which had made itself scarce for most of the meal, returned. "Right, then. Good to hear. If you're finished with dinner, shall we go meet the staff?"

Their first stop was the kitchen. Kerrick took Alastair through the back door of the dining room and into a shining, spotless space full of substantial, old-fashioned appliances and granite surfaces. Alastair was surprised at its size at first, but then remembered the table in the dining room: this place looked fully capable of managing a formal meal big enough to feed everyone seated there, with some left over.

A man and a woman, both dressed in crisp chef's whites, bustled around checking on the contents of pots, peering into the oven, and chopping vegetables. They looked up as Kerrick and Alastair entered.

"Esteban and Gretchen, this is Alastair Stone. He's Mr. Desmond's new apprentice. Mr. Stone, this is Esteban, our head chef, and Gretchen, his assistant."

"Pleasure to meet you both," Alastair said.

"You are very young," Esteban said. He looked Alastair over, then glanced at Kerrick. "He is an apprentice?"

"He is," Kerrick said firmly.

While the two of them spoke, Alastair took the opportunity to clear his mind and once again shift his perceptions to the magical realm. Gretchen's aura was a vibrant yellow-orange, similar in composition and brightness to Kerrick's. Esteban's, on the other hand, was dimmer, its yellow-green clouded in a few spots. Alastair blinked, thinking he was losing his hold on the sight, but while the spots shifted around a bit, they didn't disappear.

Kerrick gently cleared his throat, and Alastair realized he'd been staring at Esteban for far too long to even be explained by 'apprentice assignment.'

"Sorry," he said. "I'm happy to meet you, and thank you for the meal tonight. It was excellent."

Gretchen smiled at him. "Come by any time," she said. "I had teenage boys of my own—I know how much they eat."

When they were back out of the kitchen, Alastair said, "Sorry about that. I guess I need more practice shifting between the senses." He pulled out a notebook and jotted down the chefs' names and the details of their auras.

"I wouldn't worry about it," Kerrick said. "We're all used to...oddities around here. Let's go meet the maids. They should be in their quarters this time of the evening."

The maids' quarters, and presumably those of the other staff members, were on the first floor in the opposite wing of the house from Alastair's room. Kerrick knocked on one of the doors, and after a moment it opened to reveal a woman in her late twenties. Her smile at Kerrick was a little broader than one might expect from mere work associates. "Hello, Kerrick," she said. Then her gaze fell on Alastair. "Ah, this must be the new one." She chuckled. "He's just a baby."

Another woman appeared behind her: older, chubby, with an open, friendly face. She held a coffee cup. Alastair could hear the sound of a television playing softly in the background.

"These are Natasha and Marie," Kerrick told Alastair, pointing first at the younger woman and then at the older one.

Alastair nodded and quickly introduced himself. Having them staring at him like that was making him uncomfortable, so he quickly shifted over and checked out their auras. Natasha's was an attractive blue-purple, and Marie's was a solid green.

They wished the two maids a good evening and left. Once again, Alastair took the opportunity to pull out his notebook and make notations. "How big is the staff here, anyway?"

"Not as large as you might expect—at least not the permanent staff." Kerrick led him back out through the great room. "Samuels is in charge—he's got an assistant, and we have the chefs, a head housekeeper, the maids, groundskeepers, a driver...if we need additional staff, we hire them on temporarily."

"But the permanent ones—they know about magic?"

"Most of them do, yes. As you probably know, there are numerous families in Britain with some tradition of magic. Mr. Desmond tries to choose the staff from among the non-magical members of those families whenever possible."

Alastair frowned. "And...they're all right with that? They don't resent it?"

"Oh, no, sir." He chuckled. "If you'll forgive me for saying so, I suspect you've had a rather sheltered upbringing. I understand you've spent most of your life away at school, surrounded by the sons of well-to-do families. But magic doesn't respect class. There are a number of old families with members who, while they're familiar with the magical tradition, are otherwise quite pleased to accept Mr. Desmond's generous offers."

Alastair knew that was true—and he also knew Kerrick was right. He *had* spent most of his life sheltered away from the realities of life. That was something he'd need to remedy, he decided. "I suppose I've got a lot to learn."

"That's why you're here, sir," Kerrick said. "Let's continue—I'm afraid I've still got some other duties I must attend to tonight, so we'll have to move along a bit."

For the next hour, Alastair got both a tour of the vast house and an introduction to the remainder of the staff. He hadn't been exaggerating his guess about how big the place was: most of the hour was spent tramping from one hallway to the next as Kerrick showed him the various locations in its three-story space. "Of course, there are areas Mr. Desmond will have to show you," he said when they'd returned at last to the great room. "You may have seen some of them already. But these are the...mundane bits." He smiled. "I hope you have a good memory—we're fresh out of maps. But if you get lost, just find a main hallway and eventually you'll get back to somewhere you recognize."

Alastair wasn't sure if he was joking—it was certainly possible he wasn't. "I'll try not to wander off into any secret portals or anything."

"Good call. We misplace more apprentices that way..."

Alastair glanced down at his notes, which were much more substantial now. In addition to the chefs and the maids, he'd met and catalogued the auras of three groundskeepers, the head housekeeper, Samuels the estate steward, and the driver. "There's still one more, right?" he asked Kerrick. "You said Samuels had an assistant."

"Ah. Yes, sir. That's Selby. I almost forgot about him." He thought a moment. "I believe you'll find him in the dining room, polishing some of the silver. I hope you'll forgive me, sir, but I'm afraid you'll have to speak with him on your own. As I said, I've some duties I must attend to before Mr. Desmond arrives for his evening meal."

"Not a problem. Thank you, Kerrick. I appreciate that you've taken your time to shepherd me around."

"Happy to do it, sir. Have a good evening."

Alastair paused in the doorway to the dining room. As Kerrick had indicated, a suit-clad young man sat at the far end of the dining table, a wooden box open in front of him, a rag in his hand. He appeared to be in his early to middle twenties, dark-haired and slim. From the look of things, he'd either just started the polishing job or was almost finished with it.

Alastair took the opportunity to examine Selby's aura as he worked; it was a deep, reddish purple. "Excuse me…" he said softly when he finished, not wanting to startle the man.

Selby didn't look startled. In fact, he looked as if he'd known Alastair had been there all along. His gaze came up slowly, examining Alastair with an upward glance and narrowed eyes. "Got what you need?" he asked. His voice held a faint hint of a drawl; Alastair couldn't tell if it was contempt.

"I'm sorry?"

"You were staring at me long enough. Either you were looking at my aura or else you're too shy to ask me out." His smile and his eyes were coldly courteous.

"Sorry," Alastair said. "You're not my type. And yes, I was looking at your aura." What was wrong with this guy? He was supposed to be working for Desmond, but that hardly seemed the sort of attitude the mage would condone in his staff members.

"Are you finished, then? I still have the rest of the silver to do before I return to my room."

"Er—yes. Sorry. Didn't mean to disturb you."

"Not a problem. You're not planning to run back to your master and tattle on me for being less than respectful to his new child prodigy, are you?"

Alastair narrowed his eyes. "Why would I do that? And what's your problem, anyway? I haven't done anything to you."

Selby shrugged. "No, I suppose you haven't. Now run along. I'm sure you've got something you're supposed to be doing."

"I do, yes." Alastair paused to make a note in his notebook, then left the way he'd come. How odd that the young man would dislike him already, when they'd barely met. "Child prodigy," he'd called him. Did he resent the fact that Desmond had taken on someone so young? Alastair remembered what Kerrick had said about Desmond's habit of hiring staff members from families familiar with magic—perhaps Selby was one of those.

Ah, well. He could deal with it. Not everybody was going to like him, and if Selby didn't, then that was the way it was. He certainly wasn't planning to do anything to suck up to the unpleasant young man.

| CHAPTER EIGHT

THE NEXT MORNING, ALASTAIR SHOWED UP at Desmond's workroom with half an hour to spare before his lesson was due to start. He stood studying the pile of books: he'd worked hard for nearly four hours last night, so it was smaller now, and better organized. Out of the thousand-odd books, about a quarter of them were back on their various shelves, and another quarter were stacked in neat columns on the floor next to the remainder. He still had a lot to do, but at least he felt like he was making progress.

He continued thinking about the books as he grabbed a duster from the closet and ran it over the shelves and the spines of the books he'd already put on them. Even after his efforts last night, he could see he'd missed a few spots. This place was going to give him a constant battle against dust—he'd have to set aside a bit of time at the end of each session to keep it under control.

"Good morning, Mr. Stone."

Alastair jumped. He hadn't heard the door open, nor any footsteps, but there was Desmond, all the way across the room from the entrance, watching him with that severe, imperious scrutiny that seemed to be his default facial expression.

"Good morning, sir." He hurried to put away the duster, then took his place in front of Desmond.

"I trust your first day went well." His gaze flicked sideways to the pile of books. "Making progress, I see."

"Yes, sir. I should have it finished in the next couple of days. Is that acceptable?"

"Have it done by tomorrow. And remember, I will be testing you on your ability to locate particular volumes."

By tomorrow. That would be tough—he'd have to stay up even later tonight to get that done, along with his mundane studies and whatever Desmond assigned him today. "Yes, sir," was all he said.

"Were you able to complete your other assignment?"

"Yes, sir." Alastair didn't need to pull out his notebook; he'd spent a few moments this morning going over the notes to ensure he could remember everyone's details.

"Your report, then, if you please."

"Kerrick's aura is blue, sir. The maids, Natasha and Marie, are a sort of bluish purple and solid green. Selby's is reddish purple. Esteban's is yellow-green with sort of dark spots. Gretchen's is yellowish orange. Samuels's is…"

Desmond held up a hand. "Describe Esteban's again."

"Er—" A creeping sensation crawled down his back. The chef's had been one of the first auras he'd examined during his tour—had he made a mistake? Maybe the spots were just shadows from the kitchen. "Yellow-green, sir."

"What did you mean about 'dark spots'?"

"Probably just an error, sir. Shadows or something."

"Describe them."

Alastair studied him for a moment. His face, as usual, was expressionless, but something in his eyes was odd.

"There were—two or three of them, near his abdomen. They moved around. Sort of…shifted. Do they mean something, sir?"

"Did you notice anything about the relative brightness of his aura compared to the others'?"

He thought about it, trying to remember exactly what it had looked like. "It might have been a bit dimmer, sir. Or else Gretchen's was brighter."

Desmond nodded once. "I see. Please continue."

A little flustered, Alastair nonetheless took a moment to order his thoughts, then rattled off the remainder of his report on the staff and their auras.

"Well done. Do you have anything else to report?"

Alastair thought about Selby and his oddly hostile behavior, but that was between the two of them. "No, sir."

Desmond's icy eyes bored into him for several seconds, but he didn't ask further questions. "All right, then. Today we will begin with a technique that every mage should master—a shield."

"A shield, sir?" Alastair had visions of himself and Desmond standing on opposite sides of the workroom, flinging fireballs at each other and blocking them with glowing magical barriers.

"Much of what we will be working on as time goes on—particularly if you pass your probation—has the potential to be highly dangerous. You must be able to protect yourself. We will proceed no further with the practical aspects of your studies until you can prove sufficiently to me that you can do so. So it is in your best interests to pay attention and to master the rudiments of this technique quickly."

"Yes, sir. I'm ready."

Desmond waved a hand and a chair slid across the floor. It came to rest facing him, about six feet away. "Sit down."

When Alastair had done so, he gestured again and a rolling blackboard came to a stop next to him. "All of the magic I will teach you," he said, "is centered on the will. On the mastery of the forces around you. As mages, we have the ability to affect these forces—to bend them to our will. But nature, Mr. Stone, is not eager to conform to our wishes. It will fight back, and if you haven't sufficient strength of will to oppose it, you will never be more than a mediocre practitioner at best." He began to pace. "Normally, my apprentices do not even begin to perform any sort of practical magic until they have been studying theory for months. I insist on a firm theoretical grounding, and I likewise insist that their understanding of the building blocks of magical formulae be airtight before I permit them to continue."

Alastair didn't answer. He wasn't sure why Desmond was telling him this.

"Since you are on probation, I must handle you differently. I can't waste time teaching you nothing but theory, only to have you fail the first time I try you with something practical. It would waste both our time. So instead, I will teach you a small number of practical techniques to help me determine if you have the talent and the will to proceed. Do you know what usually happens to mages who have strong talent but weak will, Mr. Stone?"

"No, sir."

"Most of them fail to progress beyond the basic levels of magic. Of those who do, many of them become black mages. You do know the difference between a black and a white mage, yes?"

"Yes, sir. White mages power their own magic, and black ones take power from others."

"Precisely. None of this 'good' and 'evil' rubbish. That's simplistic thinking. Black mages, when you get down to it, don't have the willpower to trust their own resources. Do you know what happens to mages who have strong will but weak talent?"

Alastair considered. "I suppose they might find the training process frustrating."

"They often do," Desmond agreed. "Occasionally they can become accomplished mages to the limit of their talent, but I won't train them. Many teachers will, but I find they require far more instruction and handholding than their prospects warrant."

He faced Alastair again. "So, your nonstandard curriculum for this month is designed so I can determine whether your will and your talent are at the levels I require."

He began drawing a series of diagrams and formulae on the blackboard. "The shield, Mr. Stone, is a tangible manifestation of your will. With it, you can block everything from a spell to a physical attack. If your will is strong enough, a good shield can save you from significant damage. For now, we will work with relatively harmless items, but as time goes on I will expect you to be able to handle more formidable threats."

Alastair nodded. He'd heard that good shields could stop bullets, or even protect you from being hit by a car. Was Desmond planning to shoot him? If so, he hoped it wouldn't be for a while.

"You mentioned that you were successful in producing a minor ward," Desmond said.

"Yes, sir."

"The principle of the shield is similar." He turned back to the diagram and began explaining the sigils and notes he'd written. After a time, he turned back. "The secret to a good shield is to hold this pattern in your mind and then project it outward, along with your desire to repel whatever is attempting to reach you. You do this by gathering energy from your own internal reserves. Do you understand the pattern?"

Alastair studied it for a moment. Desmond was right: it *was* similar to the ward he'd created. But the ward had taken him three days. He wouldn't have that kind of time if someone was taking shots at him. "I...think so, sir."

Desmond waved his hand, and a wicker basket flew from a shadowy corner of the room and landed on a nearby table. "Then we shall find out. Gather your concentration, and project your will outward."

Alastair did as he was told, trying to hold the complicated pattern in his mind. He had no idea if anything was actually happening. He'd never done any sort of instant technique like this, and he couldn't be sure—

Something hit him hard in the chest and bounced off.

He took a step back, startled, then looked down. Whatever it was, it hadn't hurt him as much as surprised him. He bent and picked it up. A beanbag. He glanced up at Desmond—

Another beanbag hit him, this time in the shoulder.

"I don't see your shield, Mr. Stone," Desmond said. "Try again. I'll give you a moment to compose yourself."

Alastair closed his eyes, heart pounding. *Just visualize the pattern, gather energy, and project your will.* Desmond made it sound so easy! He snatched a glance at the board again, trying to force himself to calm down, to visualize the pattern, to remember how he'd done the ward and figure out how it differed from this faster, more transient application. If he could only—

A beanbag smacked him in the forehead, hard.

Growling, he knocked it away with his hand.

Damn it, I'm failing already!

Is it fair for him to expect me to do this so quickly, though?

Fair *has nothing to do with it, you idiot. He doesn't give a damn about fair. You either do it or you're going home.*

"Mr. Stone…"

"Yes! Yes, just—give me a moment, please."

Desmond didn't look angry or perturbed. "You are overthinking the process, Mr. Stone. This is not a ward. In order for a shield to be effective, it must be near-instant in its execution. Consider the way you knocked the beanbag away when it hit you. This time, I want you to do that again, but *before* it hits you. Use your hand only—no magic."

Alastair blinked. That was odd, but if it meant he wasn't getting pegged in the head, he was willing to give it a shot. He faced Desmond and waited.

Desmond didn't move. The beanbag rocketed out of the basket and flew toward him, so fast he barely had time to react.

Fortunately, although he was rubbish at sport in general, one thing he did have going for him was fast reactions. Without thinking, he knocked the missile from the air before it hit him in the face.

"Good. Now picture the pattern clearly in your mind. Keep it there. The next time the beanbag comes toward you, project your will to deflect it. It's not enough simply to *desire* to deflect it. There is a difference between desire and will.

Desire is merely emotion. Will is power. The sooner you internalize that difference, the more progress we will make. You must—"

Without changing expression or position, Desmond sent another beanbag speeding toward Alastair. Startled, he fumbled with the pattern and it slipped from his mind. The beanbag slammed into his chest hard enough to knock him backward.

Panting through clenched teeth, he glared at Desmond. Right now, if will really *was* power, he felt as if he could will the entire basket of beanbags to hit the man in the face. But even as his anger rose, he knew it wasn't at Desmond. It was at himself.

Just like the ward, but faster. He gathered the pattern again, tapping into the same reserves he'd used when casting the ward. "Throw something else," he rasped.

"Excuse me?" Desmond asked.

"Throw something else," he repeated. He realized there was a snarl in his voice, but he didn't care. "Something *real*."

Desmond didn't argue. He didn't question or protest. A small wooden footstool streaked toward Alastair, its three legs pointed at his chest.

Alastair didn't let himself think this time. He already had the pattern in his mind. He'd already pulled the power. All that was left was the will.

Go!

It wasn't a very good shield. It was small, misshapen, and flared with a bright glow only a few inches in front of him.

But none of that mattered. It was a shield.

And it worked.

The footstool slammed into it, hard enough that Alastair was sure it would have hurt a lot more than a beanbag if he'd let it hit him. The shield blazed even brighter, then winked out.

The footstool hit the floor in front of him with a crash.

He joined it an instant later as his head exploded with an agony he'd never felt before. It felt as if Desmond had buried a cleaver in his skull. For a moment, all he could process was pain as black spots and bright, pointed red spikes danced in his vision. He writhed on the cold floor clutching his head, heedless of anything else around him. Desmond could have beaten him to death with the footstool, and he'd have been powerless to stop it.

"Mr. Stone?" Desmond's voice cut into the pain.

Alastair didn't answer. He felt wetness on his upper lip and licked it, revealing the sharp, coppery tang of blood.

"Mr. Stone." The voice was sharper this time.

Alastair unclenched, slowly stretching his legs out and pulling his hands away from his head. He rolled over on his back and looked up.

Desmond stood over him, hands at his sides. Next to him lay the shattered footstool; one of its legs was broken off.

The throbbing faded, at least a bit. With tentative care, he sat up and put a cold hand to his forehead.

Desmond offered him a crisp white handkerchief. "Stay seated until you feel ready to get up. There is no hurry."

Alastair took the handkerchief and swiped it across his lower face. It came away bloody. Eyes widening, he stared up at Desmond. Had he broken something in his brain? Given himself a stroke? Had that desperate little stunt ended his magical career before it even began?

"It's just a nosebleed," Desmond said. "It won't last long. How do you feel?"

Alastair pinched the handkerchief over his nose and tilted his head back. "Like someone tried to cut the top of my skull off."

"Quite understandable. What you're experiencing is the aftereffect of attempting to channel more magical power than your body can handle, coupled with the psychic feedback from the disruption of your shield."

"I—" He glanced at the broken footstool again, as the memory flooded back: he'd done it. He'd managed some kind of shield, and deflected the thing before it hit him. "The shield—"

"Yes, Mr. Stone. The shield." He waved his hand and, a glass of water floated over from some unseen corner of the room. "Drink this."

Alastair did as he was told, draining the glass while holding the handkerchief in place. After a moment longer he removed it, relieved to see the bleeding seemed to have stopped. He handed the glass to Desmond and slowly pulled himself to his feet, noting the bright red spatters decorating the front of his white shirt. His heart still pounded fast, and a drop of sweat ran down his forehead. He swiped it away with the non-bloody portion of the handkerchief.

"Why did you tell me to throw that footstool at you, Mr. Stone?" Desmond asked.

Alastair swallowed. It was hard to think through the pounding in his head. Was this another test? "I'm—sorry, sir. I thought I might get it better if there was an actual threat."

"Your shield was far too small. It barely stopped the footstool—it would have buckled instantly if faced with a threat that might have seriously injured you. As it is, you'll need to make it significantly more substantial, to prevent the exact sort of painful feedback you experienced today."

"Sir—" Alastair protested. What did this man *want*? Was nothing good enough for him?

"However," Desmond continued, "you showed an excellent grasp of the principles involved, and you executed my instructions beyond the level I could reasonably expect of an apprentice on his first day of training. I expect that, as you continue to refine the technique, you will produce something far more impressive in the weeks to come. Well done, Mr. Stone."

"Er—thank you, sir." Alastair's mind reeled. Had Desmond just given him praise? He didn't think the man ever did that. *Don't let it go to your head.* "Shall we…try it again?" He wasn't sure he could, not with his head pounding as hard as it was, but he was damned if he'd show weakness now.

"Not today. That was more than sufficient for the practical portion of our training for this morning. You understand the principle of the shield now, correct?"

As if he could ever forget it! "Yes, sir."

"Good. We shall spend another hour going over some theory you will need for your later lessons. Your assignments for today are to continue organizing your library and tidying the workroom, completing the reading I give you following this lesson, and doing whatever portion of your mundane studies you consider sufficient. This evening, we will spend more time on the shield."

"Yes, sir." Though he was disappointed they wouldn't be getting right back on the horse with practical magical training, Alastair had to admit he was relieved as well. His head still hurt, and he wanted nothing more than to lie down in a dark room until it stopped throbbing. But Desmond had said headaches would be part of his life during his apprenticeship, so he might as well get used to it.

Besides, he'd created a shield. On his first day. That had to be worth something.

Desmond pulled a chair over with a wave of his hand. "Sit down then, and let's get started."

| CHAPTER NINE

O VER THE NEXT TWO DAYS, Alastair began settling in to life at Caventhorne. To his surprise and delight, he discovered that once he'd gotten his mind around the necessary principles for the shield and conjured a few under Desmond's direction, he quickly gained skill with it. He still wasn't anywhere near ready to have Desmond start shooting guns or throwing armoires at him, but by the end of the second day he'd gotten to where he could cast the spell fast enough to deflect the beanbags consistently. Desmond began flinging a few at him randomly during his lessons, and aside from a couple that smacked him in the head, he managed to deal with the others. Maybe not with the level of elegance and skill of an experienced mage, but for two days in, he felt he wasn't doing half bad.

Perhaps he'd be able to handle this apprenticeship thing after all. The magic part was far more interesting than tidying the workroom or doing his mundane studies, without a doubt, but at least so far he was keeping up with Desmond's expectations of him. He'd even managed to finish cataloguing and shelving all the books in the library by Desmond's deadline, and passed his first test by retrieving requested books within the time his master allotted.

Things seemed to be going well, but he was certainly busier than he'd ever been at Barrow—and the constant unspoken fear of getting chucked out if he put a toe out of line didn't make the process any less stressful. With everything he had to manage, he felt like he was spinning a half-dozen explosive plates on sticks, and if he let even one drop he'd blow himself up. But his pride at how quickly he'd picked up the shield spell carried him through the rest.

On the third morning, that pride took its first blow.

When he arrived at the workroom, Desmond was nowhere to be seen. That was odd—usually his master was waiting when he arrived a little before the scheduled time, but this time the room was empty and dark.

He switched on the lights and immediately noticed the information on the board was different from what they'd been studying the previous day. Curious, he approached it and began scanning the figures and sigils, trying to make sense of them. All he could determine was that it looked like another spell formula, and possibly had something to do with light.

"Can you make anything of it, Mr. Stone?" Desmond's voice came from perhaps three feet behind him.

Alastair whirled, instinctively pulling up his newly-learned shield.

No one was there.

He dropped the shield. "Mr. Desmond?"

A beanbag streaked from the basket and slammed into his arm. He whirled again, this time shifting to magical sight.

Desmond's now familiar gold-and-blue aura sprang into sight, but it appeared only as a man-shaped outline. The other side of the room showed clearly through the part where Desmond's body should have been.

A second later, his master shimmered into view, clad as usual in a formal suit. "Good morning, Mr. Stone. Perhaps my demonstration might have given you a suggestion as to today's area of practical study?"

For a second he was stumped, but then a slow smile spread across his face. "You're going to teach me invisibility."

"Yes. A useful skill, though many find it difficult to maintain for more than a few moments. Once you master it, I will teach you another version—less effective, but easier to sustain." His expression grew stern. "Before we begin, however, know this: I will not tolerate any misuse of either of these spells in my home. You will under no circumstances use them to deceive, conceal yourself from, or spy on any of the staff, nor will you use them in any way that does not befit a gentleman. If I receive word that you've done so, your probation will be terminated immediately. Do you understand?"

"Yes, sir. Of course." Alastair was too intrigued by learning a new spell to be offended by Desmond's words—to be fair, teaching a teenage boy an invisibility spell at all represented a great deal of trust on his master's part.

"Good. Let's get started, then. Sit down."

Desmond spent the next hour explaining what he'd written on the board. Alastair paid close attention, and grasped the concepts quickly. This didn't look difficult at all. It was simply a matter of bending light to alter the perceptions of anyone who might be watching him. He was sure he'd catch on even faster than he had with the shield, since some of the concepts overlapped.

"All right, now try it," Desmond said at last. "Visualize the pattern I've shown you here, add power, and see how you do."

Alastair nearly leaped out of his chair in his eagerness. He studied the pattern on the board a moment longer, picturing it in his mind as he had for the shield, then gathered power, closed his eyes, and concentrated.

Was it working yet? He didn't feel any different, and there were no mirrors in the workroom.

"Whenever you are ready, Mr. Stone."

He opened his eyes. "Er—it didn't work, sir?"

Desmond's arms were crossed over his chest. He shook his head once.

All right, maybe this would be a little harder than he'd thought. This time he kept his eyes open as he repeated the steps, holding his arm out in front of himself. If he were invisible, would he be able to see his own body? He wasn't sure.

He held the pattern in his mind, heart pounding, and once again added the power.

He thought he saw his arm shimmer a little, but aside from that it remained frustratingly visible.

"Be patient, Mr. Stone. This is a difficult spell, and I don't expect you to get it right away. Take your time."

But I expect to get it right away, Alastair thought. He redoubled his efforts, pausing for another glance at the board. Nothing there was beyond his comprehension, so why couldn't he *do* it?

Half an hour later, he was barely closer to achieving his goal than he'd been when he'd started. He swiped his hair off his forehead in annoyance, trying to ignore the growing dull headache that had been blooming for the last fifteen minutes.

Desmond continued watching him, his expression calm and unreadable, occasionally offering a suggestion or a bit of encouragement.

Finally, though, he held up his hand. "All right, Mr. Stone. That's enough of that for today. Continue practicing on your own time, and we'll try it again tomorrow. Don't be discouraged—every mage is different in his affinity for different types of spells. For now, we'll continue with theory." He flipped the board over and began to write.

Alastair forced himself to concentrate on Desmond's lesson and took good notes, but despite his master's words, he *was* discouraged. The shield, once he'd gotten the hang of it, had come so easily for him. So had magical sight. He'd managed to produce both a minor ward and a detection ritual on his own, with nothing but books for guidance. Why couldn't he manage a simple invisibility spell?

When Desmond dismissed him at the end of his lesson, he trudged out of the workroom and took the lift upstairs feeling like he'd failed not just Desmond, but himself. All he wanted to do was retreat to his room and spend the rest of the afternoon in front of his mirror, working on the spell until he could manage it with the same ease as he did the others.

Reluctant wisdom prevailed, however: he wasn't going to get anywhere with this headache. Not to mention, he'd once again skipped breakfast, so he was starving. Lunch first, then if he felt better he might give the spell a few tries after.

He passed Selby in the great room on his way to the kitchen. The young man looked him up and down with his cool, appraising gaze. "Rough morning...sir?"

Alastair almost snapped a sarcastic reply, but realized that was probably what Selby was trying to goad him into.

Instead, he made a noncommittal grunt and swept by without further response. Perhaps later he could ask Kerrick about Selby, if he could figure out a way to do it without arousing suspicion.

To his surprise, he'd barely entered the kitchen when Esteban approached him. "Lunch is almost ready, sir," the chef said. "But I wanted to speak with you in private for a moment, if I may."

"Is something wrong?" Alastair tried to remember if he might have done anything to offend the chef, but so far everything he'd had to eat at the house had been delicious.

To his surprise, when Esteban spoke again, his voice shook a little. "I wanted to thank you, Mr. Stone."

"For what?"

"For what you did the other day. Mr. Desmond spoke with me and told me that you had spotted something odd in my aura. He examined it himself and came to the same conclusion. He suggested I visit my physician."

Alastair stared at him. Those spots he'd noticed *hadn't* just been shadows?

"I did as he suggested," Esteban continued, "and my doctor discovered a small irregularity that could easily have become a large irregularity if not caught early. I have you to thank for that."

"I—er—I'm glad to help," he said. He'd never thought of auras as being diagnostic tools before. "You're all right now, then?"

"I will be, yes," he said. "I'll be out for a couple of days to have a minor procedure, but Gretchen and the others can easily handle my duties in the meantime." He smiled. "I don't want to keep you—I know Mr. Desmond keeps you quite busy. But thank you."

Alastair returned to the dining room feeling a good deal better than he had when he'd arrived. Perhaps he couldn't manage the invisibility spell after one day's study, and that still dug at him—but given the choice, Esteban's words had done more to raise his mood than even praise from Desmond would have.

| CHAPTER TEN

O VER THE NEXT FEW DAYS, Alastair barely had time to sit down for five minutes between magical instruction and practice with Desmond, outside study, and keeping up with his mundane lessons.

To his growing frustration, he continued struggling with the invisibility spell. It took him two days to get to the point where he could even manage it at all, and even then he could only maintain it for about five seconds before it fizzled and died.

Desmond still didn't seem disturbed by this fact. "It appears we've identified one of your weak areas," was all he'd said. "As I told you before, every mage has them. I'll teach you the less powerful version, but we don't have time during your probationary period to focus on any given spell too much. Later on, if you pass, we'll have time to devote more effort to it."

Alastair's frustration didn't last too long, though. Over the next week and a half, he was learning too many other techniques—and succeeding at them—to spend much time dwelling on the one he couldn't manage. By the end of his second week, his growing repertoire included not only magical sight and a defensive shield, but a telekinetic spell that allowed him to pick up small items and move them around the room, an analysis spell he could use to examine magical items and artifacts to determine their purpose, and a more robust version of the same detection spell he'd taught himself back at Barrow (this one worked on people as well—Desmond had tested his mastery of it by instructing him to locate Kerrick, who'd hidden on the second floor of the carriage house).

Desmond also taught him how to adjust his shield to stop magical energy in addition to physical objects; Alastair had spent most of a three-hour session conjuring shields while Desmond threw various low-powered lightning, fire, concussion, and ice attacks at him.

"I suppose you aren't going to teach me any of those during my probation period," he'd asked, feeling confident enough that day to risk what he hoped Desmond would identify as a joke.

"You suppose correctly, Mr. Stone," was all he'd said, his deadpan expression never slipping.

Alastair didn't mind. He was getting this. He was learning magic. Despite the fact that he'd known since he was a small child that it would happen someday, and despite seeing his father use magic around the house as naturally as mundanes used tools, it had always seemed to be a "sometime in the future" thing—something he'd be able to do eventually, but not for a long time. Sort of like University.

But that wasn't true anymore. He was doing it *now*. Each morning when he woke up, he still had to reassure himself it wasn't just a dream.

Sure, he wasn't great at any of the spells yet. He couldn't lift anything heavier than a large book, and he still wasn't confident his shield spell could stop anything truly life-threatening—though if a marauding beanbag-slinger came after him, he was good to go. Even though he'd shown a much stronger affinity for the lesser version of the invisibility spell (Desmond called it a "disregarding spell," because it didn't so much make the caster invisible as prevent anyone from noticing him), he didn't think he had a future as a magical spy. But none of that mattered. With the single exception of the invisibility spell, he'd taken everything Desmond had thrown at him and managed to make something of it. That was surely worth a bit of pride.

He refused to admit it out loud, but he began to think he might just pull this off. He might just pass his probationary period, impress the lofty William Desmond enough to take him on as the youngest magical apprentice ever, and end up as a fully qualified mage by the time his peers had barely entered University.

Heady stuff.

But dangerous, too. *Don't get overconfident,* he told himself for what had to be the hundredth time as he headed down for one of his morning lessons. Taking anything for granted could be disastrous. It could be that, as well as he thought he was doing, he hadn't achieved the levels Desmond would require to continue training him. He had no way to know, since his master never revealed anything about his overall progress. So far he hadn't been brave enough to ask, not wanting to sound like an overeager child.

At the end of the lesson that day, Desmond closed up his books and erased the formulas he'd written on the blackboard. "I shall be away for the remainder of the day, Mr.

Stone, so our afternoon lesson will be cancelled. For today, your assignment will be a bit different."

"Yes, sir?" Alastair leaned forward eagerly. Would Desmond give him a new technique to study on his own?

"You've been working hard over these two weeks. Your progress so far has been quite satisfactory, but Kerrick informs me that you've been devoting all of your time to your studies, often to the detriment of your sleep and meals."

Alastair frowned, tilting his head. Desmond had yet to show any interest in anything but his magical training. True to what he'd said on their first day, he hadn't made any attempt to enforce a schedule on Alastair beyond the times designated for their morning and afternoon lessons together. "I'm fine, sir."

"No doubt you are. You are young and resilient, and your dedication to your studies is admirable. But if you are to succeed in your magical career—regardless of who teaches you—you must learn balance. Otherwise, you risk burning yourself out, which will ultimately delay or even jeopardize your progress. Do you understand?"

"Yes, sir." Alastair still wasn't sure where Desmond was going with this. Sure, he was tired most of the time, and often forgot about meals while buried in the depths of some fascinating bit of magical data, but it wasn't anything to worry about. Who had time to sleep when there was magic to be mastered?

"Good. Your assignment, then, is to take the rest of the day off. No magical study, no practice, no mundane lessons. The village of Wexley is about three miles north of here. I understand you enjoy running, or I believe Kerrick can find a bicycle you can borrow if you prefer. Go into town. Spend some time outdoors, and among other people."

Alastair's frown deepened. "That's…it, sir?"

"Yes, Mr. Stone," he said firmly. He waved his hand and the books returned to their places on the shelves. "You might not believe it now, in your eagerness to learn as much as you can as quickly as you can—but there are times when merely allowing your mind to drift without any demands on it can result in improved performance. So that is your assignment. You're not to think about magic or studies for the remainder of the day. We will resume tomorrow at the regular time. Off you go, now."

Alastair glanced at him sideways, but didn't protest. In truth, Desmond's words rankled—'off you go' was what you said to a child you wanted to get rid of, not an apprentice (even a probationary one) you'd promised to treat as an adult. He wondered if his aura showed his frustration as he left the room, but couldn't do anything about it. Desmond hadn't taught him that yet. It didn't matter anyway, since he wasn't making any effort to hide it.

Wexley was, as Desmond had said, about three miles up a narrow, meandering road bounded on both sides by low stone walls separating it from lands dominated by pleasant forests and rolling meadows. Alastair paused his easy jogging pace to catch his breath as he reached the outskirts, taking in the little village.

It was indeed little; he could see most of the main street from where he stood: shops, pubs, and quaint restaurants dominated the center of town, while more utilitarian businesses and residential areas ranged out on less-traveled lanes. It reminded him a lot of the village near his own home in Surrey, except even smaller and more boring.

What did Desmond expect him to do here, anyway? He glanced at his watch; it was a little after one o'clock. Perhaps if he just found a place to have lunch and then walked around a bit looking in shop windows, he could head back to Caventhorne and use the afternoon to catch up on some lost sleep. Desmond certainly couldn't fault him for that. His mind spun with the concepts his master had taught him today, and already he itched to get back to his lessons so he could put them to practical use. He still needed more practice on the invisibility spell, and he wasn't happy with either his endurance or his mental strength when using the telekinesis. For that matter, even his physics and history reading held more appeal to him than a dull afternoon window-shopping in some backwater little town.

But...Desmond had spoken, and at least for the remainder of the month, his word was law. Alastair zipped up his light jacket and set off at a fast walk toward the center of town.

Proximity didn't improve it. He supposed, objectively, that it was a nice enough little place, its quaint buildings earning their quaintness through legitimate age rather than the trend for putting up new structures designed to look like old ones. It was Saturday, so a number of people, both tourists and locals, strolled up and down the main street taking in the day and browsing the shops. The people he passed nodded politely, though he noticed a few who looked like locals gave him discreet, odd looks. Made sense, he supposed—in a village this small the locals probably all at least recognized each other, and an unfamiliar teenage boy not dressed like a tourist would stand out.

He spotted a fish and chips shop with a small outdoor seating area—as good a place as any to grab a quick lunch. Barely paying attention to the savory aromas and vinegary tang inside, he placed his order and carried it outside, finding an out-of-the-way table where he could watch people walking by while trying to obey Desmond's order not to occupy his mind with matters of magic or study.

It wasn't working. Halfway through his lunch he was already formulating ideas for how he might be able to improve his shield and wondering if he could get away with a little telekinesis practice before Desmond returned home.

"Thought you might want this," said a voice next to him, startling him from his thoughts.

"Er—sorry?" He glanced up; a girl about his age stood next to the table, holding up a bottle of malt vinegar. She wore jeans and a pink T-shirt covered by a white apron.

She pointed at the bottle on his table. "Yours was empty." She swapped the two, but didn't leave right away.

He studied her a moment. She had shoulder-length brown hair, a dusting of freckles across a slightly turned-up nose, and wide green eyes. "Thanks."

"Haven't seen you 'round here." She pulled a rag from her apron pocket and wiped down the other side of his table. "Visiting?"

"Sort of."

"How can you be 'sort of' visiting?" Her smile was open and amused. "You either are or you aren't. You sure don't *sound* like you're from around here."

"I'm here on a sort of…study thing."

She tilted her head and put the rag back, all pretense of working gone now. "Study thing?"

He nodded in the general direction of where he'd come from. "Do you know Caventhorne Hall?"

Her nose crinkled. "That odd old place up Greybriar? You're up *there*?"

"Is that what people here think—that it's odd?"

"It *is* odd. It's like the house that time forgot or something. Couple of my friends from school know people who've been hired on for events and such up there—they say it's huge and posh and formal, like something out of a history book or a museum. That true?"

Alastair shrugged. He should be annoyed by her probing questions, but instead he found them charming. Besides, curiosity wasn't a bad thing, and nothing she'd said had been wrong. "It's fairly posh," he admitted.

She took in his light jacket, tracksuit bottoms, and trainers. "Are you some sort of athlete or something? Is that what you're studying?"

"Hardly." He chuckled. "I'm Alastair Stone, by the way."

"That's a posh name to go with a posh house, for sure. I'm Madeleine Hill. My dad owns the chip shop. That's why I'm slaving away here on a Saturday instead of off getting in trouble with my mates." She rolled her eyes and grinned. "So, what *do* you study up at that spooky old place? I'd be afraid to spend the night there. Some people say it's haunted."

"It's not haunted." Not as far as he knew, anyway. But then again, with Desmond he really didn't know much of anything for sure. His master could be hiding a whole fleet of ghosts up there. "I'm...on a short leave from my regular school down south. For some specialized study."

"Oh, you're one of those."

"One of—those?"

"You know—brainiacs. Though you don't look like a nerd." She gave him another once-over, not hiding her appreciation of what she saw.

"What does a nerd look like, then?" he asked. Impulsively, he gestured toward the seat across from him. "Do you have time to sit down for a bit?"

She was about to answer when a booming male voice came from the doorway. "Get back in here, girl! There's tables to be cleaned!"

"Sorry," she said. "Can't. I get off at four, though, if you want to pop by later." The grinned at him over her shoulder and waved as she hurried off.

Alastair watched her go, then gathered up his lunch trash and tossed it in a nearby bin.

He almost didn't go back. He thought long and hard about it as he wandered the streets of the village with aimless steps, looking in shop windows without seeing or caring about what they contained.

It would be best, he knew, to just turn around and head back to Caventhorne right after lunch. He'd done what Desmond asked of him—he'd gotten out in the sun, gotten some exercise, and interacted with people who knew nothing about magic. He'd let his mind wander, at least as much as it was possible, and tried his best not to think about spells, techniques, rituals, or even his mundane homework.

That was enough, right? If he hurried, he could get back to the house and catch a couple hours' afternoon nap before dinner, and go to bed early afterward. He'd been barely averaging four hours of sleep per night since he'd arrived at Caventhorne, so it would probably do him good. Far better than sticking around for nearly three hours waiting for Madeleine Hill to get off work, that was certain.

Probably safer, too. The one thing he could definitely not afford to do, other than break some rule of Desmond's and get himself turfed out, was to develop any local entanglements. Desmond hadn't sugar-coated it: if he got accepted for his apprenticeship, he would have no time for a social life. No dates, no "hanging out" with friends, no late-night study sessions with schoolmates. Essentially, he'd be a monk. Even military recruits would have more free time than he would. Desmond had been very clear about that.

And so what? He'd long ago accepted that he wasn't a normal boy. His devotion to magic, the thing that had spurred him to take the potentially disastrous chance of trying to learn it on his own back at Barrow because he couldn't stand not *knowing* any longer, had ensured that.

But if foregoing the pleasures of the typical teenager was the price he had to pay to excel at it, he'd long ago agreed to pay it. It wasn't any different than if he were a musical prodigy, or one of those athletes who got up at four in the morning to get their daily practice in before a full day of school. Sacrifices had to be made, and when it was all over, they'd be more than worth it.

He pictured Madeleine Hill's easy smile, her green eyes, the way her nose crinkled when she laughed.

Surely it wouldn't hurt to just chat with her for a bit. That was all it would—or could—be. Odds were good he probably wouldn't get Desmond's leave to come back to

Wexley for quite some time, so it wasn't as if they'd be sneaking off to see each other or anything. He sighed, disgusted and amused with himself for the way his thoughts were running away with him. *She doesn't even fancy you, you prat. She probably smiles like that at* all *the customers. It's her job.*

But still…she hadn't needed to tell him what time she was off. She probably didn't do *that* with all the customers.

It wasn't easy to kill time in the boring little village for three hours, but he managed. By the time four o'clock rolled around, he'd taken in a film at the tiny local cinema, made two circuits up and down both sides of the small downtown street, looked in all the shop windows, and entered a few of the shops to check out what was inside until the proprietors started giving him suspicious looks.

After that, he ranged off the main street and ambled up and down the side lanes, letting his mind wander and his thoughts go where they wanted. Unfortunately, that meant he did a lot more thinking about magic than he should have according to Desmond's strictures, but it couldn't be helped.

Madeleine Hill smiled when she looked up and spotted him entering the chip shop. "You *did* come back," she said. "I didn't think you would."

He shrugged. "Can't stay too long."

"No, I'm sure you've got to get back up to the haunted house. The ghosts will miss you." She slipped off her apron and tossed it behind the counter.

"They do get lonely sometimes," he agreed. "But they'll have to cope without me for a while. Does them good every now and then."

She laughed. She had a nice laugh, bubbly and cheerful. "Well, I suppose it's good they let you out now and then. I was gonna go meet some mates at the park in a bit. You want to come along? I could introduce you around, and the next time the ghosts let you out to play, you'll know some people in town. You play football?"

"Er—not really," he said. "I'm basically rubbish at it, actually."

"That's okay. I forgot you were a brainiac—the outfit sort of doesn't go with that, you know?" She slipped on a light jacket and called into the back part of the shop, "Dad! I'm going out!"

"Back home by supper!" boomed the same voice Alastair remembered calling to her when he'd left the first time.

"C'mon," Madeleine said, waving him toward the door. "Before he finds something else that needs washing up. Works me like a slave, he does." She rolled her eyes to indicate she wasn't serious.

Alastair followed her outside, and she set off with a confident stride down the street. "They'll be at the park in a half-hour or so. You been to the park yet?"

"No. This is the first time I've been to town, actually." He fell into step next to her, his long strides easily keeping up. It felt good to talk to someone who didn't expect anything of him.

"They *don't* let you out much."

"Well—I've only been here for a couple of weeks. They keep me fairly busy."

"The ghosts?"

"Them too."

She glanced at him. "So…what exactly *are* you doing up there? Everything I've heard from the people who get hired on for parties and dinners and such say that the place is huge and posh and old-fashioned, but they've never said anything about anybody our age being there."

"I'm the first."

"So it's not some sort of Professor Xavier's School or something, then?"

He chuckled. "No. Nothing like that. It would be a lot more fun if it were."

"No mutant powers? You aren't suddenly going to fly off, or shoot laser beams out of your eyes or anything, are you?"

"Not today." *But you're closer than you think,* he thought with amusement. Despite the ease at which he'd caught on to it, he could hardly call his minimal grasp of the levitation spell "flying," and to his disappointment Desmond had still shown no sign of teaching him any offensive magic. But perhaps magical ability *was* some sort of mutation. He'd never thought about it that way before. "Maybe in a few more weeks—if I'm still here."

"Why wouldn't you still be here? Are you leaving?"

"Don't know." He followed her as she turned on one of the side lanes he hadn't investigated on his earlier meanderings; not far ahead, the houses soon began to give way to open fields.

"How can you not know?"

"I'm sort of—on probation. I'm being tested to see if I've got enough of what my teacher is looking for that he'll take me on permanently."

"Sounds stressful. So, do you?"

"Do I what?"

"Have enough of what he's looking for."

"I guess I'll find out in the next two weeks."

"So you don't know?"

He pondered. "I think I do," he said after a few moments. "But there's no way to know for sure, because I'm not entirely certain what he's looking for."

"That's weird," she said, regarding him critically. "So what is it you're supposed to be learning? Are you one of those types who ends up going to University years before anybody else because you're too bright for regular school?"

"Sort of," he admitted. "I can't tell you exactly what it is. I guess the best way to explain it is…a combination of maths and a lot of research." The thought almost made him chuckle—that was a pretty accurate description of the kind of magic he and Desmond practiced. "And a bit of art too, I guess."

She tilted her head. "You're an odd bloke, Alastair Stone."

"I suppose I am. It's probably from spending all that time with the ghosts."

"You know," she said, stopping and fixing him with her wide, green-eyed gaze, "I almost believe you—or at least believe you think so. Which I suppose could make you mental." She grinned. "Cute, though, so I'll give you a chance. As long as you're a harmless sort of mental, and not some kind of axe murderer. *Are* you an axe murderer?"

Alastair made a show of checking his pockets. "Sorry—left my axe in my other trousers."

"You *are* mental," she said, laughing. Before he could reply, she started off again. "So you find out in two weeks if you're staying."

"At the latest, yeah. If I wash out, it will be sooner."

They arrived at the park, a wide expanse of grassy land heavily dotted with trees and split by meandering dirt paths. Off in the distance, several figures were kicking a ball around on a football pitch while others lounged along the sidelines. "Well, you're here now," she said. "Let's go meet the others."

Given his choice, Alastair would have preferred spending the next hour or so walking and chatting with Madeleine alone, and not just because he liked being around her. Large groups of people—especially people he had next to nothing in common with, beyond approximate age—made him uncomfortable. He'd never been any good at small talk, and his unusual upbringing meant he hadn't had much experience interacting with mixed groups of teenagers.

To his relief, Madeleine didn't mention anything about ghosts or weird old houses or brainiacs when she introduced him to her friends. All she said was that he was new to the area, visiting, and might be staying but wasn't sure yet. The others—a collection of boys and girls ranging from around fourteen to seventeen—greeted him cheerfully and then went back to their conversations. Madeleine waved him over to a bench and sat down to watch the football match, which consisted of a bunch of guys and a few girls. "See, they don't bite. Sure you don't want to play? I'm sure you could sub in."

"That's all right," he said. "I'm not kidding—I'm rubbish at football. They made us play at my old school, and the teams used to fight over who had to take me."

"Oh, I doubt that. You don't look like one of those blokes who trips over his own feet."

"Let's keep up that delusion, shall we?"

They settled back to watch the match for a while, though Alastair wasn't really paying attention to it. He was acutely conscious of Madeleine sitting next to him on the small bench, her warm, jeans-clad leg touching his. To stave off the sorts of thoughts he didn't want to have right now, he shifted to magical sight and watched the auras of the football players as they chased the ball back and forth across the pitch.

The auras formed a riot of bright, pulsing colors—blues, greens, golds, purples. He didn't spot any double-colored ones like his and Desmond's, though he did notice traces of red around many of those that weren't red to start with. It didn't surprise him. Get a bunch of passionate teenagers together, and of course emotions would run high. Desmond had taught him to spot the telltale signs.

He switched his attention the sidelines, scanning the group sitting on the grass or on other benches as they watched. The colors were more subdued here, still bright and pulsing but not as intense as those playing the game. Madeleine's aura was a brilliant, cheery yellow. Part of him had been convinced she was somehow having him on, encouraging him because it amused her. Some teenage girls were like that—even though he hadn't encountered many, he was well aware of the reality. But no, she seemed to be exactly what she presented herself as. He relaxed a little, letting himself savor this pleasant afternoon while it lasted. Soon enough he'd have to head back to Caventhorne and get back to his studies—he might as well enjoy this while he could.

He was about to switch off magical sight when something caught his eye, off to his right. He glanced over toward it.

A girl was walking by along the path off to the side of the pitch. He couldn't get a good look at her from where he sat, but she was of medium height and more voluptuously built than Madeleine, with long hair tied back in a ponytail.

If Alastair had merely spotted her walking by, he'd barely have noticed her; it was her aura that had caught his attention. Pale orange and close to her body, it flared in spots with reds and shifting dark areas. He thought back to Esteban and the medical issue he'd spotted in the chef's aura, but these dark spots weren't like what he'd seen then. They were larger, more diffuse, more integrated with the whole than interlopers.

"Whatcha lookin' at?" Madeleine asked.

"Oh—er—sorry." He nodded at the girl, who'd drawn closer as she continued by. He could see her better now: plain and pale, with dark hair and a shapeless sweater over her jeans. He noticed she cast a couple of nervous glances toward the pitch and increased her speed as she passed it. "Do you know that girl?"

"Who?" She followed his gaze with her own and her expression clouded. "Oh. Yeah. That's Rosemary Cooper. Why?"

He shrugged. "She just looks...off, I guess. Upset about something."

"Could be." She stared into her lap. "She's an odd one, Rosemary. Nice enough, I guess, but...a bit strange, you know? I think she might be a little slow. Doesn't go to normal school with the rest of us. She comes into the chip shop with her mum sometimes."

From the pitch, a couple of the boys yelled catcalls at the girl. She flinched, her body stiffening as she picked up her pace once again.

"Oi! Leave her alone, you lot!" Madeleine called at them. They laughed and returned to their game.

Alastair watched Rosemary Cooper until her path took her out of sight. He'd never seen an aura like hers, and wondered if it had something to do with her being "strange" or "slow." He supposed it was none of his concern, though he thought it was rude of the boys to harass her. He turned back around and returned his attention to the game.

The players didn't appear terribly interested in things like scores or strict adherence to the rules—the game seemed more like an excuse for everyone to hang out together and have some laughs than anything else. They kept going for the next hour, swapping players with the spectators on the sidelines whenever someone felt like stepping out. Even Madeleine went in a couple times. She tried to encourage Alastair to have a go, but he assured her everybody present would be better off if he just played the role of spectator. In truth, he was exaggerating his ineptitude considerably—with his long legs and agility, football was one of the few sports he could probably be decent at if he cared enough to bother with it. But he was certain if he tried it now, this would be the time he tripped over an air molecule and faceplanted into the turf right in front of Madeleine. Best not to risk it.

The game broke up shortly after the field lights switched on, and everybody began shouting goodbyes and filtering off to go home for dinner or get ready for evening activities.

"Sure you can't stick around?" Madeleine asked as they headed out of the park behind a pack of laughing, shoving boys. "Later tonight, a group of us are going to the cinema. They're playing this horror film: *They Eat Your Brain*."

The offer was tempting, even though he'd already watched the same film earlier that day. Desmond wouldn't be back until late tonight at the earliest, and he doubted anyone else at Caventhorne would care if he didn't show up for dinner. But still, this was a path he probably shouldn't venture too far down, for his own good. "Sorry," he said. "I've got to get back. The ghosts will miss me, and they get up to all sorts of mischief when they get cross." He gave her what he hoped was a charming grin.

She punched him lightly on the arm. "You know, you're not bad for a posh, mental bloke," she said, returning the grin. "You'll come back, though, right?"

"I will. If I'm allowed." He had no idea when Desmond would give him a break again.

"You tell those ghosts I'm coming up there to have words with them if they don't let you out."

"I'll pass that along." He paused, suddenly awkward. "Thanks for introducing me around—I had a great time."

Her grin sparkled. "Me too. Oh! Let me give you my number, if you want to ring me up—assuming they have telephones up at that old place." She fished in her little bag, scribbled something on a scrap of paper and offered it to him.

"Thanks." He put it in his pocket where he wouldn't lose it, realizing with some embarrassment that he had no idea what the telephone number at Caventhorne was.

Before he could react further, she leaned in and brushed a quick kiss across his cheek. "See you 'round, Ali." Then she gave him another light arm punch and took off after the crowd of boys, back toward town.

For several seconds he stood there, watching them go. He didn't put his hand to his cheek where she'd kissed him, sure that if he did she'd turn around at that exact moment and see. But he could feel the spot warming nonetheless.

He set off at a jog back toward Caventhorne, his mind far away. He barely noticed the scenery.

| CHAPTER ELEVEN

B Y THE TIME HE ARRIVED AT CAVENTHORNE'S GATES, it was almost seven p.m. and already fully dark. He jogged up the road toward the house, the damp chill in the air cutting through his light running gear. If he hurried, he might have time for a quick shower before he completely missed the dinner hour. He wondered if Desmond was back yet—he wasn't terribly hungry, so maybe he could get away with skipping dinner, or just grabbing something from the kitchen later. The shower sounded better anyway.

As he rounded the last bend before reaching the house, he was surprised to notice a faint glow coming from the wooded area off to his right. He wasn't sure what was over there—so far, the only parts of the estate he'd had time to visit were the house itself and the large freestanding building that served as both a garage and a workshop/storage area for the groundskeepers. Whatever this was, it was neither of those.

What could it be? Was there another building over there? Perhaps the groundskeepers were performing some late-night maintenance, or a vehicle was there with its headlights on. On a whim, he shifted to magical sight.

Immediately, another odd-looking light punctuated the glow—not steady this time, but flickering, sort of like a fluorescent bulb before it failed. And instead of white, this one had a distinct purple hue.

Purple light didn't usually mean maintenance, or a vehicle. Curious now, he veered off the path and headed toward the glow. Desmond had never told him he couldn't explore the grounds—only that he couldn't use magic to conceal himself or spy on the staff. Whatever this was, either it was authorized and whoever was doing it wouldn't mind him investigating, or it wasn't, in which case he should inform Desmond or Kerrick about it so something could be done.

He switched off magical sight and slowed his pace as he entered the forested area off the road, not wanting to give himself away by tripping over a root or running into something. Out here with the overhanging branches blocking out the moonlight, the only illumination came from the faint white light he'd originally spotted, barely bright enough to see through the trees and certainly not enough to navigate by. Alastair wondered when Desmond would teach him a light spell—it would have come in handy now.

A hundred feet or so in, the thick forest opened into a small clearing. A rustic little house, hardly bigger than a large shed, sat in the center, with a neat path leading off to the right and disappearing into the trees. Alastair paused at the edge, trying to figure out the purpose of the house. The curtains were drawn, but it was clear that, whatever the light was, it was coming from inside.

What was going on in there?

Ever since he was a small boy, Alastair had suffered from an excess of curiosity. He'd been the sort of child who tried the patience of most adults—too clever for his own good, preferring the company of older people to those his own age, and seeing no reason why he shouldn't ask about things he wanted to know. He'd annoyed far more than one nanny, instructor, or random adult who grew tired of responding to his barrages of questions. Eventually he'd learned to temper that curiosity as he grew older, but only in the sense that he toned down his questions and did his best to hunt up the answers in books before seeking out experts. But one thing had not changed over the years: he'd never met a mystery or puzzle he didn't have to solve.

In other words, he could no more have walked away from the strange, flickering purple lights in the little house than he could have turned his back on his magical studies.

He crept forward, approaching the house while trying to stay out of sight of the window in case whoever was inside happened to glance up and spot him approaching. When he reached the edge of the house, he glanced back to make sure nobody was sneaking up behind him. Then, still crouched below the level of the window, he sidled over, lifted his head just high enough that he could see through a small break in the curtains, and shifted back to magical sight.

For a moment, he couldn't make out what was going on inside. A single, shadowy figure moved around, occasionally bending down to adjust something below Alastair's line of sight. Its aura was hard to make out against the flickering purple light, which also seemed to be going on near the floor.

Cautiously, he raised himself up a little more so he could look down at whatever it was. When it came into view, it startled him so much he nearly lost his balance and fell against the house. He caught himself at the last moment before toppling, using one hand to brace himself while keeping his gaze firmly fixed on what he'd seen.

Whoever was inside the little building, they'd constructed a magical circle on the floor. Alastair couldn't see it well enough to recognize its purpose, but the basics were obvious and unmistakable: carefully drawn sigils, lit candles, glowing crystals placed at various points around the outer perimeter. The purple flickers danced from one crystal to another, casting eerie patterns on the bare walls.

As far as he could see, the circle was of a low power level, carefully constructed but simplistic, and not even at the level of the one he'd done back at Barrow. But it was still a magical circle, and that wasn't the sort of thing he'd expect to see in a remote outbuilding in the middle of Desmond's estate on a random Saturday night. Especially not when Desmond was away.

Leaning closer to the window, Alastair tore his attention reluctantly from the circle to focus it on the figure, who was across the room now and appeared to be consulting an open tome on a small table. A tiny reading lamp provided illumination for the tome and revealed the figure to be tall, slim, and male—definitely too slim to be the broad-shouldered Desmond.

As the unknown man stepped back away from the light, Alastair got a better view of his aura.

It was a dark red-purple.

Alastair stared into the room in shock as he realized who the figure was.

Selby.

What was Selby doing out in the middle of nowhere in the middle of the night?

Or perhaps the more important question was: how was he doing magic?

| CHAPTER TWELVE

F OR A MOMENT, ALASTAIR'S BRAIN FROZE. What should he do? Should he confront Selby? Ignore him and go back to the house as if he hadn't seen anything? Inform Desmond, or at least ask Kerrick what he should do? It seemed quite odd and more than a bit suspicious that Selby would wait until a night when Desmond was away to do...whatever he was doing.

Alastair leaned in a little closer, pressing his face against the window to get the best view of the circle. Even with magical sight up, he still couldn't quite make out its purpose. It looked similar to the tracking ritual he'd conducted back at Barrow, but much less sophisticated in design and potent in power. Was Selby trying to find something?

Selby turned back around to the circle. Before Alastair could pull back, the young man's gaze traveled across the window, then locked back on it. He frowned, his expression darkening. Then the magical light abruptly fled the circle and Selby was striding toward the door.

For a moment, Alastair almost spun and sprinted back toward the house. He was fast and could probably make it before Selby caught him.

But then he stopped. Why should he run? He had every right to be here. He hadn't done anything wrong—he hadn't used any magic to spy on Selby (magical sight didn't count—Desmond had encouraged him to spend time exploring his surroundings to identify how different auras looked). All he'd done was to spot an unusual phenomenon in one of the estate's outbuildings and investigate it. If anybody was doing anything wrong, it was Selby.

So he held his position, standing up and facing the angry assistant steward as he came around the corner, glaring.

"I thought it was you," Selby said with a sneer. "Sir," he added after a beat, and it was unlikely he could have infused any more sarcasm into the word.

Alastair's heart pounded, but he stood straight. "What were you doing in there?"

"Is that any of your concern?"

"I don't know. You tell me."

Selby's sneer didn't fade. "I suppose you're going to trot back up to the house like a good little boy and tell Mr. Desmond everything you saw here."

"I don't know," Alastair said again, keeping his voice even. "I suppose that depends, doesn't it?"

"On what?"

He glanced back toward the house. "On what you were doing."

"I don't have to justify myself to Mr. Desmond's golden boy," Selby said. He glanced at his watch. "You've missed dinner. Shouldn't you be up at the house doing homework or something?"

Anger rose, and Alastair fought to keep it under control. "What is your problem, anyway? I haven't done anything to you. We barely speak to each other. Why have you got such a problem with me?"

Selby looked as if he was trying as hard as Alastair to keep his tone civil. "As a part of Mr. Desmond's staff, I'm required to treat anyone he brings into the house with courtesy," he said in a tight tone. "But that doesn't mean I have to stand for having my activities questioned by *children*."

Alastair almost rose to the bait, but caught himself and gave Selby a cold smile instead. "Is that it, then? You've got a problem with my age?"

"I've got a lot of problems with you," he said. "But don't worry—none of them will affect my work." He nodded over his shoulder toward the main house. "So, are you going to tattle on me to Mr. Desmond?"

"As I said before: I don't know." Alastair crossed his arms. "Are you going to tell me the truth?"

"About what?"

"Does he know you've got the Talent?"

Selby snorted. "Mr. Desmond? Of course."

Alastair watched his aura. To his surprise, while it still billowed with anger and frustration, it didn't budge at his last statement. Desmond had another mage in the house—working as part of the staff, even—and he hadn't mentioned it? "So why are you doing it out here, then? Why not use the circle in the house?"

"Because I'm not permitted to." Selby let his breath out, and some of the anger dissipated from his aura. "Staff is not allowed in Mr. Desmond's workroom. As you should well know, since he's got you cleaning it. Only Mr. Desmond, his guests...and his apprentices." Once again, sarcasm suffused the final word as he looked Alastair up and down with a slow gaze dripping with contempt. "Or reasonable substitutions, anyway."

"If that's supposed to be an insult, it won't work. I know that's all I am, at the moment," Alastair said. He tilted his head, still watching Selby. Keeping magical sight going was starting to give him a dull headache, so he dropped it.

"Wait a minute..." He remembered something Kerrick had told him. "I'm starting to get it now. You're from one of those magical families Mr. Desmond employs on his staff, aren't you? Did you want to apprentice with him? Is that it?"

It was hard to see Selby clearly in the darkness, but the anger in his carriage was clear as he tensed and stepped forward. For a second, Alastair thought he might attack him. But then the air went out of his posture and he retreated again.

"Score one for the Boy Wonder. Go on, then—say what you want to say and get it over with. I've got to clean up here before I'm needed back at the house."

"What do I want to say?" Alastair asked, confused.

"Have a go at me about being a failure—we can't all be child prodigies like you, after all, can we?"

Alastair stared at him, even more confused. "Why would I do that?"

Selby didn't answer him. "Are you going to tell Mr. Desmond you found me here?"

"I told you—that depends on you."

"How?"

"Tell me what you were doing in there. Show me."

Some of the old sneer came back. "Why should I?"

Alastair was getting the impression Selby had issues that had very little to do with him, and he'd just blundered into a

R. L. KING

minefield he'd never been meant to encounter. "Because," he said patiently, "I'm not Mr. Desmond's apprentice. Not yet. I'm on probation. You might not believe it, but I've got no real desire to get you in trouble for whatever you're doing out here. I don't care what you're doing—it's none of my business. But," he added as Selby started to speak, "there's no way I'm putting my apprenticeship at risk for somebody I barely know and who seems to hate me for things I didn't even do. So I guess it's up to you, isn't it? Tell me what you're doing out here, or I *will* ask Mr. Desmond about it at our next session."

Once again, Selby's eyes glittered and his posture stiffened, and once again he deflated. "Fine," he said, resigned. "I'll show you, if you insist. Come on." He gestured back toward the little house.

Alastair followed him, wondering briefly if he was making a mistake. If Selby really did have it in for him, and if he was a more talented mage than he was letting on, this could be a potentially bad decision. Hell, Selby was bigger than he was and could probably overpower him physically, if it came to that. These thoughts lasted only a second, though— his curiosity about what the man was doing in there swept them away.

Selby went in first, paused to light a couple of candles on another table just inside the door, then stepped aside. "There. Take a good look."

Alastair stopped just inside the door, where he could get the best view of the room. Selby had pushed the meager furniture against the walls, clearing space for a circle about six feet in diameter. He'd drawn the circle itself with chalk; it included intricate sigils around the outer diameter, with lines radiating out toward crystals and candles he'd placed around the perimeter.

As Alastair had noted from his glimpse from outside, it was a simplistic thing, but constructed with obvious skill. He'd been wrong about the purpose, though—he could see that now, on closer inspection. He paced around it, examining the sigils with more care and trying to reconcile them with what he'd studied in his theory lessons with Desmond. "This is a...you're trying to connect with the ley lines, aren't you?"

Selby blinked. "Not bad," he admitted. "Maybe you do live up to some of your reputation after all."

Alastair continued studying the circle. Desmond had told him during one of their early lessons that Caventhorne was constructed on land intersected by five ley lines, which made it one of the most magically potent locations in England. This didn't surprise him—he knew his own house in Surrey was at the confluence of three, which was why things like the wards around the house didn't require periodic refreshing, and why magical workings done there tended to be more powerful than those in other areas. "I'm not sure I understand why, though. You say Mr. Desmond knows you're doing this?"

"He does, yes. And I don't care if you mention it to him. It's not a secret. There's no real *why* to it—it's an introductory technique. Mr. Desmond gives me a bit of instruction when he has free time, and I spend some of my time off practicing." He crossed his arms. "There. Satisfied I'm not trying to summon a Great Old One or something?"

Alastair nodded. "I'll go now. Sorry I interrupted you." He turned toward the door, then turned back. Selby was gathering up the candles and crystals around the outside of the circle. "I'm not your enemy, you know. This whole thing isn't exactly a walk in the park for me, either. You think I don't know everyone's expecting me to fail because of my age? I don't even know if I'm doing what Mr. Desmond expects—he never tells me how I'm doing. So every day this month, I'm just waiting to see if I do something wrong and he chucks me out on my arse. You glaring at me from the shadows because you're jealous of something I can't help isn't making it any better, and it can't be much fun for you either. So just—you leave me alone, and I'll leave you alone. Fair enough?"

Selby's steady, appraising gaze settled on him for a moment, and then he nodded once. "Fine. Fair enough." Then he returned his attention to what he was doing.

Alastair had made it a few steps out into the clearing when Selby called to him. "Mr. Stone?"

He stopped and turned back. What was it now? "Yes?"

"You should be careful."

"Careful?" Alastair blinked and tensed. That had almost sounded like a threat. "Of what?"

"Magic." Selby leaned in the doorway; his pose was casual, but his aura wasn't. "Just a bit of…friendly advice. Respect it. Never take it for granted."

What an odd, sudden thing for him to say. "Er…right. I won't. I never do."

Selby held his gaze for a moment longer, then spun without another word and disappeared back into the little building, leaving Alastair to regard the space he'd just occupied with confusion.

| CHAPTER THIRTEEN

THE NEXT MORNING, he showed up as usual for his lesson. Desmond was waiting for him when he got there. "Did you do as I instructed yesterday, Mr. Stone?"

"I went into town, yes."

"No studies?"

"No, sir."

"Did you enjoy your break?" Desmond directed gestures at various books and reagents, settling them neatly on the table in front of him.

Alastair thought about his time with Madeleine Hill. He'd enjoyed chatting with her, but he had no illusions that anything further would come of it. He wondered what it would be like to have a girlfriend, like most guys his age did. It was a remote concept, sort of like wondering what it would be like to live at the bottom of the sea. "Honestly, sir—I think I'd rather have stayed here and worked on my magical studies."

"Oh?" Desmond's eyebrows rose.

"Well—it was good to get some exercise, and I met a girl at a chip shop and we chatted for a bit. But my mind kept going back to magic."

Desmond didn't seem disturbed by this. "Mr. Stone, your devotion to the Art is admirable, and I certainly understand how you want to focus on it to the exclusion of all else, especially during this probationary period. But learning to clear your mind of distractions is a vital part of magical training. Especially if you want to reach the highest levels of skill."

Easy for *him* to say—his position was secure, and he didn't have to worry about what might happen if he let his mind wander too far from the areas he was supposed to be concentrating on. Last night, for example, his dreams had been decidedly non-magical in nature, having a lot more to do with Madeleine Hill than constructing ritual circles. "Yes, sir," was all he said.

"Good. If you pass your probationary period, I will expect you to allow time in your schedule for such breaks. You won't have a great deal of time for recreation, so you'll need to make the best of what you do have. Now let's begin today's lesson."

To Alastair's disappointment, Desmond didn't teach him any new techniques today. Instead, his master focused the first part of the lesson on refining the telekinesis spell so he could begin both to lift heavier objects and to exhibit greater control over them. The second half was devoted to work on the massive circle in the middle of the workroom, as Desmond stood back and watched while he attempted to set up a ritual designed to aid his concentration, using nothing but what he could find in the books in his library.

By the end of the session he'd barely begun the actual construction of the circle; he'd spent most of his time running back and forth to his bookshelves, trying to find the correct references to show him what he needed to do.

As usual, Desmond didn't seem bothered. "Your homework before this evening," he said, "is to continue consulting your reference books to finish as much of this as you can for our next session. As a more ongoing project, I want you to practice the telekinetic spell. Try lifting different things of increasing weight, holding them aloft as long as you can, and moving them around. It will be tiring. It will probably be painful. But this sort of thing is similar to training physical muscles. You have the ability, but you'll never progress if you abandon your efforts when they become difficult. Do you understand?"

That was definitely Desmond's pet phrase, Alastair had decided a while ago. "Yes, sir."

Desmond didn't turn to leave yet. "Mr. Stone?"

"Yes, sir?" Alastair had been about to head back to the bookshelf; he stopped and waited.

"You've seemed distracted about something today. Is your mind perhaps on something other than the lesson?"

Damn. That was one unfortunate thing about learning magic—and especially about learning it from somebody as good at it as Desmond. He wondered if that was why his master hadn't taught him to conceal his aura yet: so he could keep an eye on it for potential problems.

For a moment he didn't answer, but then he let his breath out. "I...suppose it is, sir."

"Would you care to tell me what it is? Did something happen during your time in the village yesterday?"

"No, sir...not exactly. It was actually on my way back." He paced, feeling stuck between two equally undesirable courses of action. Despite Selby's surly personality, Alastair didn't want to get him in trouble. But even more than that, he hadn't been kidding when he'd told Selby there was no way he'd put his potential apprenticeship with Desmond at risk by withholding information from his master.

He brought his gaze up to meet Desmond's. "As I returned last night, I was scanning the grounds with magical sight, and I spotted something odd—a sort of glow coming from one of the outbuildings. When I investigated, I discovered Selby there, setting up a magical circle—and actually making it work. He told me you were aware of it."

Desmond's expression didn't change. "I am."

"Right." Alastair shelved a book and looked away. "Then it's none of my business, I suppose."

When Desmond didn't reply, Alastair turned back around. The man was watching him intently; he wasn't sure if Desmond was simply scanning his aura or trying to read his mind. As far as he knew, mages couldn't read minds—but Desmond did seem to break quite a few of the established molds. "Sir?"

Desmond remained silent for a moment longer, then waved Alastair toward a chair. "Sit down, Mr. Stone."

Alastair did as he was told, perching on the edge of the hard-backed wooden chair. He waited.

Now it was Desmond's turn to pace. "You are curious about Selby."

He couldn't exactly deny it. "Well...yes, sir. But I assumed it wasn't my concern, or you'd have mentioned it before."

"I didn't mention it before because he prefers to keep his magical abilities to himself, and I respect his request. But now that you've discovered the truth, I think it best that you know the whole story. I despise rumors and half-truths—nothing more quickly upsets a smoothly running system."

He continued pacing as he spoke, pausing on occasion to examine something on the chalkboard, or a book on one of the shelves. But even when his back was to Alastair and he spoke softly, Alastair had no trouble hearing him. "Selby is, as you might have suspected, a member of one of the magical families whose members I sometimes employ on my staff. I find it easier to maintain the household when my staff members are familiar with the Art—that way, there is no need to conceal its existence from them. As you well know, even among families with a strong magical tradition, the Talent is relatively rare. In many cases, that leaves a number of individuals who are familiar with the existence of magic without the ability to practice it themselves."

"I wondered about that," Alastair admitted. "Doesn't it cause resentment to be surrounded by something they might have had? Isn't the constant reminder difficult to handle?" He knew it would be for him—if it had turned out for some reason that he didn't have magical ability after all, the last thing he'd want to do was stay in a situation where he had to watch other people practicing it every day. It would be a lot like employing an alcoholic behind the bar at a pub, except at least the alcoholic could choose to take a drink if the temptation grew too strong.

"Most of them don't care, surprisingly," Desmond said, his tone suggesting he sympathized with Alastair's point of view. "You might understandably find it difficult to believe, but there are actually many people who have no interest or desire to possess magical talent. The fact is, I pay my staff handsomely—far more than they might expect to be paid in any other similar situation—and they are given opportunities for study, education, and enrichment outside their normal duties. If any of them are unsatisfied in their situation, they know they have only to inform me and I will provide them with whatever assistance they might require in obtaining another position. I have not had any issues with this practice for many years, and none of my staff have opted to leave my employ."

Alastair nodded. He wanted to ask another question, but hesitated.

Desmond's gaze grew stern. "Mr. Stone, I value curiosity more highly than almost any other trait in a student. I will never punish or chastise you for asking questions. I might refuse to answer, or inform you that the answer is not your concern, but if you have any hope of becoming my apprentice, you must get over this reluctance."

"All right, sir." Alastair sat up a little straighter. "Do other members of the staff have magical abilities as well?" Had Kerrick been hiding his talent all this time? Could the maids check out his aura as easily as he could theirs? Was Gretchen the assistant chef casting magic circles in the back corner of the kitchen?

"No."

"So Selby's the only one."

"Yes."

He pondered that, thinking back over what Selby had said last night. Now came the time to test Desmond—could he *really* ask any question he liked? "He mentioned something about being a 'failure.' Was he to be apprenticed to you, then?"

For the first time that day, Desmond didn't look stern, imperious, or unreadable. He sighed, and for just a second dropped his gaze. "That was his hope." To Alastair's surprise, he sounded tired.

"He didn't succeed at the training?" That didn't seem so unusual to Alastair—from everything he'd heard or understood, Desmond didn't take many apprentices, and he considered only the strongest talents. Though it was possible to improve it with study and practice, a person's natural level of magical talent was something he or she was born with, like the potential to be a top athlete or a musical prodigy. There was certainly no shame in discovering you didn't possess that level of inherent ability.

"He didn't even begin," Desmond said. "I evaluated him because I am familiar with his family, but unfortunately he possesses only a minimal level of natural talent. Nowhere near the minimum I require of my potential apprentices."

Alastair frowned. "But...you're not the only teacher available. Surely he could have found another—"

Desmond shook his head. "You don't understand, Mr. Stone. When I say 'minimal,' I don't mean simply below what I would consider a satisfactory level. I mean low enough that no reputable teacher would take him on. It would simply be a waste of time for both the teacher and Selby."

"So..." Alastair paused, thinking. How horrible it must be to have the Talent, but at such a low level that you couldn't even convince anyone to take you on as an apprentice. In a way, that would be worse than not having it at all. He remembered more of Selby's words. "Ah, I see now. He said you've agreed to teach him a few things when you have time, so he decided to stay on here."

"Yes. It is not an optimal solution, but given our unique location at the ley line confluence, it's possible for him to progress further here than he might do somewhere else. I am sure your presence has caused him no small amount of discomfort, but that is the way of things. He must cope." He glanced up. "He hasn't treated you inappropriately, has he?"

Alastair shook his head. Given new information, he could hardly blame Selby for being resentful of this underaged interloper showing up and getting a shot at everything he so desperately wanted for himself. "He's...fine, sir. No problems."

"Good." He tilted his head. "You say you found him working on a circle in one of the outbuildings?"

"Yes, sir."

"What sort of circle? Did you see?"

"Yes, sir. He showed it to me. He didn't tell me what it was, but I could see. He was trying to tap into the ley lines. He claimed it was an introductory technique you taught him."

"It was indeed, though I had no idea he was working on the practical aspects." Desmond returned the book he was holding to the shelf. "Was he successful in doing so?"

Alastair considered his answer. "The structure of the circle was a bit simplistic, sir, but I did spot it with magical sight from the road. He'd gotten it powered, at least."

"Excellent." He turned briskly back toward Alastair with an air of dismissal. "Thank you, Mr. Stone. That will be all. Get something to eat if you wish, then work on your own circle here. I will see you this evening."

Alastair watched him go. He almost called after him, but didn't. That was enough questions for today—but he couldn't shake the feeling that there was more to Selby's story than either Selby or Desmond was telling him.

| CHAPTER FOURTEEN

THE NEXT FEW DAYS PASSED, taking Alastair over the two-week mark of his probationary period. He refused to let himself grow overconfident, but with each new technique Desmond taught that he grasped with minimal difficulty, he began allowing himself to believe—just a little—that he might actually be making a go of this.

Nothing was easy—that wasn't it. Between his twice-daily magic lessons, the copious amounts of reading Desmond assigned, his mundane studies, tidying the workroom (he hadn't yet located the dust generator, but he was certain there had to be one in there somewhere), finding time to go for runs around the estate to keep himself in reasonable shape, and carving out enough sleep to keep from falling over in the middle of his sessions, he had to maintain a delicate juggling act and develop the skills of a master scheduler in order to fit everything in. He ended each late night by tumbling into bed for a few quick hours, usually with a headache. His mind still whirled with whatever he'd learned that day, trying to place the new puzzle pieces into the larger whole that was his growing magical knowledge.

None of that mattered, though, because he was *doing* it. With the single exception of the invisibility spell, which he still couldn't get the hang of maintaining for longer than thirty seconds or so, he grasped everything Desmond offered him. Some techniques were easier than others—he took to levitation, for example, like he was born to it—while others, like basic healing, were more difficult. But on the whole, while he certainly wasn't anywhere near the level of mastering any of the techniques in such a short time, he felt he'd caught on to them well enough to satisfy Desmond.

Not that Desmond ever said anything about it, beyond a general "well done" when he did a good job at something, or tips and encouragement when he took a bit longer. It was maddening in a way, because despite his own confidence in his progression, he had no way to know if it was good enough to get him to the next stage.

The thought plagued him on more than one occasion: what would he do if, despite his best efforts, he *couldn't* manage to perform at the level Desmond expected of his apprentices? What would his father do with a son who knew too much magic to simply let it languish for the next three years, but not enough to be allowed to practice it safely without guidance? Alastair had already decided that if Desmond cut him loose, there was no way he was going to wait three more years before continuing his studies, no matter what his father said. He'd find a teacher willing to take him *somewhere*. Or, if he couldn't do that, he'd figure out a way to continue his studies on his own. It wouldn't be fair to open up a world like this to him and then slam the door shut because he failed to meet some impossible taskmaster's unattainable standards.

But that was getting ahead of himself. He hadn't failed, and for all he knew, he was doing fine. Desmond hadn't given him any indication of this—but he also hadn't given him any that he *wasn't* doing fine. Alastair remembered back to their first discussion: Desmond had said if he wasn't performing up to snuff, he'd be cut loose immediately. No waiting until the end of the month to get the bad news.

So if he was still here, things were still good, right?

Selby, for his part, essentially ignored him. They hadn't spoken for several days beyond the minimal interaction required when they encountered each other in the house, and it seemed to Alastair that the assistant steward was going out of his way to avoid him. That was fine with him, so he did the same. Desmond didn't comment on it, and while Kerrick gave him occasional odd looks and appeared a couple times to be on the verge of asking him a question, he didn't do so.

Occasionally he thought about what an odd life he was leading. Most boys his age were in school, worrying about the sorts of things normal teenagers worried about. Sure, they might be concerned about getting kicked out of school if they failed an exam or got into trouble with girls or booze or drugs, but they didn't have to consider what might happen if their magical ability didn't live up to expectations, or if they failed to perform to the standards of a teacher who made the worst drill-sergeant instructor at Barrow look like a pussycat by comparison.

Alastair smiled as he hovered three books over his head while lying in bed late one night , moving them in a slow circle a few feet above him. His skill with the levitation and telekinesis spells was growing with each passing day, and he always tried to get in a bit of practice every night to supplement what he was doing in the workroom.

His thoughts turned to Madeleine, as they often did lately. He wondered when he might have a chance to see her again. Perhaps they could go for a walk together, and even possibly find a nice, out-of-the way place to—

The books wobbled, crashed into each other, and hurtled toward his face.

Without thinking, he formed the shield pattern in his mind, bringing it up to protect his head, then reached out to re-establish his grip on the books. They shuddered to a stop inches before they hit the shield, then rose back up to their former height.

Alastair gaped, eyes wide, and almost lost control of both spells. Two spells at once—he'd never done that before! He knew it was possible, since the reference material Desmond had given him to read explained the process, but Desmond hadn't actually taught him how to do it yet.

He grinned. It wasn't a new skill—he knew both spells, of course—but still, this could definitely prove useful.

Tiring, though. He carefully lowered the three books to his nightstand, then dropped the shield. He'd have to show that one to Desmond.

He got his chance the very next day.

Desmond began the lesson, as he almost always did, by flipping over the blackboard to reveal a series of complicated diagrams. He started his lecture as soon as Alastair was seated, and Alastair had to scramble to get his notebook and pen out of his bag before he missed anything.

He was just about caught up, glancing at the board to make sure he'd gotten a sigil right, when suddenly three

R. L. KING

missiles came hurtling at top speed from the far sight of the room, headed directly for his head.

Alastair didn't think, but only reacted. It all happened in the space of less than two seconds. With one flick of his mind his shimmering shield appeared, deflecting the three bean-bags before they hit him. Grinning, he visualized the second pattern, just as he'd been doing in his bedroom the previous night, and superimposed it with the first. The beanbags stopped before they hit the floor and sped back at Desmond.

Alastair knew he'd done something wrong the instant he saw the expression on his master's face.

At first, everything seemed fine: Desmond's shield came up even faster than Alastair's had, halting the three missiles and dropping them to the floor. Alastair's triumphant grin faltered as Desmond's shield came down, revealing his master fixing him with a cold stare that could have bored its way through solid diamond.

"…Sir?" What could be wrong? He'd done the techniques perfectly, just as he'd visualized them, just as he'd done them during his practices in his room. It couldn't be possible Desmond was so petty that getting smacked with a few beanbags would anger him…could it?

Desmond's expression did not warm, and his tone, if possible, was even colder. "Mr. Stone. What was that I just observed?"

For a moment, Alastair had no idea how to answer. Hadn't it been obvious? That wouldn't be a good way to respond, though. When in doubt, stick with the facts. "Er…I summoned the shield to stop the attack, and then sent it back at you, sir. Did I do something incorrectly?"

"No, Mr. Stone. But would you care to inform me—you may consult your notes if necessary—where during your lessons I taught you what you just did?"

Alastair frowned, more perplexed than ever. "Sir, I don't understand. I've been working on the shield since our first lesson, and the other is simply the telekinesis technique you've had me practicing."

Desmond could have been a statue. He stood, arms crossed, and continued to fix his penetrating gaze on Alastair. "When did I teach you how to use the two of them together?"

"You...didn't, sir. Not specifically. But in the supplemental reading you gave me, it mentioned visualizing multiple patterns to produce more than one spell effect at a time."

"And you worked out how to do that on your own?"

"Well...sort of. It followed logically from what you taught me. I discovered it when I almost dropped something on my head while practicing a shield in bed last night, and just...went with it," he finished lamely.

"You...'went with it'." Desmond's patrician tones twisted the words into something shameful.

"Er...yes sir." Alastair's heart pounded faster. "Did I do something wrong?"

Desmond began to pace. "Mr. Stone. Do you remember what I told you on our first day together?"

"There were quite a lot of things, sir. Could you be more specific?"

"Let me refresh your memory. I am referring to the part where I informed you of the most reliable way to terminate your probationary period."

Alastair's whole body grew suddenly cold as his mind returned to that day. It seemed so long ago now, but Desmond's words were fresh. *No...please...* "I...You...told me I wasn't to pursue any outside study beyond what you taught me." He struggled for a defense. "But sir—you *did* teach me those techniques. And the bit about visualizing multiple patterns was in one of the reference books you assigned. I didn't think—"

"No, Mr. Stone. You didn't think." Desmond's words rose in volume, cutting Alastair off. For the first time, a hint of visible anger showed on his near-impassive face. "I understand your desire to impress me. I understand that you are under a great deal of pressure to perform to my standards. But one thing I expect and require of my students at all times is obedience to the rules I set. And yet you have chosen to disobey."

"Sir—" Alastair thought his racing heart would leap free of his chest. Sweat beaded on his forehead, and his mind refused to lock on to a thought. Would it all come to this? He'd been doing so well, grown so confident in spite of his fear of doing so—was this to be the end, all because he'd done *more* than Desmond expected of him?

"Do you deny it, Mr. Stone? Had you perhaps forgotten my instruction?"

Alastair swallowed hard. "I—hadn't forgotten it, sir. It...honestly didn't occur to me in this case, since the techniques were things you'd already taught me."

"But yet I specified that you were not only forbidden from exploring new techniques on your own, but also from supplementing anything I taught you. Did that fail to occur to you as well, Mr. Stone?"

Desmond hadn't raised his voice again. Aside from the initial flash of anger that showed on his face, he hadn't changed expression. He continued to regard Alastair with the stern, unblinking gaze of a judge facing a suspect who had no defense.

"I—" Alastair struggled to get his thoughts to respond, to find anything to say that would convince Desmond not to give up on him.

But nothing came. He had no way to counter Desmond's words, because there *was* no way to counter them. Desmond had made his requirements crystal clear during their first meeting, and Alastair had failed to meet them.

"I—" he said again, then bowed his head and let his breath out. "No, sir. You're right. It should have occurred to me." He drew in another deep breath and forced himself to raise his eyes to his (likely former, now) master. "I'll—go pack my things, sir, if you'll excuse me."

"I will not."

Alastair blinked. "Sir?"

"I will not excuse you, Mr. Stone."

"I—don't understand."

Once again, Desmond began pacing in front of Alastair. Something about his expression changed, but it was difficult to identify. "Sit down," he said at last.

Alastair, growing more confused with each passing moment, did as he was told. He pulled up one of the wooden chairs and dropped into it, never taking his eyes off Desmond.

This time, Desmond didn't watch him back. As he spoke, his gaze ranged out over the workroom as if he were speaking to some unseen audience instead of the boy seated in front of him. "I told you, Mr. Stone, on the day before I informed you of the rules you would be expected to follow, that one of my failed apprentices died. You do, I trust, remember that."

"Yes, sir. I've never forgotten it."

"You were curious about the circumstances, but you didn't ask me. Kerrick informs me that you asked him, but that he told you, properly, that he wasn't permitted to discuss it."

"Yes, sir. I'm sorry if I spoke out of turn."

"Mr. Stone, I told you only yesterday that it is never wrong to ask a question, even though you won't always get an answer. I do not fault you for your curiosity. The details were simply not a subject I felt it necessary to discuss with you." He turned back around to face Alastair and stopped. "However, I have changed my mind. I *am* going to tell you how my apprentice died."

Alastair held Desmond's gaze, not daring to breathe or reply.

Desmond resumed his pacing, and once again seemed to be speaking to the room in general rather than to Alastair. "My last apprentice was a brilliant young man from a family with a long history of magical talent. He was much like you, in fact, though he was older—he didn't begin his apprenticeship until he was eighteen—and unlike yours, his family's magical pedigree was considerably more unpredictable, and his social circumstances considerably more modest. I agreed to apprentice him because I saw great potential in him.

"For the first two years, he did not disappoint me. His magical talent was prodigious, and his devotion to the Art was greater than that of any previous apprentice I had ever taught. Whatever task I gave him, or whatever technique I introduced to him, he performed them with skill and confidence. Given that my previous apprentice had failed to complete his training, I dared to hope that this time I might be training a practitioner who had the potential to not only be my equal, but perhaps even my superior, in magical ability."

He walked over to the circle and began gathering the crystals, candles, and other paraphernalia Alastair had been using for his lesson that day, magically directing each to its proper cubby. When he finished, he stopped and looked over the circle, his faraway stare suggesting he was seeing something in his mind's eye. When he resumed speaking, his voice was even and emotionless. "I began teaching him the rudiments of summoning magic. Summoning is not difficult in and of itself—given the proper materials and incantations, even some mundanes can summon beings and entities from other planes. The difficult part is *controlling* what is summoned. Most of those mundanes and many of the mages who manage it are killed instantly—either because whatever they attempted to summon wasn't what they ultimately got, or because the summoned being was stronger than they expected."

He paused a moment, then walked back until he stood six feet in front of Alastair. "If my apprentice had any fault, it was overconfidence, and perhaps more than a bit of arrogance. These are common traits in our kind, as I'm sure you're aware. But they're quite dangerous in an apprentice who hasn't been fully instructed in the techniques he might be tempted to try."

Alastair had nearly forgotten to breathe as he listened to Desmond's tale. He was sure he saw where this was going now, at least in a general sense.

Desmond's gaze locked in on him. "Can you guess what my apprentice did, Mr. Stone?"

"Yes, sir," he said softly. "He...tried summoning something, and couldn't control it?"

Desmond inclined his head. "He took it upon himself, in an attempt to impress me, to design his own summoning ritual." He indicated the area above them with a hand gesture. "By that time I had given him access to my own library, and he located some advanced reference material. One night following our lesson, he remained in the workroom and spent most of the night casting his circle. I believe his intention was to present the results of his labor to me when I arrived the following morning."

Alastair continued to listen in silence, never taking his attention from Desmond. A chill of dread rose in him.

"The ritual was intricate and complex—far more so than I had expected him capable of managing at his stage of training. The circle must have taken him hours to produce. It was perfect—with one exception. He'd made a small but critical error with one of the symbols. Possibly it was because he was tired from working on it all night following a full day of training. Possibly he was not as careful as he should have been. Possibly he mistakenly chose the wrong symbol because he misread it. I will never know."

Now, he began pacing again, this time circling Alastair's chair. His voice grew softer and even more inflectionless. "When I arrived at the workroom that morning, it was already too late. He had obviously begun the summoning only a few moments earlier, intending to reach out to a powerful but relatively benign entity useful in assisting with study. But the thing that came through was—horrific."

Desmond's voice and his steps both stopped behind Alastair.

He twisted around in his chair and was surprised to see his master standing still, fists clenched, facing away from him. It was hard to tell for sure, but he thought he detected a faint tremor in Desmond's hands. Suddenly he wasn't sure he wanted to hear all the details. "Sir—"

Apparently, however, Desmond had now determined it important for him to do just that. He turned back around, composed now, and unclenched his fists. "Horrific," he said again. "Before I could act, it grabbed my apprentice and pulled him back through the summoning portal. I still hear his screams sometimes in my nightmares. Yes, Mr. Stone, I do have nightmares sometimes. And you will too, as your training progresses, if you don't already."

Once more he resumed his pacing and came back around to the front of Alastair's chair. "The portal didn't fade right away—it took several seconds before it disappeared. The creature ripped my apprentice to pieces directly in front of it. It wanted me to see what it was doing. I tried to intervene, but it was already too late. There was nothing I could have done at that point, beyond hasten the closing of the portal. I disrupted the ritual, and the feedback from doing so rendered me unconscious for several minutes. By the time I awoke, the portal was gone, and no trace of my apprentice remained."

Slowly and with deliberate calm, he walked over until he stood only a step from Alastair, looming over him. "Do you see now, Mr. Stone, why I do not permit my apprentices—and especially my barely-trained probationary apprentices—from practicing unauthorized magical techniques?"

Alastair nodded, still afraid to let his breath out. "Y...yes, sir. I do." He couldn't help picturing his version of what Desmond had described—the screaming apprentice being ripped limb from limb, blood everywhere... "I'm...sorry, sir."

Desmond held his gaze for several seconds, then nodded once. "I think you are, Mr. Stone. I think I've successfully impressed upon you the reasons for what might seem like arbitrarily draconian rules."

Abruptly his entire demeanor changed, returning to its normal brisk formality. He summoned a book, which hovered in front of Alastair. "Continue with the techniques you've been working on, and read the first hundred pages of this book by tomorrow morning. If you like, you may continue practicing the technique you demonstrated today, but *only* with those two spells. Do you understand?"

Alastair gaped at him. "Er...no, sir. I don't understand."

Desmond's brow furrowed. "Was I not clear, Mr. Stone?"

Could Desmond hear his heart pounding? He swiped sweat off his forehead and ignored the book suspended in the air in front of him. "You said—if I broke your rules—"

"Yes. I did. And if it happens again, there will be no appeal. So I suggest you watch yourself, and consider carefully both the letter and the spirit of my rules before attempting any other unauthorized techniques." He indicated the hovering book. "If you wish to impress me, you will have ample opportunity simply by mastering the methods and techniques I teach you. I suggest you focus on that."

"Er—" Alastair, hardly daring to believe what he was hearing, plucked the book from the air and put it under his arm. He struggled for a moment with what to say, knowing all too keenly how close he'd come to messing up everything he'd been striving for ever since those nights in the attic at Barrow, and how fortunate he was that William Desmond did apparently possess at least a shred of humanity under that hard-assed exterior. "Thank you, sir," he finally said.

"Don't thank me, Mr. Stone. Or rather, thank me by doing as I ask."

"I—I will, sir." He was stammering, but he didn't care. His body felt like he'd just put it through a marathon followed by an ice-cold shower followed by a quick trip through an industrial clothes-ringer. He took a deep breath, almost said something else, then spun and hurried off toward the workroom door.

When he reached it, though, a final thought occurred to him—one piece of the puzzle he didn't have. Did he dare ask, after such a close call? Desmond had said he would never punish him for questions—this would be the real test. "Mr. Desmond?"

Desmond had turned away and once again appeared to be watching some film unspooling in his mind's eye. He started slightly, then looked up. "Yes, Mr. Stone?"

"This apprentice—who was he?"

Something flashed across Desmond's eyes—was it surprise? It was too far away to tell for sure. For a long time, he didn't answer. Then: "His name was Gareth Selby. He was Selby's older brother."

| CHAPTER FIFTEEN

ALASTAIR DID HIS BEST, but despite his efforts he couldn't put his troubled thoughts aside over the next couple of days. Between coming far too close to having his probation terminated due to his unauthorized experiments and the cold realization that it genuinely hadn't occurred to him they were unauthorized at all (which meant it was possible he could screw up again without even knowing he'd done it), he was constantly watching himself to make sure every bit of magic he practiced was something Desmond had specifically taught him.

Even with all that, though, it wasn't the thing causing him the most stress.

He couldn't get his mind off what Desmond had told him about Gareth Selby.

His master hadn't said anything else after revealing his name, and hadn't brought the subject up again. At the lesson following their conversation, he'd picked things up as if nothing had changed—either Alastair's screw-up or the talk about dead apprentices. Alastair had been aching to ask more questions, but he held his curiosity, not wanting to set Desmond off again so soon after such a close call.

He'd only seen Selby once in those two days, directing some workmen doing repairs in the east wing of the house. He met the assistant steward's gaze for perhaps a beat or two longer than necessary, then hurried off before Selby could ask him any questions.

He wondered if Desmond had told Selby what he'd revealed. And even more, he wondered how Selby felt about the situation. Did he even know? If this had been several years ago, Selby would have been a teenager, or even a child, when it happened. Had they told him the details? If they had, how could he stand to work here, surrounded by terrible memories?

Finally, he couldn't do it anymore. He was getting to the point where the distraction was affecting his work, and he was sure Desmond had noticed.

"Sir," he said as he levitated his books over to re-shelve them after a morning lesson. "May I ask you a question?"

"Of course, Mr. Stone."

Alastair put the books away and walked back over to where Desmond waited. "I've been thinking about what you told me the other day—about Gareth Selby."

"I rather thought you might be. In fact, I would be surprised if you weren't."

"Well—yes. Of course I'm thinking about what happened. But there's something else, too."

"Yes?"

"I'm wondering—well—does Selby know? His brother, I mean. Does he know what happened to Gareth?"

Desmond's expression was, as usual, unreadable. "He does, yes."

"He knows the details?" Alastair asked, surprised.

"He knows that his brother attempted an unauthorized summoning ritual that went awry and died as a result, yes. He was young at the time—a bit younger than you are now."

Alastair nodded, looking down at the floor, trying to formulate his next question.

"Is there something else?" It was a question, but not really. Obviously Desmond knew there was.

"I—" He looked up to meet Desmond's gaze. "I'm just wondering how he can stand to be here, after—"

"After his brother was killed during his apprenticeship?" When Alastair nodded, he spread his hands. "Gareth knew the dangers of what he was undertaking. I make sure all my apprentices thoroughly understand that studying with me—with anyone who teaches complex magic—entails a degree of risk. I try to minimize that risk as much as possible with rules such as the one you ran afoul of the other day, but I can't control everything an apprentice does when he or she is outside my presence."

"Yes, but that was Gareth. Selby—his brother—"

"His given name is Roderick."

"Roderick lost his brother. And he doesn't resent that?" Alastair wondered, now, if that were another of the reasons Selby always came across as so surly and brooding.

"No, Mr. Stone. He doesn't. Do you think he would have begged to apprentice with me if he felt his brother's death was my fault?" He shook his head before Alastair could answer. "No. After I turned him down for an apprenticeship and offered him the position here at Caventhorne and the opportunity for supplemental instruction, I examined his aura thoroughly while asking him some pointed questions about just that. I suspected the same thing you did. But the truth, Mr. Stone, is almost always one's best defense against misunderstanding. I did not withhold any facts from him, or from his parents. The only exception being that I did not deem it necessary to describe Gareth's death in detail. That would have done nothing but cause unneeded pain."

Alastair pondered that. He didn't have any siblings, so it was harder to put himself in Roderick Selby's position, but he wondered if he wouldn't harbor at least a few lingering subconscious resentments of Desmond. Had the master pushed the student too far? Had he failed to provide enough feedback, spurring Gareth to try more ambitious methods of impressing him?

He didn't know. He probably wouldn't ever know. He swallowed and let his breath out slowly. "Thank you, sir," he said at last.

"You're still not convinced, are you?" Desmond asked. His tone was quiet and even.

Alastair shrugged. "I don't know, sir. It seems hard to believe, but if you say it's so—you know the situation better than I do. I don't think it would be a good idea to ask Selby about it, so I suppose I should just let it go."

"You are correct that it probably wouldn't be best to discuss it with Selby." Desmond returned a group of candles to a table with a gesture. "He is a good man, Mr. Stone—loyal and exceptional at his job. I understand that there might be some friction between the two of you due to your unusual circumstances, but I trust that both of you are mature enough not to allow it to affect your work."

"Yes, sir." He was right—regardless of what had happened to Selby's brother, and how Selby felt about his own situation, he didn't intend to let it affect his shot at apprenticeship. "I'd best get going—I've got quite a lot to do before our next lesson."

Desmond didn't stop him. He took the lift back upstairs, still thinking about Selby. He did feel better, though—even if Desmond couldn't read minds, exactly, he was bloody good at reading auras. If his master wasn't concerned about any lingering bad feelings on Selby's part, he supposed he shouldn't be either. As he'd told Desmond, there was no way he was going to approach Selby himself about it.

CHAPTER SIXTEEN

ONCE AGAIN OVER THE NEXT THREE DAYS, life returned to normal for Alastair—or at least as normal as it ever got at Caventhorne—and once again, he began to entertain the faint stirrings of hope that he might succeed in passing his probation.

Desmond did not bring up his mistake again, and Alastair remained vigilant to give careful consideration to any magic he wanted to try. He even made a point of running a couple of ideas past Desmond to ensure that they were within acceptable parameters. Sure, he felt a bit like a child who had to run to Teacher every time he wanted to try something new, but better safe than sorry. He could put up with anything for another week, if it meant studying formally with Desmond.

Eyes on the prize—that was what it was all about.

He didn't think Desmond had told Selby about their conversation. He continued avoiding the assistant steward whenever possible, directing his non-magical requests to Kerrick. Selby, for his part, made himself scarce most of the time when Alastair was around, appearing only when something was required of him and leaving as soon as it was finished. On the few occasions they were required to briefly interact, he was scrupulously polite and courteous. Alastair noticed a few faint twitches in his aura indicating that he might feel otherwise, but feelings were irrelevant. The guy didn't have to like him to do a good job.

He thought about Madeleine Hill more than he wanted to. It wasn't a problem—despite the fun he'd had talking with her during their afternoon in Wexley, he was pleased to discover that magic remained his first priority. He'd been a little concerned about that, after seeing a few boys with promising futures at Barrow brought down by relationships with girls they'd met in town or during events with other schools. Since he'd had very little experience in that area, he sometimes worried he wouldn't be immune if he should ever meet someone he fancied enough to take his mind off his studies.

But no, the memory of his afternoon with Madeleine remained in a pleasant corner of his mind, something to pull up when he was alone or just needed to be reminded there was a real, normal world out there that he'd be returning to someday. But such thoughts eventually and inevitably drifted back toward the latest magical techniques he was trying to master. He considered it a fair balance, especially since Desmond hadn't commented on it.

On the first day of his final week of probation, Desmond waved him toward the familiar high-backed wooden chair at the end of their morning session. "You have one more week to go in your probationary period, Mr. Stone."

As if he hadn't been keeping track of the days! "Yes, sir. I know."

As was his habit, Desmond began pacing the room. "Tell me—how do you think you are performing?"

Alastair froze. It seemed a simple question, but all he could picture was a field of landmines, or a room full of rocking chairs and nervous, long-tailed cats. He had no idea how Desmond expected him to respond.

Desmond stopped in front of him. "There is no wrong answer, Mr. Stone. It's not a test. I merely want your self-evaluation. You've been here three weeks now, you've had a good taste of my methods of instruction and the sort of life you'll have if we formalize our situation, and I suspect you've entertained a few thoughts about your performance. I want to know what you think."

Alastair swallowed. It occurred to him that never, not once during the entire three weeks he'd been at Caventhorne, had he ever seen William Desmond smile. He wondered if the man was even capable of it. "Er—" he began, angry with himself at how tentative he sounded. *You're supposed to be an adult, damn it. Act like one!* "Well, I think I've done a fairly good job mastering the techniques you've taught me. Except invisibility," he added quickly, in the interest of fairness.

"Indeed. I would not be too concerned about your failure to grasp the nuances of invisibility. As I told you before, every mage has areas of strength and weakness."

Alastair thought about asking what Desmond's areas of weakness were, but decided not to. Instead he said, "I think I've settled in here well enough, and I've been keeping up with the assignments you've been giving me."

"Quite true. I must admit, I've been impressed at your devotion to your work. There have been times when I've assigned you more than I thought you could handle, and each time you've proven that you were up to the task."

"Thank you, sir." *Don't get yourself excited. Just stay calm.*

"However," Desmond added, his expression growing more severe, "you must remember that during your probationary period, you have not been required to pursue your mundane studies except to keep up with your current workload on your own. If you remain in my apprenticeship, your father will provide you with a tutor who will conduct your mundane lessons during the part of the day when you are not studying with me. That will put yet another demand on your limited free time."

"Yes, sir."

"If—and I emphasize again, it is still *if* at this point—I do accept you as my apprentice, our studies will increase in difficulty, requiring more outside work on your part. This will be in addition to whatever homework your mundane tutor assigns you. You might be fortunate to find an hour or two during the week when your time is your own. Do you understand that, and are you willing to accept it?"

Alastair hardly dared to breathe. Despite Desmond's talk about "if," it certainly sounded to him like the man was well on his way to making up his mind. "Of course, sir. I knew that was the way it would be going in."

Desmond once again held his gaze for several long, uncomfortable seconds. His eyes were the pale blue of ice, intense and probing. Alastair was sure his teacher was studying his aura, but not for the first time he wondered if Desmond really *had* worked out a way to read minds.

Eventually, Desmond nodded once. "All right, then. I will be away for the rest of the day and will return late tomorrow afternoon, so our remaining session today and the one tomorrow morning will be cancelled. Spend as much time as you deem necessary working on our current techniques, your mundane assignments, and tidying the workroom. You may have the evening off if you wish. I will see you tomorrow afternoon at the usual time."

"Yes, sir. Thank you, sir."

Alastair headed for the door, making sure he was fully turned away from Desmond before he allowed himself to grin.

For the rest of the day, nothing seemed difficult to him. He grabbed a quick lunch and went back down to the workroom for a few hours to focus on his current magical techniques, then spent two more in his bedroom catching up on his mundane reading. He had to fight a bit to keep his mind from wandering, but he treated it as a challenge and used meditation to compartmentalize the elation he felt at Desmond's words this morning.

He was going to make it!

He was sure of it now. Desmond was clearly pleased with his efforts and his diligence. Apparently, his innate talent was strong enough, and his study habits had passed his master's stringent standards. He rolled onto his back on his bed, idly levitating three of his schoolbooks in a magical imitation of juggling, and smiled. A week from now, he'd officially be William Desmond's apprentice—and the youngest apprentice anybody he knew, including Desmond himself, had ever heard of. In four years he'd be a fully qualified mage, ready to start University when most of his peers were barely a year into their apprenticeships.

He wondered what his father would say when he found out. Surely he'd be proud. Alastair remembered the day back home when his father had told him he'd be studying with Desmond. Orion Stone was not generous with praise, and that simple "well done" had sustained Alastair far more than a whole batch of effusive compliments from more emotionally demonstrative instructors back at Barrow.

And perhaps not best of all—the sheer joy of learning magic was the best, no denying it—but still important: he wouldn't let the family down. He *would* be the sixth in that unbroken line of Stone mages.

He let his breath out in a satisfied sigh and lowered the books into a neat stack on his nightstand. That was all for later, though. First, he had to get through this last week of probation, and four grueling years of apprenticeship.

But for now…he'd finished everything Desmond had told him to do. He'd practiced the new techniques until he had them down, and actually read ahead in his mundane books. He'd tidied up the workroom until it shone, making use of the extra jolt of energy he'd gotten from Desmond's words.

He glanced at his watch: it was a little after five o'clock. He had the evening ahead of him, and nothing he was required to do.

He rolled over on the bed and opened his nightstand drawer. Inside, next to a couple more books and a notepad, lay the scrap of paper Madeleine Hill had given him back in Wexley. The one with her phone number on it.

Should he do it? Would she even want to see him again? Was it wise to pursue something he couldn't maintain, and was it even fair to Madeleine to try? He knew, once he started his true apprenticeship, he wouldn't have time for her, or any girl.

The thought gave him a twinge of regret, but it was true. Desmond hadn't hidden anything from him, and one or two hours' free time at unpredictable intervals wasn't enough to keep a proper relationship going. Not to mention he couldn't afford to let his concentration get fragmented. He wasn't naïve: he was a fifteen-year-old boy, complete with the same raging urges nearly every fifteen-year-old boy in the history of time had to deal with. It was difficult enough to ignore them when he didn't even have any female friends his own age, let alone someone who could potentially develop into more.

He wasn't sure if it was even true anyway, or just wishful thinking—he barely knew her, and as far as he knew she could already have a boyfriend. Maybe she'd considered their afternoon together to be nothing more than a bit of harmless fun, and she'd laugh in his face if he suggested there might have been more to it than that.

Then again, she *had* kissed him. On the cheek, not the lips, but still. A kiss was a kiss.

He sat up and grabbed the slip of paper. Tonight, perhaps for the last time in a long while, he was free. He was going to take full advantage of it. If she laughed at him, it was probably for the best anyway. At least then he'd know for sure.

But if she didn't...

His bedroom didn't have a telephone, so he found an empty guest room that did, ducked inside, and locked the door. This would be hard enough without Selby popping in on him in the middle of the conversation.

He sat on the edge of the bed and stared at the phone. With more than a bit of wry amusement, he realized he was facing this simple call with more trepidation than he had all the techniques he'd been studying with Desmond.

Learning magic? *Pfft, easy-peasy.* Trying to satisfy a taskmaster instructor who never gave you any feedback? *No problem.* Keeping up with a rigorous mundane workload on top of a full slate of magical training at the same time? *Bring it on.*

Calling a girl he barely knew and asking her out?

Basically terrifying.

It was after five. Maybe she'd already had dinner. Coffee, perhaps, or ice cream? Did they even *have* an ice cream shop in Wexley? Another trip to the cinema? The only other film playing was some romantic comedy thing he'd ignored in favor of the horror show. But girls liked romantic comedies, right?

She's probably busy anyway. She probably has loads of guys asking her out.

He pulled the slip with her number on it from his pocket and put it on the table. *Just do it, you prat. She's not going to bite you.* He thought of Selby, and what he might say if he found out—especially about his nervousness. He could practically picture the sly grin and hear the drawling, deceptively courteous comments.

"This is stupid," he muttered, and snatched up the phone. Before he lost his nerve, he punched in the number and settled back to wait.

It rang three times, then picked up. "'Lo?" It sounded like a young boy, maybe ten or so.

Great. Now he had to get past the gatekeeper. "Yes. Er. Is Madeleine there?"

"Who's callin'?"

"Alastair Stone."

"Who?"

"Alastair Stone," he repeated more slowly, suddenly thinking this had been a bad idea.

"I don't think Maddy knows no Al-ster Stone," the voice said dubiously.

"It's all right," he said. "I'll ring back lat—"

There was the sound of a scuffle, muffled voices, and then Madeleine was on the line. "Ali. Hi! How are you?"

"I'm good." He hoped he'd managed to sound casual.

"I didn't think you'd call," she said. "Sorry about Charlie—he's a twerp."

She sounded a little shy, which surprised him. Could she be nervous too? She'd seemed so confident before. Oddly, her hesitation emboldened him, driving off the last vestiges of his own nervousness. "The ghosts have let me off for the night. I was wondering—well, if you'd like to go somewhere with me this evening. If you're not busy, I mean. Dinner, or coffee, or the cinema or something?"

The pause was long enough he began to fear she was looking for a polite way to decline, but then: "Yeah, I'd like that. I'd have to ask Dad, though. And I've already had dinner—had it at the shop after I got off work."

"What about a film, then?"

"That would be great. Already saw the horror one, but there's another one. Some romantic thing. Probably bore you to death, though."

"It's all right," he said. "Do you want to?"

"Sure. Sounds like fun. Let me ask Dad. Hold on."

She disappeared for several moments, then returned. "He says it's fine as long as I'm home by ten. School night."

"Brilliant. Shall I come by your place, or meet you there?"

"Meet me," she said. "At seven, okay? I'll have Dad drop me off, and you can walk me home after."

"It's a plan."

"See you then," she said, and he could hear the smile in her voice as she hung up.

He waited a few minutes to calm down before heading downstairs. Once again, he dreaded running into Selby, especially now that he knew the assistant steward could probably read auras. He'd be sure to notice something and comment on it, and Alastair didn't feel inclined to mess up his good mood by dealing with that.

Selby was nowhere to be found, though, as he reached the ground floor and hurried off in search of Kerrick. He found him in one of the sitting rooms, reading a newspaper.

"Oh, hello, sir," Kerrick said with a smile, looking up. "Haven't seen much of you today. Mr. Desmond got you busy while he's gone?"

Alastair nodded. "All day, but he's given me the evening off. I'm going into town for a bit—just thought I'd let someone know in case I'm needed for anything."

Kerrick's smile widened. "Good to see you getting in a little time to yourself. That's something you'll need to learn to do if Mr. Desmond takes you on. You'll work like a dog, but you still need a bit of relaxation."

Alastair noticed Kerrick didn't ask where he was going or what he'd be doing in town. He could get to like this whole 'responsibility' thing—back at Barrow, leaving the school was a big deal requiring permission slips, along with careful reporting of where you'd be, who you'd be with, and when you'd be back. And that was only for the older students. Even when he was home for holidays, he had to report his comings and goings to Aubrey.

"Do you need a ride?" Kerrick asked.

He hadn't thought about that. Last time he'd gone into Wexley he'd been running, but it wouldn't do to show up coated with sweat. He couldn't exactly take Madeleine to a movie wearing a tracksuit, anyway, and walking would be too slow. "Mr. Desmond said someone around here might have a bicycle I could borrow…"

"Are you sure I can't give you a ride, sir? It's no trouble, I assure you."

"No, thanks—I'm not sure when I'll be coming back, and I don't want to wake anyone up."

Kerrick put down his paper, thought a moment, and then smiled, raising a finger. "I've got it," he said. "Give me a moment to check something—I might have just the thing."

Alastair pulled up in front of the cinema an hour later, which was twenty minutes before he was supposed to meet Madeleine. That was all right, though—it would give him time to get collected, and perhaps convince himself he had no reason to be so nervous. She was just a girl. An attractive girl who seemed to fancy him, but that was all. They'd have a pleasant evening together and that would be that.

He had to admit the little green Vespa scooter Kerrick had talked one of the groundskeepers into lending him was much better than a bicycle, or walking. It had taken him a few minutes of instruction to get the hang of riding it, but by the time he zipped off down the road toward the gate, the scooter's owner was no longer casting dubious looks at him and wincing every time he hit the brakes.

He liked the thing, he decided as he parked it under a streetlight a few doors down from the cinema entrance. Maybe after he passed his probation, he'd ask his father if he could have one of his own. He rarely asked for material things since he didn't care much about them in general, but his father had never turned down a reasonable request.

Madeleine showed up at five minutes to seven, as Alastair loitered outside the cinema house studying the movie posters. "Hi!" she called, coming up behind him.

He turned. "Hi." She was dressed casually, in a sky-blue, scoop-neck T-shirt, faded jeans, and boots, which made him glad he hadn't shown up in a suit. He still felt overdressed in a button-down long-sleeved shirt with the sleeves turned up and the most casual pair of trousers he'd dared bring along, but it wasn't as bad as it could have been. Still, he caught her looking him up and down.

"Sorry," he said, indicating his outfit. "Mr. Desmond isn't much for jeans. He thinks they're vulgar or something. Had to leave all the good stuff at home."

She laughed. "I wondered if you owned any," she admitted. "So formal all the time."

Her laugh warmed him. For now—just for the next two or three hours—he wouldn't think about magic, or Desmond, or his father, or all the things he'd have to deal with in the weeks and months to come. For now, all he wanted to do was sit next to Madeleine and watch some fluffy romantic comedy film he probably wouldn't remember a bit of tomorrow.

Just…be normal for a little while, for one last time before everything changed.

"You sure you're all right with this one?" she asked as they waited in the queue to buy tickets. "I could see the horror one again. You'd like it, I think."

"It's all right. I actually saw it the other day. Let's watch something new."

She gave him a sly grin. "Or, you know…*not* watch it."

It was a good thing they'd reached the front of the queue by that point, so he could hide the sudden full-body tingle that rushed through him by dealing with the ticket-seller.

They got a tub of popcorn to share and drinks the size of small buckets, and he let her choose where they sat. She trooped all the way up to the back row and dropped down into one of the middle seats. "This okay?"

"Brilliant." The theater was old and smelled strongly of popcorn, with just a hint of musty funk. The seats were narrow and covered in a tatty red velvet-like fabric, rubbed smooth by thousands of customers' backsides over the years. He settled in next to her and tried not to think too hard about the implications of her choice of location. Maybe she just liked sitting in the back row.

Since it was a weeknight and the film had been out for a while, there weren't many other people in the theater. Alastair watched as a few others drifted in and found seats: mostly couples, a few groups of women, a mother and her adolescent daughter. He amused himself for the moment looking over the auras—the blazing nimbuses that glowed around each person still fascinated him. He wondered if he'd ever get used to them, and wished he could show them to Madeleine.

"So," she said, "Has your teacher decided yet if he's keeping you around?"

He switched off. "No—not quite yet. Though I'm starting to think I might be okay."

"What makes you think so?" She grabbed a big handful of popcorn and munched on it, turning a little in her seat to face him.

He shrugged. "I think I'm doing what he expects. And today he sort of started talking like I might have a future. I don't know—I don't want to jinx it by getting my hopes up."

"Well, I'd like it if you stayed. The boys around here are all right, but they're a bit boring, you know? I've known most of them all my life. Could use a bit of new blood, couldn't we?"

He didn't answer. He wanted to tell her that even if he did stay, he probably wouldn't be able to see her anymore—at least not often enough to develop any sort of real friendship. He was struggling for something else to fill the silence when she gripped his arm and pointed toward a couple coming in.

"That's Rosemary Cooper," she said under her breath. "With a *bloke*." Her surprise came though even in her whisper.

Alastair followed her gaze. Sure enough, it was the same nervous girl he'd seen at the park a few days ago. Behind her was a shadowy figure he couldn't make out clearly in the dim light.

He switched back to magical sight. Rosemary's aura was the same orange as before, but less disturbed; the darker patches were still there, but the aura had a bouncy quality to it that hadn't been there before—and a few bright red patches indicating she might be more interested in the guy she was with than she was letting on. She seemed happy, anyway. Behind her, her date's aura was green and steady. "Is that odd?" he asked as the two of them sidled down one of the rows halfway up and took seats in the middle.

"Well...yeah. I've never seen Rosemary with a guy. Thought she was too shy, or her mum wouldn't let her. I don't recognize him, though—maybe he's her cousin or something. He looks older than her."

Alastair doubted it. The red flashes didn't fit with a cousin. He watched them for a moment, but at that point the lights dimmed and the screen lit up with trailers.

He didn't pay much attention to the movie. For a while he sat, arm pressed against Madeleine's, as they took turns dipping into the tub of popcorn. He watched Rosemary Cooper and her date several rows in front of them; about a quarter of the way into the film, they leaned closer to each other and the guy slipped his arm around Rosemary's shoulders. She rested her head against him.

Alastair wondered how Madeleine would react if he put his arm around her, or perhaps held her hand. He pondered that as he took another handful of popcorn.

"Bit boring, isn't it?" Madeleine whispered.

194 |

He turned toward her. She was watching him, her eyes glittering in the dimness. He could just make out her sly smile.

"Bit," he admitted.

She pressed her arm a little harder into his, leaning in until her upper arm was against him too. When he glanced at her aura, he saw definite signs of red flashes around the edges of the sunny yellow.

Taking a chance, he leaned in a little closer to her. He figured if she wasn't interested, she'd pull back, maybe on the pretense of grabbing more popcorn.

She didn't pull back. She tilted her face closer until it was barely an inch from his.

Okay, even with his minimal experience with girls, that was a hint Alastair couldn't miss, or misinterpret.

He kissed her.

She kissed him back. Her lips were soft and hot, and she tasted like popcorn and cherry lip gloss.

Neither one of them watched the rest of the movie.

Afterward, Alastair didn't tell Madeleine he'd arrived on the Vespa. Part of it was that it didn't really have the seating for two, but most of it was because walking her home would allow him to spend more time with her.

"Want to stop for a coffee or something?" he asked as they left the theater. His mind refused to stop replaying the last couple of hours, most of which had been spent in deep—albeit mostly gentlemanly—exploration of Madeleine's charms. Considering she'd cheerfully given as good as she got and nobody came by with a flashlight to kick them out, he counted the evening an unmitigated success. Even if he didn't get to see Madeleine again for a long time, those memories weren't going anywhere. The taste of her lips, the light floral scent of her hair, her soft skin as he'd slipped his hand under her shirt to rub her back as they kissed and she gently encouraged him to move it around to the front…those would all be pretty much on permanent rotation for the foreseeable future. The problem would be getting rid of them when he was supposed to be thinking about other things—like magic.

"Probably shouldn't," she said with some regret, glancing at her watch. "It's already almost nine-thirty, and Dad won't like it if I'm home late." She brightened. "Some other time, though, okay?"

He didn't reply to that. It might not be strictly the most honorable way to handle things, but he wanted to wait as long as he could before telling her that the "other time" might be a long while in the future—if ever. He'd take her home first, and tell her when they got there. "Where are we going, then?"

"C'mon. Best way is to cut through the park. More private, too." She took his hand and tugged him down the street.

The park—the same one where they'd observed the football players the other day—wasn't well lit this late; the pitches were dark, and only a few pole lamps lined the meandering paths.

Madeleine didn't seem worried, though. She squeezed his hand. "I had a good time tonight."

"So did I." He thought about the benches near the pitch, and how nice it would be to just sit down there with her for a while to continue what they'd been doing at the theater— and perhaps even a little more, if she was willing and

R. L. KING

enthusiastic—but he drove the thought back. *Better get used to it now,* he told himself. *Magic and girls don't mix, and you've already made your choice. Go take a cold shower and get over it.*

Her house, a small, older two-story, was on a narrow lane a couple blocks from the park. "Here we are," she said, coming to a stop in front of it. "Now you know where I live, so it's only fair that I expect an invitation to come meet the ghosts some time."

She was smiling, but he couldn't tell if she was teasing. "We'll—see," he said. "They're a bit…touchy sometimes."

"That's all right. I like touchy." Now she really was grinning. She squeezed his hand. "Thanks for a great time, Ali."

Normally he'd find the shortening of his name annoying, but from her he didn't mind. "Thank *you,*" he said.

"Ring me again?"

He sighed, and let go of her hand. "If I can. I—don't know how things will go, going forward. I might not be able to come to town very often."

She looked down. "Well…okay. If you can, then."

He leaned closer to her, giving her plenty of time to back up. When she didn't, he gave her a gentle kiss, far less passionate than what they'd shared in the back row at the cinema. "I'd—better go now. Don't want your dad to get upset."

"No…Don't want that." She pulled back then, squeezed his hand a last time, and turned and hurried up the walk toward the front door. He didn't miss the look of disappointment in her eyes before she did it, and magical sight revealed a dimming in her aura to go with it.

Alastair remained there watching until she'd opened it and disappeared inside, then watched for a few moments more before turning to head back the way he'd come.

All at once, all the good feelings he'd been enjoying all night flowed away, leaving him distracted and disassociated.

He knew he was doing the right thing. Magic was all he'd ever cared about from the time he'd been a small child and found out it existed. He knew pursuing it would mean sacrifices.

He just hadn't—not until tonight anyway—encountered one of those so-called sacrifices that actually meant something to him.

| CHAPTER SEVENTEEN

A LASTAIR DIDN'T HURRY BACK TO THE VESPA. He didn't see any need to, since he was in no rush to get back to Caventhorne. His thoughts were a muddle, warring between pleasant recollections of the evening they'd shared and the sinking feeling that, even if somehow he were able to find enough free time to give Madeleine a call again in the near future, whatever might have been growing between them had already begun to cool. Even though he knew it was ultimately for the best, that still didn't make it hurt any less.

The most direct way back to the center of town was to re-trace his steps through the park. He walked with his hands stuffed in his pockets and his head down, barely paying any attention to his surroundings. The park was deserted at this hour, the intermittent light poles along the path providing small pools of illumination at widely spaced intervals. A cou-ple of the poles were dark, their bulbs either burned out or vandalized. Alastair trudged on, not caring whether he walked through light or darkness. It was all the same to him right now.

The best thing to do, he knew, was to go back to Cav-enthorne, take a good long shower, and try to forget about the whole thing.

Best for who, though? a little voice in the back of his mind asked.

Best for him, no doubt about it. In his logical, analytical mind, he knew it. Magic was his passion, his love, and his life. Anything that took his mind off that was bad for him. Anything that tempted him to stray from his single-minded focus on being the best mage he could possibly be could derail his progress for the rest of his career. He was poised to get the chance of a lifetime—the opportunity to study with the best of the best. The chance to have his magical future shaped by one of the strongest talents and most brilliant magical minds in the world.

How could he even consider putting all that at risk so he could snog a chip-shop girl in the back row of a tatty old cinema?

No...it didn't matter how she looked at him with those wide green eyes, or the way her lips felt on his, or her humor and quick wit. It didn't matter how her nose crinkled when she laughed, or the way her warm, willing body felt under his hands.

Magic, Stone. Magic. He almost growled as his thoughts turned once again to his evening with Madeleine, and his body betrayed his mind with a whole collection of stirrings that were frustratingly difficult to ignore.

No, it was settled. Much as he hated it, much as his body and his inconvenient urges were trying to convince him otherwise, he'd have to be done with Madeleine. With all girls, in fact. It was only for four years, after all—maybe not even that long. Once he was really Desmond's apprentice and he'd earned his master's respect, maybe he could risk it. Maybe in a couple years, he could let his guard down a little, and

R. L. KING

maybe meet someone who enjoyed spending time with him. But not now. The price for failure was simply too high. The sooner he realized it—the sooner he truly accepted it—the better off he'd be.

He'd made it halfway through the park when a sound off to his left jolted him from his brooding thoughts.

He stopped, listening harder. He'd definitely heard something, but he couldn't identify what it was. Probably an animal, or maybe the far-off laughter of some couple making out on one of the benches. *Good that* somebody *is,* he thought morosely. He almost started moving once more when he heard it again.

Voices. At least three, maybe four—he couldn't tell for sure. One of them was female, the others male. He closed his eyes to focus more tightly on the sounds, and froze.

"No—please—" The female voice sounded muddy and slurred, but shook with fear.

The response was deep male laughter, followed by some words Alastair couldn't make out. All of the sounds were coming from an area hidden by trees and darkness, well off the path.

He switched to magical sight, and immediately spotted several auras filtered through the scattered trees and bushes. They were different colors—orange, green, blue, yellow—but all four were in chaos, tinged with bright, flaring red.

"No! Let me go!" the female voice called again, pitching louder. "I don't want—"

Her voice was suddenly muffled, as if someone had clamped a hand over her mouth.

Alastair froze. Whoever she was, she was in trouble. And here in the middle of this deserted park, he might be the only one who'd heard her cries for help.

The male voices laughed again. One, as slurred as hers had been, said something, but all Alastair could make out was, "...know you want it," and "...leadin' me on, little bitch." He sounded older than her.

Alastair didn't think. He didn't consider his actions, or any possible danger he might be putting himself in. Instead, he ran toward the voices, with no idea what he'd do when he got there. In only a few seconds, he burst through the trees into a small clearing.

He stopped in shock.

The faint moonlight revealed two large, male figures standing back from another one, who was bent over a prone woman. They appeared to be cheering their friend on as he fumbled at her clothes. The stench of cheap liquor hung in the air, strong enough Alastair could smell it from several feet away.

That wasn't the worst of it, though.

The worst was that he recognized two of the figures. It was too dim to see them clearly, but that didn't matter: their auras were clear as day.

The sobbing girl on the ground was Rosemary Cooper, and the guy bending over her, laughing drunkenly along with his two cheering mates, was her date from the cinema.

For the second time in less than a minute, he reacted without thinking. "Get away from her!" he yelled. Heart pounding, he gathered magic to him and flung the man looming over Rosemary aside. His control wasn't the best and the man was heavy, but he succeeded in shoving him sideways enough that he stumbled and crashed to the ground. His drunken state probably made it easier.

"What the 'ell?" one of the others yelled, whirling toward Alastair.

The third and final man also turned, fixing a cold glare. "Off you go, kid. This ain't your concern." He seemed somewhat less drunk than the other two, but still swayed on his feet.

On the ground, Rosemary continued sobbing, scrabbling feebly to cover herself with the remnants of her torn sweater.

Alastair was sure if they could read auras, they could see the bright red of terror blooming around his. But they couldn't. He held his ground and forced himself to keep his tone even. They'd only know he was scared if he let them see it. "Get out of here. Leave her alone."

"Who's the twerp?" Rosemary's original date asked as he scrambled awkwardly back to his feet. His belt and the front of his jeans were undone. "Bugger off, kid. She wants it. Stupid little tart's been askin' for it all night."

Alastair kept a close eye on all three of them. He had no idea what they might do next, and he had little confidence that his underdeveloped magical abilities would be able to hold all three of them off if they decided to rush him. As sometimes happened when he was stressed or angry, though, his mouth took over before his brain caught up. "You lot are pathetic. You so hard up you have to force yourselves on a girl before she'll notice you?" He glared at Green Aura. "What'd you do, spike her drink back at the cinema?"

"Hey, wait—" the guy said, squinting to get a better look at him in the dim light. "You're that little wanker in the back row, aren't you? The one feelin' up the chip-shop bird?"

Rosemary moaned. "Please...please...I want to go home..."

"Let her go," Alastair said. "Get the hell out of here."

"Or what?" the more lucid of the other two demanded, balling up his fists. "Skinny kid like you gonna take all of us on? If you're lucky, we'll just kick yer arse."

The third one brayed drunken laughter, which abruptly morphed into a roar of rage. "Get 'im!" he yelled, and charging forward. "Kick 'is arse!"

The other two added their yells to their friends' and both surged after him.

Alastair did it just like Desmond had taught him. He focused on the pattern, gathered magical energy, and projected his will outward into a glowing shield that shoved the three men violently backward. They tumbled in a tangled heap of flailing arms and legs and shouted curses, then tripped over each other as they tried to get back to their feet.

"What the bloody 'ell?" one of them shouted. He didn't sound quite as drunk now. He sounded scared, and he was staring at Alastair with wide-eyed disbelief. "What did you do?"

The other two weren't yelling. They were still trying to get up, their feet slipping as they tried to gain traction on the damp grass.

"Hey!" another voice—older, authoritative—yelled from the trees, and the piercing beam of a flashlight split the darkness. "What's goin' on over there?"

"It's the cops! Run!" Green Aura yelled. He slipped again, recovered, and took off into the night. His friends both quickly followed.

Alastair, panting, hurried over to Rosemary. "Over here!" he yelled to the voice behind the flashlight. Then, to the sobbing girl: "It's all right. You're all right now."

She threw her arms around him and continued crying into his shoulder. He smelled alcohol hovering around her as well, and thought his initial idea that her "date" had spiked her soda back at the cinema had been correct.

A figure burst through the trees, and the harsh flashlight beam pinned Alastair and Rosemary. "Get away from her!" the man ordered. "Now!"

Alastair disentangled himself from Rosemary as gently as he could and got up, pointing. He couldn't see the man with the light glaring in his eyes, but he was sure he had to be a policeman. "They went that way! There were three of them."

"Get away!" the cop ordered again, coming closer. The flashlight beam moved off Rosemary, who was still trying to fix her sweater, and settled on Alastair.

All at once, Alastair froze as he realized that, based on the scene he'd encountered, the cop might think *he* was the one who'd attacked Rosemary. "Officer—it's not me. There were three of them. They ran off when you yelled."

"Don't you move, boy." The cop held him in the bright beam for a second longer, then shifted it so it illuminated the clearing and muttered something into his radio.

Now that his eyes weren't dazzled, Alastair could see he was right—it *was* a cop. Big, beefy, maybe mid-thirties. "Officer—"

"I said don't move." He hurried over to Rosemary and crouched down next to her. "It's all right, luv," he said in a more gentle voice. "Everything's all right now. Did he hurt you?"

For a moment, Alastair was terrified that the "slow" and "strange" Rosemary wouldn't—or couldn't—reveal the truth, which would put him in a lot of trouble. But she shook her head violently, her slurred, muddy voice bubbling through her sobs. "No...no...wasn't him. He helped me. Was Bobby...and his mates."

The cop's brow furrowed. He glanced at Alastair, then back at Rosemary, and frowned, sniffing the air. "You been drinking, luv?"

"I think he spiked her fizzy drink," Alastair said. "Back at the cinema. Her name is Rosemary Cooper."

Another flashlight beam appeared through the trees, and a moment later another cop—a woman this time—broke through. "You stay put," the male cop told Alastair, then patted Rosemary on the shoulder. "Everything's fine now, honey. This lady here will help you, all right?"

Rosemary nodded, but didn't look up. She'd gotten her sweater back to as much order as she could manage, and now stared at her hands in her lap as she sat against the tree.

The male cop motioned Alastair over to the other side of the clearing. "Right, then," he said. "She right? You helped her?"

Alastair nodded. "Yes, sir." Now that it appeared he wasn't about to be arrested, the adrenaline from the scene was draining away. His heart pounded, and so did his head from the magic. That had been a big shield he'd cast, bigger than he'd ever done before.

"You been drinking?"

"No, sir."

He shined the beam around—with the female cop's added in, the clearing was much better illuminated now—and it fell on a couple of bottles the three attackers had dropped when they'd taken off after Alastair had hit them with the shield. "So those aren't yours?"

"No, sir. Like I said—there were three of them." He paused a moment, trying to get his spinning thoughts under control so he could present a coherent story. "I was at the cinema earlier—I saw one of them with her there. I don't know who the other two were."

"Can you describe them?"

"Not really. It was dark, and I didn't see the one at the cinema very well." He couldn't exactly tell him about the green aura, after all.

As the cop wrote something in his notebook, Alastair glanced over toward where the female officer was chatting softly with Rosemary. The girl had stopped sobbing now, and appeared to have gone back to her shy, uncommunicative self. Occasionally she glanced over toward Alastair and mumbled something he couldn't hear.

"How did you see them here?" the male cop asked. "What's your name, by the way?"

"Alastair Stone."

He frowned again. "Stone. Don't know that name. Haven't seen you 'round town. Where do you live?"

"I don't live here in Wexley, sir. I'm—studying here. Up at Caventhorne."

"Got some ID?"

Alastair pulled out his wallet and handed over his ID card.

The cop shined the flashlight on it, his gaze flicking between the photo and Alastair's face. For a moment it appeared he might say something, but then he shook his head and handed the card back. "Okay. Okay. So what were you doing in the park this late?"

"I was at the cinema with a girl. Madeleine Hill."

"Oh, yeah, I know Maddy's dad. Owns the chip shop downtown."

"Yes, sir. I was walking her home after, and then I walked back through the park to where I'd left my Vespa in town."

The cop wrote that down, then waved over toward where the scene had occurred. "How did you notice them?"

"Heard something. It sounded like a girl needed help. So I investigated."

"And you say there were three of them?"

"Yes, sir."

The cop eyed Alastair, looking him up and down. "Skinny kid like you fought off three big blokes?"

Alastair swallowed. "No...no, sir. I didn't fight them off. They were drunk. I yelled, and they ran off. Probably didn't want to get caught."

For a moment, it seemed the cop would challenge his words, but finally he just closed his notebook. "Okay. You'll have to come back to the station and give us a statement, and we'll have to call your parents."

Great. Things were about to get uncomfortable again. "You...can't do that, sir."

"What do you mean, I can't?"

"My father's away, sir. We live in Surrey normally, but he travels. You can call Caventhorne if you like. My ma—er—teacher is away for the evening, but you can ask for Kerrick. He'll vouch for me."

Alastair had hoped he could handle this without involving anybody at Caventhorne, but it didn't look like that would be the case. He shouldn't have been surprised, he supposed—despite the fact that everybody at Caventhorne treated him like an adult, down here in the real world he was still just a fifteen-year-old boy.

Once again the cop looked suspicious, but finally sighed. "Right. Give me the number, and I'll do that when we get back to the station."

Great. This night just kept getting better and better. "I—don't have it, sir."

"You don't *have* it?"

"No, sir. I've only been there for three weeks, and I haven't had any reason to call there."

The cop's expression suggested he was trying to determine if Alastair was being a smart-ass. "Then you'll have to come—" He paused as yet another policeman came through the trees and beckoned to him. "You stay here," he told Alastair, and moved off to confer with the new cop.

Alastair waited, hands in his pockets against the growing damp chill of the night. His adrenaline surge was almost completely gone now, leaving him twitchy and shivering; the persistent dull ache in his head wasn't getting any worse, but it wasn't getting any better either. Now that he knew Rosemary was safe and would be taken care of, all he wanted to do was get back to the Vespa and home to Caventhorne. Would they want to take him back to the station? Would they keep him there all night?

The cop came back over. "They've picked up three blokes tryin' to make a run for it. Drunk as lords, they were. Crashed their car into a hedgerow and took off across a field, but we got 'em." He paused, and Alastair got the impression he wanted to say something else.

"That's—good news, right?" he ventured.

"Yeah. Good news. They'll take 'em to the station, get a statement from the girl. Got 'em for public drunkenness and drink driving, minimum, and once the Cooper girl tells 'er story, should be open and shut." He tilted his head at Alastair. "There's just one thing weird."

"Sir?"

"They all said the same thing—said some skinny dark-haired kid yelled somethin' at 'em, then waved his hands and some glowin' thing shot out and knocked 'em on their arses. You got any idea what they were talkin' about?"

Alastair wondered if the cop could see his heart pounding; to him, it felt as if it might leap directly out of his chest and make a run for it. He forced himself to keep his tone even—this might be the most important acting job he'd ever done in his life. "Er—no, sir. No idea. They were all pretty drunk, though. Tripping over their feet. I don't think they expected anyone to bother them while they were—" He nodded toward Rosemary, who was being led off by the female cop.

The cop held his gaze for a few more seconds, then sighed. "Yeah, that's probably it. Bloody idiots were so blotto they were probably seein' pink elephants." He closed his notebook.

"So…do I have to go to the station, then?"

He considered. "Got your name and where you're stayin'. Cooper girl says you helped her, and I don't smell any booze on you. I think it'll be okay for you to go home for the night. If we need you, we'll call this Kerrick tomorrow. You need a ride?"

Relief—momentary relief, anyway—washed over Alastair. "No, thank you, sir. I've got to pick up the Vespa downtown. I borrowed it, so I need to get it home."

"Right, then." He paused a moment, then his expression softened as he clapped Alastair on the shoulder. "Good job, boy. That girl would have been in a world of trouble if you hadn't come along. I'm sure her mum will want to thank you."

Alastair nodded, but didn't reply. When the cop waved him off, he trudged back through the park and back downtown, finding the Vespa right where he'd left it. He glanced at his watch: barely ten-thirty. So much had happened over the last hour, it felt a lot later.

When he got back to Caventhorne after a brief but chilly ride, he managed to hurry up to his room without seeing or talking to anyone. He'd have to do it tomorrow, of course—there was no avoiding it. He was sure the police would call Kerrick, but probably not until the morning. And then there was Desmond himself, who would no doubt hear about it as soon as he got home. But for now, all Alastair wanted to do was sleep.

Sleep, however, did not come easily. He lay in his bed for hours, staring up at the ceiling and trying to will his mind to let go of the images of the three men laughing around the terrified Rosemary Cooper, and the memory of her cries and the stench of alcohol. Every time he almost dropped off, another memory would jolt him back to full wakefulness. By the time his exhaustion finally got the better of him, it was well after four a.m.

Even then, his sleep was uneasy, his dreams haunted by jumbled images of Madeleine Hill, Rosemary, and, hovering above them, the looming, dark figure of William Desmond.

| CHAPTER EIGHTEEN

ALASTAIR WOULD HAVE PREFERRED to sleep late, but awakened before seven a.m. For several moments he lay in bed, looking up at the same ceiling he'd been staring at for most of the night, and allowed himself to hope that everything that happened last night had been a dream.

Well, *almost* everything. His time with Madeleine Hill, despite their bittersweet parting, was a memory he didn't want to forget. But as for the rest—life going forward would be a lot easier if the whole thing had been nothing more than a product of his overactive imagination.

But no—there were his clothes from last night hanging over the chair next to his bed, and there were the keys to the Vespa on his desk. He'd have to return those to the groundskeeper.

He drifted through his morning routine of showering, dressing, and preparing for the day in a kind of fog, his mind torn between horror at what had almost happened to Rosemary Cooper, dismay about what *had* happened with Madeleine, and pride that he'd managed to stop those three louts before they'd done something terrible. That situation could have turned out a lot worse than it had: if his magic had faltered, either because of fear or simple lack of experience using it in real-world situations, he had no idea what those three men might have done to him. Beaten him up, at minimum—possibly even killed him, in their drunken state. And Rosemary would have been hurt too. What they'd been intending was horrific enough, but three guys like that could have done serious damage to her without even intending to. Or even panicked and killed her to keep her from talking.

No, he thought as he headed downstairs to dust the workroom—despite wishing none of the night's events had ever happened, he was convinced he'd dealt with them in the best way he could have.

He lingered perhaps a little longer than necessary over the dusting. He straightened books, lined up the room's few chairs neatly along one wall, and checked the circle to make sure no signs of the design he and Desmond had been working on remained. It was only when he stood in the middle of the vast room and admitted to himself he was stalling that he finally headed back to the lift and ascended to the ground floor.

Kerrick was waiting in the great room. He had a duster in his hand and appeared to be deeply interested in one of the paintings hanging on the near wall, but Alastair wasn't fooled. A quick glance at the tension in the man's blue aura confirmed it.

Alastair took a deep breath, let it out slowly, then spoke. "They rang, then, did they?"

Kerrick turned and set down the duster. He didn't have his usual cheerful smile, but neither did he look angry. "They did, yes." He nodded at the dining room. "Will you have breakfast with me, sir? I assume you've some things you'd like to talk about?"

Inexplicably nervous, Alastair joined Kerrick in the dining room. He thought he shouldn't be, since Kerrick had no authority over him, but nonetheless he'd grown to associate the man with a pseudo-parental role over the past few weeks, sort of like he did with Aubrey back home. Neither William Desmond nor Orion Stone—despite the fact that Stone was Alastair's actual parent—gave any impression that they'd be willing or interested in dealing with their young charge's day-to-day problems, so in both cases, in the rare instance when he needed such a thing, Alastair had found it elsewhere.

Now, he and Kerrick faced each other across the table after Gretchen brought in several plates full of various breakfast dishes. It was far more food than they usually served, and Alastair wondered if Kerrick had requested it on purpose. It didn't matter—the last thing he wanted to do right now was eat.

"I—" he began. "So the police called?"

"Yes, sir. They wanted to check your story, and they'd like you to come into town a bit later to give them a more detailed statement."

He glanced up. "How's Rosemary?"

"She'll be fine. Shaken up, of course, but that's to be expected after what happened. They had her checked for injuries, and her mum picked her up."

Alastair noticed something odd in Kerrick's tone. He tilted his head. "So…she wasn't hurt? He spiked her drink…"

"He didn't…" Kerrick said gently. "The police told me the whole story, sir. They found out after they talked to the girl and her mum some more. She'd been sneaking out to see the young man—his name is Bobby Portman, and he's nearly twenty. She says she went with him to the park willingly after the film. They had some drinks together, and then…well, his mates showed up and things got out of hand."

Alastair stared at him. "So she—"

"Apparently, she's been chafing against her mother's overprotectiveness for some time, and when she met Mr. Portman in a shop a few days ago, he decided to take advantage of that. She waited until her mum was out for the evening, and sneaked out. Apparently she didn't realize what was happening, what he had in mind, since the idea of having someone pay attention to her—" He shook his head. "Sad situation."

"She didn't deserve *that*," Alastair said, clenching his fists.

"Of course she didn't," Kerrick agreed. "It was a good thing you came along and frightened them off, sir. The girl's mother would like to talk to you, when you're feeling up to it."

"We'll see," he said. Suddenly, he had no desire to keep dwelling on the situation. He hadn't done anything heroic. Hell, he'd been terrified the whole time. Rosemary was fine, and that was all he cared about. He'd have to go talk to the police later today, no getting out of that, but being away from the house for a while might be a good thing. It would save him moping around like one of the ghosts he'd joked with Madeleine about until Desmond got back.

He brought his gaze up again. "Does everyone know?"

"Not yet, sir. I took the call in private. But Wexley is small, and the staff will hear eventually."

He knew it was true. Nothing moved faster in small villages than gossip. "And Mr. Desmond."

Kerrick nodded. "He is responsible for you while you're here, so he'll have to be told. But you've nothing to be ashamed of, sir. To the contrary—what you did was admirable. The policeman who rang was quite adamant about that." He pointed at the array of food. "You should eat something, sir. I'm sure last night was quite harrowing."

Alastair picked at a piece of toast to satisfy him, but barely finished half of it. His body was hungry; both the stress and the magic had indeed taken a lot out of him. But he was afraid if he ate anything more substantial he'd be sick.

Finally he sighed. "I think I'll go back into town and talk to the police, to get it over with. Do you think Max will mind if I borrow the Vespa again?"

"Would you like a ride, sir? I'd be happy to—"

He stood and tossed his napkin on the table. "No, thanks, Kerrick. I appreciate it, but I think I just want to be alone for a while."

"As you like, sir." Kerrick eyed him with some concern, but didn't comment further.

As he left the dining room on his way back to his room to retrieve the Vespa's keys, Alastair noticed a shadowy figure in one of the halls. A quick shift to magical sight confirmed it was Selby, but as soon as the assistant steward spotted him, he turned abruptly and hurried away.

Alastair spent longer in Wexley than he'd intended.

It didn't take long to give his statement to the police; he found the tiny station tucked away on a side street and explained to them why he was there. The cop he'd spoken with last night wasn't present, but once he gave his name everybody on the small force knew who he was.

They seemed surprised that he'd come alone, but didn't say anything about it. He supposed since he was only giving a statement and not under suspicion for anything, he didn't need a guardian or a solicitor present before they could talk to him. Instead, an older, fatherly man in a suit, who introduced himself as Detective Inspector Ulney, took him into a room and asked him several questions about what had happened. He answered them to the best of his ability and recollection, and the detective wrote his answers down in his notebook. Ulney did ask about the strange "glowing thing" Bobby Portman and his friends claimed pushed them over, but he said the same thing he had last night—that he had no idea what they meant, and that they'd been very drunk at the time. Ulney seemed satisfied with that.

Eventually, after a few more questions about what why he was in Wexley, who his family was, and what he was doing up at Caventhorne, Ulney let him go. "You're a good lad, Stone, though that was a dangerous thing you did. If you should ever come upon a situation like that again, call the police. That's what we're here for. Don't try to be a hero—you could have been badly hurt, and so could Rosemary. Got it?"

"Yes, sir. Though I hope I never have to do that again."

Outside, the day was gray and drizzly. He glanced at his watch: it was after eleven already. The police had asked him questions for nearly an hour. He paused outside the station, trying to decide what he wanted to do.

He still had a few hours before his session with Desmond this afternoon. He could stay in town, perhaps try to find lunch somewhere, since his hunger at this point was overwhelming his lingering stress from last night. Or, he could head back to Caventhorne and spend the time working on his magic, so he'd be well prepared to show Desmond his progress.

Time to get back on the horse, he told himself firmly. The events of the past couple days had done a good job of showing him why he should keep his mind on his magic. He was glad he'd been able to help Rosemary, but from now on it was probably best to just keep his head down and his focus on his studies.

He got back on the Vespa and putted off toward the main street, which would take him back to Caventhorne.

"Ali!" a familiar voice called as he stopped at the corner and waited for a chance to make a right turn.

He turned to see Madeleine Hill hurrying toward him; only then did he realize the chip shop was only two doors down from the corner. He pulled over and waited for her to approach.

She skidded to a stop in front of him, flushed and puffing. "Oh, my God! I just popped by the shop for lunch, and I heard about last night—about Rosemary! Is it true?"

"Er—" he began.

"Did you really save her from being gang-raped by four blokes in the park?" Her eyes were wide, but her expression showed fear, not prurient interest. "I heard one of them was the bloke at the cinema last night!"

"I—didn't really save her," he said. "I just scared them off when I stumbled in on them. It was the one from the cinema, yeah. But there weren't four. Only three."

"Oh, my God!" she repeated. She stared at him with wonder. "That's—amazing. You could have been killed."

"It wasn't like that," he said, suddenly awkward. He knew, in a small town like this, what had happened was a big deal that would likely be the talk of many pub nights and study-hall discussions for weeks to come. But right now, he didn't want to think about it anymore, let alone discuss it. "Really. They're making it sound like more than it is. She's fine. I'm fine. They arrested the guys. That's it."

She eyed him again and her posture changed, as if she'd just remembered how things had gone last night when they'd parted. "Well," she said, more restrained, "it's still amazing. You should be proud of yourself. Really."

"I suppose I should. Doesn't feel like it, though."

A long pause hung between them, as both looked anywhere but at each other. "I...guess I should get back, then," she said, pointing over her shoulder. "Need to get back to class. But when I saw you, I just wanted to—"

"Thanks," he said.

"Yeah."

She held his gaze for a moment longer, her green eyes troubled. "See ya, then." She turned and started to walk away.

"Madeleine?" he called.

She turned back. "Yeah?"

"Rosemary. She..." This was unfamiliar territory for him, and he had no idea how to navigate it. Still, he felt he had to say something. "Well, I think she could use some friends.

R. L. KING

Girls, you know? To help her...so she doesn't..." Damn, this was awkward. He sounded like a stammering idiot!

But Madeleine seemed to get it. Her expression softened a little. "I'll see about that. Talk to her. Maybe invite her to the shop or something. Okay?"

He nodded. "Yeah. Okay."

She lingered a moment longer; when he didn't say anything else, she spun again and trotted back toward the shop.

Alastair waited until she'd disappeared inside, then pulled the Vespa back into the sparse traffic and resumed his trip back to Caventhorne.

| CHAPTER NINETEEN

WHEN HE GOT BACK, Kerrick was waiting for him. "Mr. Desmond rang," he said. "He said he'll be a bit late this afternoon. He wants you to meet him in his study at four o'clock."

Alastair frowned. In his study? "Not the workroom?"

"No, sir. He specified the study."

"Does he…know about what happened?"

Kerrick nodded. "I've explained the situation to him, sir."

"Er…right. Did he say anything else?" Despite Kerrick's neutral expression, Alastair felt as if the temperature in the room had chilled by several degrees. An uncomfortable knot formed in the pit of his stomach.

"No, sir. I'm sure he'd like to discuss the situation with you."

Of course he did. It made sense—Desmond was his temporary guardian, after all. "I'll be sure not to be late. I think I'll head down and work on some things downstairs until then."

It appeared that Kerrick was about to say something, but then he merely nodded. "Yes, sir."

❖

Alastair arrived at Desmond's study at three fifty-five that afternoon. The door was closed. He lingered there, glancing at his watch and wondering if he should knock or wait for the door to open on its own. *Stop it,* he told himself angrily. *Everything's fine. He might ask you to stop seeing Madeleine, but you were going to do that anyway.*

He'd spent the last few hours in the workroom, going through all the techniques Desmond had taught him over the last three weeks, one after the other. He practiced the shield, the invisibility spell (which he was still terrible at), levitation, telekinesis, and magical analysis. He practiced the combination of shield and telekinesis that Desmond had given him leave to work on. He read ahead in several of his reference books and finally, forty-five minutes before he was due to meet Desmond, he did a quick last-minute dusting job and headed upstairs for another shower and a change of clothes.

The most important thing was to keep moving, to keep his mind occupied. The one thing he didn't want to do—couldn't afford to do, if he didn't want to drive himself mad with stress—was to think about why Desmond wanted to meet him in the study instead of the workroom, and what his master planned to say to him.

He couldn't know that, so there was no point in obsessing about it. He'd find out soon enough. He leaned on the wall outside the door and checked his watch again.

Three fifty-eight.

How could two minutes grind by so slowly?

The door swung open as the ancient, massive grandfather clock in the hall struck four. "Come in, Mr. Stone," Desmond's familiar voice called from the dimness inside.

Stop getting nervous, Alastair firmly ordered himself. *He's always like this.*

He stepped inside and the door closed behind him.

Desmond didn't look any different than usual: he sat behind his ornately carved desk, dressed in his usual immaculate suit. His hands rested on the desktop; the room's only illumination came from the late-afternoon sunlight filtering in through a narrow opening in the heavy drapes behind him, and a small lamp on a table nearby. "Sit down, please." He indicated a nearby chair.

Alastair, feeling very much like he had during one of his first meetings with Desmond in this very room, lowered himself to the edge of the chair and waited.

"Kerrick has informed me about your activities last night, Mr. Stone."

"Yes, sir. He mentioned that."

Desmond leaned back a little. "First, let me say I am pleased you were able to prevent a terrible crime. It was fortunate you were in a position to do so."

"Thank you, sir."

"Regarding your—other activities last evening, while I don't necessarily approve of your carrying on any sort of romantic relationship during the apprenticeship period, as long as you conducted yourself as a gentleman and didn't allow it to affect your studies, it was none of my concern."

Alastair thought about what he and Madeleine had done in the back row of the cinema and wasn't sure it exactly qualified as 'conducting himself as a gentleman,' but he wasn't about to tell Desmond that. "It—won't be a problem, sir. I've already decided to stop seeing her, to prevent any...distractions."

"Very wise, Mr. Stone." Desmond took a deep breath, and Alastair was sure he saw a fleeting look of disappointment pass across his face. "Unfortunately, what you do with your time will cease to be any of my concern after today. It is with great regret that I am terminating your apprenticeship, effective immediately."

| CHAPTER TWENTY

ALASTAIR WENT STIFF, his breath catching in his throat. For a moment his brain refused to connect to his mouth. He felt as if Desmond had just hit him in the gut with a battering ram.

No.

It couldn't be! Not after all this time—not after how hard he'd worked—

"Sir—please—" He leaned forward, his voice shaking with desperation.

Desmond held up a hand. His gaze was hard, but not unkind. "No, Mr. Stone. There will be neither argument nor appeal to my decision. I was very clear on that from the beginning."

Alastair's mind whirled. "But—sir—what did I do wrong? You said what I did at the park was—"

"Mr. Stone, please. When I agreed to take you on as my apprentice, you agreed to certain rules. I allowed myself to be swayed, against my better judgment, when you skirted the edge of breaking them before. I did this because of your potential, which I felt was significant. But now I see that my original assessment was correct: your talent is prodigious, your intellect impressive, and your devotion to the Art is strong. But you are simply too young—too immature—to pursue serious magical study yet. Perhaps if you were to approach me again when you are of age, I might consider entering into an arrangement with you. That assumes, of course, that you still wish to do so, and I am not otherwise occupied at the time."

Alastair clutched at the edge of the desk. *Breathe.* 'Too immature,' Desmond had said. 'Too young.' But he'd been doing so well, learning nearly everything his master had thrown at him, and learning it fast. How could Desmond—

"Sir, please. If this is about Madeleine, I told you, I've—"

"I do not know who 'Madeleine' is, Mr. Stone. If she is the girl you have taken to seeing then no, this is not related to her." He pulled a piece of paper to him and glanced down at it. "As your temporary guardian, I received the report from the police regarding what occurred last night." His gaze came up. "The men who attacked the young lady reported that a dark-haired young man shouted something at them, waved his hand, and a—their words—'big glowing thing flew out and knocked us on our arses.'" He looked down at the paper again, then fixed a hard, probing stare on Alastair. "The police were inclined to discount this testimony, attributing it to the men's state of inebriation at the time. You and I know better, do we not, Mr. Stone?"

Alastair couldn't meet his gaze. "Yes, sir."

"Despite my making it abundantly clear that you were not to use magic outside what I have directly taught you or assigned you to practice."

Alastair didn't answer.

"Do you deny using magic against these men, Mr. Stone, against my orders?"

Suddenly, anger rose in Alastair. He brought his gaze back up and glared at Desmond. "No, sir, I don't deny it. What should I have done? There were three of them, and they were all bigger than me. There's no way I could have gotten them away from Rosemary without using magic."

"You should have done what any mundane faced with the same situation would have done." Desmond's face could have been carved from stone, for all the reaction that showed on it. "You should have sought out a police officer, or a telephone to report the crime."

Alastair's anger grew. Was Desmond kidding? He hadn't been there—he hadn't observed the scene in the dark, deserted park. "No one else was around. I didn't see any phones. If I'd yelled, those guys would have heard me and come after me. I had no idea if any policemen were close enough to hear me even if I did."

He focused his own gaze in a fair imitation of Desmond's own. "Are you saying I should have run away to try to find someone who might not even have been there? That even though I had the power to stop them, I shouldn't have used it? What's the point of knowing magic, if you can't use it when you need to?"

He leaped up, still gripping the table, and leaned farther over Desmond's desk. "Is that what you're saying, Mr. Desmond? That I should have let them *rape* Rosemary because of your *rules*?" Adrenaline surged through his body, driving way any last vestiges of fear or hesitation.

"That is *enough*, Mr. Stone!" Desmond thundered. "Sit down this instant!"

"I don't think so, sir." Alastair had felt this way occasionally before—it was one of the few things that had gotten him into trouble at Barrow and with his father. It was as if some other force had taken control of his body and his mouth, while his wiser consciousness hovered overhead, powerless to intervene. "You said it yourself—you're turfing me out because I broke your rules. That means I'm not your apprentice anymore, so you can't give me orders. You told me before that I should act like a gentleman. I don't bloody see how running off like a coward and leaving a girl to get raped by three guys is acting like a gentleman, do you?" He was nearly shouting, but he no longer cared what Desmond thought of him.

Desmond didn't answer; his gaze was colder than Alastair had ever seen it.

Part of Alastair's brain was yelling at him to stop, but he wasn't done yet. "You taught me the most important thing about magic is willpower. But what kind of willpower would I have if I rolled over and did something I knew was wrong, just to follow some arbitrary rule you made because you're too scared you might lose another apprentice? I can't believe you'd even respect me for that!"

Still, Desmond didn't respond. He remained behind his desk, still as death, his eyes fixed on his now-former apprentice.

Alastair stood there a moment longer, fists clenched at his side, breathing hard, his whole body singing with energy and anger. When he finally spoke again, his voice shook with it. "It's all right, sir. It's probably best I found this out now. If those are the kinds of rules you want me to follow, then I don't want anything to do with them. You might be the best magic teacher around, but some things are more important than magic. I might have to wait until I'm eighteen before I can find another teacher, but at least this way I'll be able to live with myself."

Desmond continued watching him for several seconds, unmoving. When he spoke, his voice was calm and steady. "It is too late for you to leave tonight, Mr. Stone, and in any case, I have an engagement that will take me away for the remainder of the evening. Please pack your things, and I will call your father in the morning when I return."

He stood, and sighed. "I truly regret that it had to end this way, Mr. Stone. As I said, your potential is immense—possibly the strongest I have ever seen, and that includes Gareth Selby. You will make a fine mage someday, when you learn to control your passions. I wish all the best to you and whomever is fortunate to be your teacher, when you are old enough."

On a whim, Alastair switched to magical sight. To his surprise, he saw a hint of unrest around Desmond's normally unflappable aura. It lasted only a second, and then it was gone. Already his surge of adrenaline was starting to fade, giving way to the cold, gray rise of despair, disappointment, and regret. He wanted to take back some of what he said—but not all of it. He didn't regret what he'd done last night, Desmond's rules be damned. He'd do it again if faced with the same situation.

But none of that mattered now—he'd done it, he couldn't take it back even if he wanted to, and his days as the youngest apprentice of the finest magic teacher in Britain were now at their end.

"Yes, sir," was all he said. Then, before Desmond could say anything else, he turned and left the room, closing the door softly behind him. The old-fashioned way.

CHAPTER TWENTY-ONE

KERRICK HAD TO KNOW WHAT HAD HAPPENED, because he was once again loitering in the great room as Alastair came striding through, head down, eyes focused, and fists clenched.

"Sir—" he called softly.

Alastair wasn't sure he could speak to anyone right now without screaming, or saying something he'd regret, or possibly even bursting into frustrated tears. "Not now, please, Kerrick," he muttered without stopping. All he wanted to do was get back to his room, lock the door, and close the world out.

"Sir, please—" Kerrick's tone was gentle, almost fatherly.

Alastair stopped and whirled on him. "You don't have to call me 'sir' anymore."

"Why wouldn't I—"

"He's chucked me out!" His voice came louder than he wanted it to, and even if Kerrick might not have noticed the shake in it, he did. "I'm not his apprentice anymore. I'm done. So just—please, leave me alone. I've got to go pack."

Kerrick looked shocked. "Mr. Stone, please, stop for a moment. You say he's terminated your apprenticeship?"

"He didn't tell you?" Every nerve in Alastair's body was shrieking, demanding that he *move* or he might simply fly to pieces. "The way you looked at me before, I thought you knew." He forced his voice down to something close to calm—it wasn't great, but it was the best he could manage right now.

"No, sir. He didn't. I thought he might not approve of your visits with the young lady in town, but—"

Alastair almost laughed; the whole thing was so absurd. "Madeleine? No, he was fine with her. As long as she didn't affect my studies, anyway. No, apparently he thinks I should have run off and let a girl get raped rather than break his stupid rule against using magic he didn't authorize." He clenched his fists tighter. "If that's how he feels, then it's good I found out now."

Kerrick's expression grew more shocked, and then he raised his hands. "No...sir...that can't be what he said. I know Mr. Desmond. He wouldn't have—"

"Look." Alastair took several deep breaths in an attempt to calm himself. It didn't work. "I don't give a damn what happened to Gareth Selby, okay? I'm not Gareth Selby. I tried to obey Desmond's rules. I did the best job I could. I wanted this more than anything in the world, and I was willing to give up everything to get it. At least that's what I thought." He glared at Kerrick. "But I was wrong, wasn't I? I *wasn't* willing to give up everything—not quite. I might not be William Desmond's golden-boy apprentice anymore, but at least I've still got my self-respect. Now, will you let me go, please? I've got to pack before tomorrow, and I don't really want to talk about it anymore."

"Of course, sir." Kerrick's expression had shifted from shock to sadness. "But if you'll permit me to say one more thing before you do…"

"*What?*" Alastair hated the harsh impatience in his tone—out of all the people in this strange, almost otherworldly place, Kerrick had been the one who'd made the biggest effort to make him feel normal. The man didn't deserve to be on the receiving end of his misplaced wrath.

Kerrick approached him slowly, as if he were a skittish animal in the forest who might bolt away if frightened. When Alastair didn't move, he reached out a tentative hand and put it on his shoulder. "I'm so sorry this happened, sir. I want you to know that. I was looking forward to having you here. But please believe me—Mr. Desmond isn't a tyrant, or a cruel man. Of course he wouldn't have wanted that poor girl to be hurt. But—and he wouldn't want me to tell you this, so I ask that you don't reveal that I did—he took Gareth Selby's death very hard. It devastated him—and more to the point, it frightened him to his core. Why do you think he hasn't taken another apprentice in so many years?"

He tightened his grip a little. "I wondered at first why he might have decided after all this time not only to take another one, but one far younger than any of the others he's trained. Would you like to know the conclusion I came to?"

Alastair still wanted to dash up the stairs and disappear, but Kerrick's soft words piqued his curiosity. "What is it?" he asked, looking at the floor.

"I think…I think perhaps he thought that with a younger student—someone with the talent he required, but with less life experience—he might be able to ease back into teaching with an apprentice who'd be less inclined to defy him and thus put him- or herself at risk. I'm sure he would deny that, but as I said, I've known him for many years. I might not have a shred of magical talent, but I still see things."

Alastair didn't shrug off Kerrick's hand on his shoulder. "That didn't work out so well for him, did it?" he asked with a soft, bitter laugh.

"No, sir. I think perhaps you might have been a bit more than he expected."

"Yes…well…it doesn't matter anymore, does it? It's over. Thanks for everything, Kerrick. Really. It was good to know you, and I appreciate your trying to make things—well, normal—for me while I was here." He could feel himself shaking now. He had to get away before he did something he'd regret.

"Goodbye, Kerrick," he mumbled, and then darted up the stairs before anyone else could show up.

The last thing he wanted right now was for Selby to turn up to gloat.

| CHAPTER TWENTY-TWO

H E DIDN'T ENCOUNTER ANYBODY ELSE on his way back to his room—whether that was by accident or design, he neither knew nor cared. He flung open the door, shut it hard behind him, and flipped the lock. Then he flung himself onto his bed face-down, his whole body still thrumming with energy. He gripped the pillow so hard his fingers almost tore through the pillowcase.

What had he *done*?

Three solid weeks of hard work and exhaustion—not to mention everything he'd done back at Barrow—and now, in an instant, it was all over. Just like that, his dreams of being the youngest apprentice ever, of studying with the best teacher in Britain, were gone like so much smoke drifting away on the wind. This time tomorrow, he'd be back home in Surrey, facing his father.

A failure.

But he *wasn't* a failure! He threw himself over onto his back, his glare boring into the ceiling even though he wasn't truly seeing it in the dimming late-afternoon light.

Sure, he'd failed to obey Desmond's rule—his arbitrary, draconian prohibition against any kind of originality or initiative from his apprentices. The rule that had been established because, years ago, another apprentice had over-reached while trying to impress his teacher. But that wasn't what Alastair had been trying to do. Maybe the first time, with the shield-and-telekinesis combo. He'd deserved what he'd gotten for that, and he hadn't argued with the dressing-down he'd received over it.

But last night—no. That wasn't failure. That was being a decent human being, and using whatever resources he had at hand to deal with a bad situation.

He sighed, thinking. Was Desmond right? *Was* there something else he could have done, without breaking the rule? He hadn't even stopped to consider it at the time, but merely acted without any thought. What would he have done if he'd been a mundane and didn't have magical power to fall back on? There *had* been a policeman nearby, though he hadn't known it at the time. If he'd yelled, maybe the cop would have heard him and come running.

Or, more likely, those three drunken louts would have heard him first. They'd have come after him. He might have been able to outrun them—he was fast and agile, and they'd been pissed off their arses. But if they'd caught him, they'd probably have beaten him badly.

But so what? If they had, it probably would have given Rosemary time to run away. Maybe the cop would have noticed the commotion and turned up before things got too badly out of hand. Weren't a few bruises or even broken bones worth that?

Was he a coward? Had he taken the easy way out, using magic instead of risking injury like a mundane? Was that what Desmond had meant about his being too young—that he wasn't mature enough to know when magic was the proper response to a situation, and when it could better be handled with mundane methods? Could it be, now that he had this most wondrous of hammers at his command, that every problem suddenly looked like a nail?

He let his breath out in a loud *whoosh* and slumped back into the pillows. He didn't know. But in any case, it didn't matter. Desmond wasn't going to change his mind. Not if he apologized, not if he tried to explain, not if he begged.

Not that he'd do any of those things, of course. The situation was already bad enough as it was, without crawling back to Desmond like a sniveling coward.

It was over.

He'd made his choice, and now he'd have to accept the consequences.

He was done, at least for the foreseeable future.

He had no idea what his father would say, or what his opinion would be of Alastair's reasons for what he did. He wasn't even sure he'd listen to them. There was a lot he didn't know about his father—he hadn't quite realized how much until recently. Would Orion Stone send him to another school? Try to find him another master? See if he could convince Walter Yarborough to take him on three years early, after he'd washed out with Desmond?

He had no idea, and that was what scared him the most.

He couldn't give up magic. Not now. Not after all he'd learned.

There was no way he would allow the adults in his life to give him this tantalizing, intoxicating view of a world full of wonders, then slam the door shut on it for three more years.

He'd figure out something. He had time. But for now—

For now, he had to pack.

He glanced at the clock on the nightstand: it was four forty-five. He still had plenty of time to pack before tomorrow. That was the one good side of not being allowed to bring much with him, he decided: it wouldn't take long to stuff it into boxes and get it ready to go. A twinge of regret struck him as he remembered he'd have to leave the magnificent library downstairs—especially after he'd spent all that time organizing it. Maybe, once his father forgave him for failing with Desmond, he might be allowed to use the one back home.

Suddenly, his thoughts turned to Madeleine. Even though he'd already decided to break off whatever budding relationship he might have been developing with her, right now he wished she were here, just so he could have someone to talk to who wasn't part of the Caventhorne freak show. He wasn't an apprentice anymore—it didn't matter if seeing her affected his work, because he didn't *have* any work. For a few moments, he entertained the idea of sneaking out of the house and heading into Wexley to find her before he left tomorrow. He could pack later, when he got back. Maybe they could spend a couple of hours together before he had to leave, and he could say a proper goodbye to her instead of slinking off like an awkward idiot.

It was a tempting thought. But as he lay there on the bed, a fog of exhaustion settled over him. He hadn't gotten much sleep lately, and between the events of last night and his confrontation with Desmond, he'd used reserves of adrenaline that he hadn't had much time to replenish. His head hurt, his body ached, his stomach rumbled, and fatigue held his limbs down to the bed sufficiently that even thoughts of Madeleine weren't enough to rouse him to action.

I'll just stay here for a bit and rest...I can always go later on, in an hour or so, and then pack when I get back. That way, Desmond will be gone and I won't have to answer to anybody.

He didn't even notice when he drifted off.

| CHAPTER TWENTY-THREE

WHEN HE AWOKE, IT WAS DARK.

He sat up quickly from his splayed sprawl and switched on his nightstand light so he could see the old-fashioned clock (nothing as modern as a digital alarm clock had ever passed the doors of Caventhorne, as far as he knew).

Nine-thirty.

Bloody hell, he'd slept for nearly five hours!

He must have been more tired than he'd thought. He swung his legs around, ran a hand through his hair, and contemplated his room as all the thoughts from the past day came crashing down on him at once.

For a brief moment just as he woke, he'd prayed everything he remembered might only have been the worst nightmare ever—worse than the one where you showed up for a final after forgetting to attend any of the classes, or even the one where you realized you'd somehow ended up at school stark naked.

But no, he'd have taken either of those in an instant over the reality of losing his apprenticeship. And now, because his exhausted body had betrayed him, he wouldn't even have time to say goodbye to Madeleine before he'd be packed off back to Surrey tomorrow. Even if he could sneak out, it was far too late for him to show up on her doorstep.

He looked around his small, cell-like chamber. He still had to pack, and suddenly a job that had looked quick and easy at five o'clock seemed far more daunting at closer to ten.

Best to get started, he supposed. It wasn't as if he was going to get any more sleep tonight, after all.

His stomach rumbled again. He'd missed dinner; he wondered if Kerrick had come up and knocked softly on his door, but left again when he didn't answer. He hadn't heard any knock, but that wasn't a surprise. He'd slept so deeply he didn't even remember any dreams this time.

He thought about going downstairs to see if he could find something in the kitchen, but decided not to. Too much chance of encountering somebody, and the last thing he wanted to do was talk to anyone now—not even Kerrick. He wondered if they'd all be lined up tomorrow morning to see him off, and dreaded the thought. Walking a gauntlet like that would be the final indignity, even if they did mean well.

Still, he supposed they would want to say goodbye. He'd developed good relationships with most of them during his stay, and he thought they liked having him around. Esteban sometimes prepared special treats for him, while Gretchen treated him with brisk motherly affection. Max had lent him his Vespa, and Kerrick...well, he wondered whether he'd have made it through his last three weeks without Kerrick serving as a self-proclaimed "buffer" between him and the intense, formidable Desmond. He'd always be grateful for that, and hoped he might see the man again someday.

At least he wouldn't miss Selby.

He pushed himself off the bed and retrieved his large suitcase from his armoire, then began robotically pulling clothes from his dresser drawers and stuffing them in. No, he wouldn't miss Selby. After his talk with Desmond about the assistant steward's situation, he felt he *understood* Selby a little better, and sympathized with his situation, but that didn't mean he felt any more comfortable around the prickly young man, who always seemed to be simmering with resentment and veiled anger.

He finished emptying the dresser drawers, folded up a few pairs of trousers to fill the suitcase, and snapped it shut, then spread two garment bags on the bed and put his suits and jackets in them. He hadn't even had a chance to wear a suit past his first day—Desmond hadn't taken him anywhere, let alone anywhere requiring more formal attire. Perhaps instructing him to bring them at all had been wishful thinking, in anticipation of his passing his apprenticeship.

Alastair dropped to his knees and dug three broken-down boxes from under his bed. *Was* Desmond disappointed that he'd failed? Alastair had seen some oddness around the man's aura there at the end—had he been hoping his would-be apprentice would make it through the trial period too? The thought seemed strange; William Desmond was even more of a force of nature than his father, and it hardly seemed possible that the man had desires, hopes, and dreams like a normal person.

He had to, though. *He's just a man,* Alastair thought as he taped up one of the boxes and began carefully filling it with books from his shelves, starting with the Barrow texts. He wondered if Desmond had ever been in love, ever been married—if he had children of his own. They'd probably be grown by now, if he did. What had his own apprenticeship been like? Had he been as willful and headstrong as Alastair?

All of that was intriguing to think about, but ultimately pointless. He might see Desmond again—someday, when he was older and fully trained. Magical society in Britain was fairly small and insular, so it was almost inevitable they'd encounter each other again at some point. But would he choose to study with the man again if he could? Would he go back when he was eighteen and try to get another shot? It appeared to him that Desmond had left the door open to the possibility—but would he take it?

He didn't know. He couldn't honestly say.

He finished packing the Barrow books and reached to the top of the shelf where he kept his magic books. He set aside three that belonged in the downstairs library, lingering his hand on the stack for a moment. He'd never have the chance to finish reading them, unless perhaps his father had copies.

Finally, his gaze fell on the books his father had given him, and a twinge of regret so strong it was almost physically painful ripped through him. He pictured his father's face when they saw each other—stern, cold, disappointed at his only son for failing to meet his expectations. Orion Stone had been so proud of him for securing this chance at such a young age, and now that pride would be no more. Alastair had no idea what he would say to his father when he arrived back in Surrey. That, without doubt, would be the hardest part of this whole thing.

He packed the books lovingly, one at a time, in another box. Would his father make him give them back? Would he forbid him from practicing any more magic until he was old enough to be a proper apprentice? He paused, gripping the edge of the desk, his hands shaking, before returning to his task.

As he finished packing the set, he paused.

One of them was missing.

For a moment he couldn't remember what he'd done with it—he scanned the rest of the shelf in case he'd misfiled it, but there weren't many unpacked books left and it clearly wasn't among them. And then it came to him—he'd taken it down to Desmond's workroom last week, to show his master a bit of research related to what they'd been working on at the time. Now that he remembered, he could picture it clearly, sitting on the end of one of the stuffed shelves of his library.

His *former* library, now.

He sighed. He didn't want to leave the room and risk encountering anyone he'd be forced to talk to, but he had to get it back. The only thing worse than facing his father tomorrow in Surrey would be facing his father and admitting he'd lost one of the priceless reference books he'd been entrusted with.

Sure, he could probably retrieve it in the morning before he left, or ask Desmond to send it to him, but why? He had no reason to be reluctant to go down there and get it himself. It wouldn't take long—he could just run down, grab it, and get back up here to finish packing before anybody realized he'd left. This late, the staff would probably all be in their rooms in the other wing of the house anyway.

That decided, he opened the door a crack and peeked out. The hall was empty, lit only by dimmed sconces at wide intervals. He paused a moment to listen, but heard nothing— no footsteps, no voices, no sound of human habitation. His mind flitted back to the "ghosts" he'd teasingly discussed with Madeleine, and wondered again if the place really did have any. It was certainly old enough.

And even if it did, they probably wouldn't want to talk to him.

He hurried down the hall and stopped at the top of the stairs, pausing to switch on magical sight. He still saw no sign of life. Just in case, though, he cast the disregarding spell he'd been working on. Invisibility would have been better, but this one was still a lot easier. And since he was no longer Desmond's apprentice, he no longer had to obey the "no sneaking around the house" restriction. He still didn't intend to spy on the staff—that would be rude—but this way he'd be even less likely to be noticed.

He descended to the first floor, keeping the spell going. All he'd have to do now was head to the hall where the lift was, get to the workroom, get the book, and get back to his room. Five minutes tops, if he hurried.

A chill passed over him, and something flitted by in the periphery of his vision, off to his left.

He stopped, stiffening, and glanced quickly in that direction.

Nothing was there—only the dimly-lit great room, just as it had always been.

He shifted back to magical sight, glancing around almost idly, not expecting to see anything.

A faintly glowing trail, indistinct as smoke, snaked across the floor and disappeared down another hallway near the back side of the great room.

Alastair frowned. That was odd indeed. Desmond had taught him that magic left traces, but that they didn't last long unless the magic was extremely powerful. That had to mean this trail either represented something potent, or something that had occurred very recently. Desmond was away, and he himself had been in his room up until five minutes ago.

If Desmond had told him the truth, that left only Selby as a possibility...unless someone else had gotten into the house.

Alastair's sense of cold dread deepened. If it was Selby, why would he be doing magic inside the house? If he was practicing his circle, shouldn't he be out in the shed where he'd been working before? The trail didn't lead toward the front door, or any of the other exits Alastair was aware of. It led back toward a part of the house he'd seen only on the initial tour Kerrick had given him. He struggled to remember what that area contained—some large rooms, if he recalled correctly. A music room, perhaps, and another big, mostly empty hall that was kept closed except during events.

Had some other mage broken into the house? It seemed unlikely—Alastair knew Caventhorne had significant warding to prevent anyone unauthorized from getting in—but not impossible. If something *had* managed to get in, it would have to be something of an impressive power level. Had the shadow he thought he'd seen had anything to do with it, or had it been a product of his own imagination?

He barely realized it, but as he'd been thinking, he'd been slowly crossing the great room, still following the faint and dissipating trail. It led where he'd expected to, down the hallway that ran along the back part of the house, and disappeared under the door to the rarely-used hall.

Heart pounding, Alastair paused only a moment to consider what he should do. His first thought was to contact Desmond. He had no way to do that, though, since he didn't know where he'd gone. Perhaps Kerrick would know, but Kerrick's rooms were clear over on the other side of the house. By the time he got there and back, the rapidly fading trail would be gone.

He crept up to the door and put his ear to it, but if anything was going on in there, the door was too heavy to hear it through.

He had to know. He'd just use his brief invisibility spell, take a quick look, and if it was anything bad, he'd close the door and track down Kerrick so they could contact Desmond for further direction.

Alastair took a deep breath, gathered his focus, and settled the spell over himself. Almost immediately he could feel it draining his energy. He'd have to act fast. With a trembling hand he gripped the knob, hoping the door wasn't locked. Desmond hadn't taught him how to unlock doors with magic yet.

The knob turned easily in his hand. The door swung open on silent hinges. He pushed it open just enough to get a look inside, then peered through the narrow crack.

When he saw it, he froze. An electric sense of panic gripped him, and for a moment he could do nothing but gape. His invisibility spell dropped away.

A large and elaborate ritual circle lay spread out in the middle of the cleared floor. All around it, broken crystals, burned-out candles, and smudged areas bore witness to the fact that, whatever it had been intended for, it was dead and inert now. But none of that was what had captured Alastair's horrified attention.

Next to the circle lay the sprawled, broken form of Selby, the spreading pool of blood beneath him gleaming black in the room's faint light.

| CHAPTER TWENTY-FOUR

ALASTAIR COULDN'T MOVE. He stood gripping the doorknob, stunned. He wanted to run forward, but his feet were rooted to the floor like in those dreams where the massive monster was bearing down on you and all you could do was look on in horror.

A moment later, a soft moan broke Alastair's immobility. His breath caught. Selby was alive!

He flung the door open and hurried inside, skidding to a stop next to the assistant steward, his feet slipping in the pooled blood. "Selby!"

The battered man's eyes cracked open. His mouth worked as he tried to speak, but nothing came out.

Alastair dropped down alongside him. "Selby! What's happened?" He darted a quick glance around the room, but saw nothing else moving. If anything else had been in here, it was gone now.

"Mr...Stone..." Selby whispered. "I'm...sorry...so sorry..."

"What did you *do*?" Alastair demanded. Terror gripped him as he shook Selby.

"Gareth…" he whispered, gesturing feebly toward the blasted circle. "He…appeared…I…thought he was…still alive…"

"Gareth? You saw your brother?"

Selby nodded weakly, apparently too distracted by his injuries to wonder how Alastair knew about his brother. "He appeared… in my circle…last night. Told me he was… stranded…all these years… That he hadn't been killed…"

"So you tried to bring him *back?*" Every nerve in Alastair's body was on edge; any second, he was sure something would jump him from behind.

"He… showed me how…"

"And you didn't tell Mr. Desmond about this? You waited until he was gone to try it?" Alastair let out a loud, frustrated breath. The apple certainly didn't fall far from the tree in the Selby family, apparently. "Why in here? Why not out in the shed where you had the other circle?"

"Too small…" Selby whispered. He gripped Alastair's arm. "It wasn't Gareth…"

You think? Alastair thought, but didn't say it aloud.

"It's in here now…Mr. Stone… It's loose… I was a fool. Such a fool…"

That shadow thing I saw… Alastair remembered what he'd spotted from the corner of his eye earlier. "What does it want? Will it try to get out?" When Selby didn't answer, he shook him again. "Tell me, Selby! What does it want?"

"To kill." Selby's voice was barely audible. "To feed…I barely…drove it off…"

A chill lanced through Alastair as he thought about the rest of the staff, oblivious to the danger, and defenseless against it. "Oh, gods… the others… And if it gets out…"

"Won't..." Selby said. "Can't...the wards..."

"The wards will keep it in?" Alastair's brain felt static-charged as he tried to come up with a plan. Desmond's powerful wards on the house were designed to keep things like whatever Selby had summoned *out*—but apparently summoning it inside the house meant it was now stuck inside.

With all of them.

He had to get them out, and he had to find a way to contact Desmond. He gripped Selby's arm again. "Can you walk? How badly are you hurt?"

"I'll try... I don't know..."

Alastair leaped to his feet and grabbed Selby's arms, trying to haul the larger, heavier man up. Selby did his best to help, but he was clearly weakened from loss of blood. As he rose and stood swaying, Alastair could see three deep slash marks on his back and along his side.

That wasn't good. Whatever this thing was, it wasn't just a shadow. It could affect the physical world.

He slung Selby's arm over his shoulder. "Where's the nearest exit?" he demanded, dragging him toward the door. He wasn't familiar with this part of the house, and he didn't want to have to lug Selby any farther than he had to. If he could get the injured man outside and away from the threat, he could go back in, locate the others, and lead them to safety. He hoped. "Do you know where Mr. Desmond's gone?"

Selby's hand fluttered. "Exit... that way... and no. I don't know."

Alastair continued dragging Selby in the direction he'd pointed. He remembered now—there was an exit door at the end of the hall. His gaze was never still, trying to spot any sign of a moving shadow as he went, but he saw nothing with normal or magical sight. Damn, but Selby was heavy! His heart thudded hard and his shoulder ached under the weight, but he couldn't stop now.

He reached the door after what felt like forever, shifted Selby, and tried to fling it open.

It didn't budge.

Of course—the lock! He flipped it and tried again.

Nothing.

What was going on? Why wouldn't it open? Was he turning the knob the wrong way? He rattled it and shoved hard, growing increasingly panicked when it still failed to open.

Then he shifted to magical sight again, and gasped.

Some kind of energy hovered around it—a dark, roiling energy he'd never seen before. Certainly not the crisp, or- dered lines of Desmond's powerful wards. "I can't get it open! It's—blocked somehow."

"No…" Selby moaned, slumping. "It's trapped us… This is all my fault…"

Think, Stone! Alastair lowered Selby into a nearby chair and clenched his fists, trying to come up with a solution. If they couldn't get out of the house, that meant two things— whatever Selby had brought over was powerful enough to block their exit, and whatever plan he came up with, it had to happen in here.

But if the creature—or whatever it was—was stuck in here with them and they couldn't get out, where could they hide? He was sure there must be parts of the house with bet- ter protections—Desmond's private chambers, most certainly. But Alastair didn't even know where those *were*, let alone if he could get inside them. He didn't have time to go running around the house looking for them. And there was no way he could construct a ward of his own, even if he had hours to do it—and any delusion that a student like him could build one strong enough to keep out something this tough.

There *had* to be a solution. *Think!*

And then he had it.

He grabbed Selby's arm again and flung it around his shoulder. "The workroom!" he said. "It's warded. If there's any place we'll be safe, it's there." He hoped he was right—he knew the staff weren't allowed in the workroom, but he didn't know if the prohibition was merely verbal or if Desmond had actually warded it so they physically couldn't enter.

For that matter, he might have tweaked the wards so Alastair himself couldn't get in anymore, before he left. It made sense— an angry, passionate, barely-trained mage left alone in the house after having his apprenticeship terminated could cause a lot of damage. Never mind that it wouldn't even occur to Alastair to do such a thing—Desmond didn't know that.

Still, it was the only solution he could think of, the only safe place inside the house he and the others might have access to. He had to try. He had get Selby there, and then find the rest of the staff before the creature killed them all.

If it hadn't already.

He had to hurry. So far, adrenaline was still carrying him on, but he knew that wouldn't last forever. "Come on," he urged Selby. "Try to help me. I've got to get you there and find the others."

Selby, pale and sweating, did the best he could, but it wasn't much. Most of his weight still settled on Alastair's shoulders as together they dragged themselves back through the great room and toward the hall leading to the workroom lift. Alastair continued his hyper-vigilance, switching to magical sight every few seconds and scanning the area for any sign of the creature. Was it hiding? Was it off in the other part of the house, feasting on Kerrick and Gretchen and the others? Not knowing made the whole situation even worse.

Part of him—a small, perverse part—was tempted to leave Selby where he was and concentrate on the other staff members. Let him drag himself to the workroom on his own—this whole thing was his fault anyway. If he hadn't tried such a monumentally idiotic stunt, none of this would have happened. He didn't deserve to live if it meant his foolishness got the others killed. The rest of them had done nothing wrong.

But he didn't listen to that part. Everybody did stupid things sometimes, and if whatever Selby had summoned had managed to convince him his brother *was* still alive and trapped in another dimension for all these years, he could hardly blame him for taking a chance. Even if he hadn't told Desmond—regardless of anything else, that part *had* been stupid.

He trudged on, dragging a barely-mobile Selby with him, hoping the man wouldn't pass out from blood loss—or even die—before he got them to the workroom.

There it was: the lift doors were just ahead! Now was the moment of truth, when he'd find out if Selby could get past the wards. Or if *he* could. Puffing with exertion, he stabbed the button and waited.

The door slid open, revealing the familiar tiny cubicle.

Alastair dragged Selby in, sat him down against the wall, and pushed the *Down* button.

After an agonizing several seconds that seemed to stretch on forever, the door slid closed and the lift descended. A few seconds later, the door opened on the hallway leading to the workroom.

Alastair had gotten a bit of his wind back from the brief rest. He grabbed Selby and dragged him out into the hall. So far, nothing impeded them. He shifted to magical sight, and slumped in relief when he saw the familiar lines of Desmond's wards, their ordered, mathematically-beautiful structure glowing and unbreached around them.

They'd made it! If the wards were strong enough to keep the creature out, they'd be safe here.

"Okay," he said, puffing. "You stay here. I'll go find the others and bring them back. If there's anything else you can tell me about this thing that might help, now would be a good time."

Selby gripped his arm. "I think…it wants Mr. Desmond. I think…that's why it…wanted me to summon it inside the house."

Bloody brilliant. So the thing's plan, apparently, had been to kill Selby and then lie in wait until Desmond returned home, but his appearance had spoiled its surprise. That meant it would be after him at minimum, but probably the others too, to ensure nobody tipped Desmond off. This just kept getting better and better.

"Stay here," he said again, even though it was unnecessary—Selby wasn't going anywhere anytime soon.

Selby sagged against the wall. "Be careful..." he whispered.

"Yeah." Because a barely-trained mage who knew about five spells total was going to be any use at all against some kind of super-powered shadow-thing he had no idea how to find. He stepped back into the lift and pressed the *Up* button, wondering how this whole situation could get any worse.

The lights went out, and the lift shuddered to a halt.

CHAPTER TWENTY-FIVE

ALASTAIR STOOD IN THE DARK and tried not to panic.

His first, visceral thought was, *It's in here with me.*

He pressed his back against one of the walls and quickly shifted to magical sight. The thing had left traces before, so he hoped that meant it couldn't hide completely.

No traces, and no glowing aura, appeared in the tiny space.

How had it shut off the lights?

It doesn't matter. They're off. You've still got a job to do, so get going.

The lift shuddered again and slowly began to descend, until it settled back to the bottom of the shaft.

That was great—he wasn't stuck between floors, which would have been even worse, but he was still stuck back at the bottom. He stabbed the button in the hope that whatever backup system had lowered him down would also take him back up, but apparently it didn't work that way. How was he going to find the rest of the staff while stuck in the dark, inside a lift barely bigger than a phone box? Even if he could get the doors open, it would do him no good if he couldn't get out of the lower level.

He had to try, anyway. He slipped his fingers into the crack between the two doors and tugged. After a moment, they slid a few inches apart, and magical sight revealed his fear was real: Selby's flickering, fading aura glowed against the wall of the workroom hallway.

Okay, the lift was stuck, and the doors would be no help. He paced the tiny confines, thinking. The cubicle didn't have an intercom or a telephone to reach anyone—he'd used it plenty of times, and certainly would have noticed such a thing. His telekinesis magic wasn't strong enough to raise the entire lift to the ground floor. So how was he supposed to get out?

His thoughts returned to one of the mindless television shows he'd watched while relaxing in the common room back at Barrow. It was some kind of spy thriller thing, and the heroine had gotten trapped in a lift in an office building. She'd escaped by going through an emergency hatch in the ceiling, and climbed the cable to the next floor up.

Did this one have a hatch like that? He realized he'd never even looked; it wasn't something you normally did, and in any case he was fairly sure that under normal circumstances, nothing in Desmond's house would ever have the nerve to cease functioning properly.

He reached up, but even with his arms fully extended his hands didn't touch the lift's ceiling. There was nothing to stand on, so if he wanted to get up there, he'd have to use levitation.

The good news was, it was one of the spells that came easiest for him.

The bad news was, being scared he was about to be jumped by a bloodthirsty shadow-thing as soon as he poked his head up through the roof didn't make concentrating on magic easy.

Just get on with it. They're counting on you.

He took a few deep breaths to calm his pounding heart, and closed his eyes even though it was so dark he couldn't see anything but blackness. After a moment, he felt his feet leave the floor, and a moment after that, his outstretched hands pressed up against the lift's ceiling. To his relief, the panel gave way to his push, shifting upward with ease. *Score one for bad telly, I guess.*

Catching hold of the edge, he used a combination of levitation and muscle to squeeze through the small opening, and a moment later he was standing on top of the lift. It was just as dark in the shaft as it had been in the cubicle, and he couldn't see any sign of light filtering in through a crack in the ground-floor doors. *Probably means the lights are off up there too. Maybe in the whole house.* That was great—he had no idea where flashlights were kept, and the only candles he knew of were back down in the workroom. He wished again that he'd asked Desmond to teach him a light spell, but right now he didn't have time to dwell on what he couldn't do. He had to get upstairs.

Another levitation spell took him up until he brushed against the ceiling—apparently the lift only extended as far as the ground floor, and didn't reach the upper parts of the house. He held the spell steady and felt around until he found the crack between the ground-floor doors, then shoved them open as he had down below. It was harder this time—not only did he not have anything to brace against, but he had to hold his concentration on the spell to keep from plummeting down while simultaneously pushing on the doors. By the time he stepped out into the hallway, he was puffing with exertion again, and sweat trickled down his back. Quickly, he shifted to magical sight to scan the area.

He spotted it an instant before it was upon him.

| CHAPTER TWENTY-SIX

I F IT HADN'T BEEN FOR ALL THE DRILLS Alastair had done with Desmond, conjuring faster and faster shields to stop surprise beanbag attacks, it would have gotten him. As it was, he got a brief, flashing impression of something vaguely humanoid but with too-long arms and legs and a gaping, tooth-filled mouth leaping at him from halfway down the hallway. The thing itself was as pitch-black as its surroundings, but a jagged aura glowed red around it. It moved in utter silence.

Alastair acted without thought, the pattern coming to his mind instantly as he'd been taught. A glowing shield sprang up between them, lighting up the area perhaps a foot or two in front. The creature slammed into it, its raking claws digging shallow furrows that sent blasts of painful feedback straight into Alastair's brain. He winced and staggered back, but didn't drop the shield.

Think! Alastair pressed himself against the wall, panting and terrified, as the creature came in for another shot. He couldn't just stand here and let it pound on the shield until it came down or his concentration failed. If he was going to get out of here, he'd have to come up with another plan. But how could he attack it? He couldn't hit it with his fists, and

R. L. KING

Desmond hadn't taught him any offensive spells. His mind raced over his limited repertoire: *Invisibility won't fool it. Neither will disregarding. Levitation won't help. Telekinesis—*

That was it! The thing had to be solid to attack him, which meant it might be vulnerable to physical attacks.

It sliced at the shield again, its claws long and pointed. The barrier's bright glow flared and began to fade, sending another spike of pain into Alastair's head. It had to be now!

In the shield's faint illumination, his gaze fell on a heavy marble statuette on a table across the hall, off to the creature's right side. He'd only have one chance at this.

Doing it just as he'd practiced, he held the shield while forming the second pattern in his mind. He gripped the statuette and flung it with all his strength at the creature's head.

Direct hit!

If the thing had been human, the missile would have impacted with a satisfying, melonlike *thunk*. Instead, it smacked into the creature with no sound at all. For an agonizing second, Alastair thought he'd missed.

Then the thing shrieked, a high, keening sound that sliced through Alastair like a whole room full of children running their fingers down blackboards at the same time. He cringed backward, almost losing his grip on the shield, as the weird jagged aura around the creature split, fragmented, and changed into something more liquid and indistinct. The shadowy form flowed off and disappeared into the darkness.

For a moment, all Alastair could do was stay where he was, slumped against the wall, panting as his heart thudded in rhythm with the pounding in his head. He swiped his hand across his forehead and it came away soaked with sweat, and he tasted the faint, familiar tang of blood.

But it was gone, at least for now. Had he hurt it? Scared it off? He didn't know, but it didn't matter. He was sure it wouldn't be gone long. He'd have to find the others and get them back to the workroom before it did.

He wished he had a real weapon. Apparently the thing could be hurt while in physical form, and while he had no combat experience beyond getting beaten up by bullies a couple times when he was younger, having something he could use to fight back without expending magical energy would be welcome. The problem was, he couldn't think of anything like that. Not in the dark, anyway. Trying to find a knife in the kitchen would be next to impossible and take far too long, and he couldn't remember seeing any old swords or other weapons hanging on the walls anywhere, even if he could spot them in the darkness. If only he had some kind of magical weapon—

Wait!

He didn't take his meals in the formal dining room very often, since Desmond was usually busy and he preferred grabbing something quick in the kitchen. But the few times he had eaten there, he'd seen it hanging on the wall across from him. Now, he pictured the strange-looking object—halfway between a spear point and a dagger, and made of some weird, multicolored metal—and remembered the glow he'd seen around it when he'd looked with magical sight.

He had no idea what it was for or if it had any additional powers, but it had to be better than nothing. If nothing else, its glow meant he'd be able to find it in the dark.

The dining room was off the great room, between where he was now and the staff's quarters on the other side of the house. If he hurried, he might be able to make it before the creature decided to have another go at him.

If it hadn't already changed targets and decided to go after the others instead.

A chill shuddered through him as another thought occurred to him: since the lights had gone out, one or more of the staff might have already ventured out of their rooms to find the source of the problem. He'd counted on finding them in their quarters—if they spread out and ended up all over the mansion, he'd never find them all before the creature did.

If only he had a way to get hold of Desmond! He had to find Kerrick—if anyone would know where Caventhorne's master had gone, it would be him.

Alastair set off at a fast walk down the hallway toward the great room, running his hand lightly along the left-side wall as he went to keep himself oriented. Even though it hurt his head to do it, he kept magical sight running at all times, and glanced over his shoulder periodically to make sure nothing was bearing down on him from the rear. It was exhausting, but there was no alternative. He remembered Desmond's words during one of their lessons, when he'd warned that learning magic would be painful. *You'll get over it,* he told himself. *Just suck it up and hurry.*

He reached the end of the hall, stopping before he stepped into the wide-open space of the great room. He'd be more vulnerable there, but he'd also have more room to maneuver. He paused a moment to gather energy, taking a quick look around the vast space. He didn't see any auras—creature or human. If anybody had ventured out of their rooms, it would probably either be to hunt for the fuse box (where would such a thing even *be* in a house this huge? He didn't even know where it was at his own place, but assumed it was somewhere in the basement) or merely to come out into the hall to chat with others. He hoped it was true, anyway.

No more time to waste. Out here, he could see a little better due to the faint moonlight filtering in through the windows. He took off at jog toward the dining room, staying close to the wall instead of cutting across the center. His every nerve was on edge as he remained ready to fling up the shield at the first sign of the creature.

He wasn't sure what made him look up as he drew near the doorway leading to the dining room. Perhaps it was a change in the air, or some kind of instinctive, developing sense of magic around him. Either way, he glanced upward just as he was about to pass through.

The ink-black shadow creature was hurtling toward him, leaping down from one of the heavy beams high up in the great room's ceiling.

This time, he didn't even have a chance to get the shield up. He moved without thinking, diving toward the doorway in a desperate attempt to get clear of the creature's claws. Pain lit up his back and he felt his shirt tear as they raked across him, but his last-second move saved him from the worst of the impact. He rolled, leaped to his feet, and grabbed one of the heavy chairs to put it between himself and the stalking creature, giving him time to get the shield up again. Before the thing could attack once more, he threw himself sideways and ripped the dagger-thing from the wall.

Instantly, he felt it thrum in his hand, as if it had an electrical current running through it. He wasn't sure if he should somehow activate it, or even if it was the sort of thing he'd *need* to activate. Keeping his gaze fixed firmly on the creature, he experimentally fed power into the weapon, the same way Desmond had taught him to do when powering a circle.

The blade began to glow brighter. It was still a faint glow, nothing impressive, but the shadow-creature hesitated. It made a growl that Alastair felt more than heard, and its attention (as much as it was possible to tell with a creature that had no proper face) seemed to be fixed on the weapon.

With another growl it went liquid again, flowing into a true shadow on the wall and disappearing around the corner back toward the great room.

Alastair let his breath out, wincing. He could feel something warm trickling down his back and was sure he was bleeding, but the pain wasn't too bad yet. It didn't matter if it was, though—he couldn't stop now. He had a weapon. He had to move.

Impulsively, he gripped the dagger in one hand and, with the other, snatched the tiny shield-thing off the wall as well. He had no idea what it did—it looked comically small to be useful as any kind of protection—but one thing he'd learned all his life was that when you were dealing with magic, things were almost never as they seemed. Maybe it would help him.

He was almost there. All he had to do now was get through the great room and down the opposite hall to the staff's quarters, and then—

Someone screamed.

CHAPTER TWENTY-SEVEN

LASTAIR DIDN'T STOP TO EVALUATE the situation, or to consider the possibility the creature might be laying a trap for him. Gripping the dagger in one hand and the tiny shield in the other, he pelted out of the dining room in the direction of the scream, which seemed to have come from the doorway at the other side of the great room.

He spotted the slumped figure on the floor before he'd made it halfway across, but couldn't identify it from that distance. All he could tell was that the scream had sounded like a man. *Kerrick?*

He skidded to a halt as he drew closer. The shadowy thing was crouched on top of the fallen figure, digging at it with its wicked claws—claws now soaked in blood.

Oh, gods, no—I'm too late!

"Get away from him!" he yelled, brandishing the dagger. His arm shook and fresh sweat broke out on his forehead as he got a clearer view of its impossibly long limbs, the gaping, fang-filled mouth that took up most of its otherwise featureless face, and the way its edges seemed to shift nauseatingly in and out of focus. It looked like something, not out of his worst nightmare, but out of a nightmare no sane mind could ever conceive of having.

"*I'll have you all...*" it whispered, more in Alastair's mind than in his ears. Its voice sounded like sandpaper scraping against rough rock. It leaped off the figure toward Alastair, claws extended.

He reeled back, tripping over his feet in his haste to get out of the way, and went over. That might have saved his life. With a roar, he slashed upward with the dagger and felt resistance as he crashed to the floor and the creature sailed over his head. Pain spiked through his back where the claws had found him before.

The thing's shriek of pain this time was even louder and more unsettling than when the statuette had hit it. It landed awkwardly on its side, then leaped up on all fours like an animal and disappeared into shadow again.

More voices were coming from the hall where the staff's quarters were, getting closer. Alastair scrambled to his feet and hurried over to drop down next to the fallen figure.

He didn't need the flashlight beam that shined over his shoulder a moment later to show him who it was: the familiar tall, stout form of Samuels, the estate steward, lay before him, his throat ripped and bleeding. He was obviously beyond help. Alastair sagged in shock, barely catching himself before he fell.

"Oh, dear God," a voice gasped from behind him.

"What's going on?" another demanded, and then, "No! Not Samuels—"

More voices. "Mr. Stone—?"

"You're *bleeding!*"

"Oh, God, is he dead?"

"What's *happening*?"

Alastair forced himself back to his knees, gripping the dagger and the shield. There was nothing he could do for Samuels now, but if he kept his wits about him and didn't panic, he might be able to get the others to safety. "Listen," he said, but his voice came out as a harsh croak. The hubbub of voices continued as if he hadn't spoken.

"Listen!" he said again, louder. "Quiet, please!"

A couple of them muttered indignantly, but gradually they all quieted down. Alastair took them all in with a quick sweep of his gaze, both magical and mundane. He saw Esteban, Gretchen, the maids Marie and Natasha, the head housekeeper whose name he could never remember, and Max, the groundskeeper who'd lent him the Vespa. All were out of their uniforms or formal working clothes, clad casually or even in robes. Esteban and Natasha held flashlights. All of them had the wide-eyed, terrified look of incipient panic as their own gazes kept darting down toward Samuels and his bloody, ruined throat.

"Something's in here," Alastair said, his voice shaking. He climbed to his feet with effort, turning slowly in place so he could scan the area with magical sight. "Something magical, and dangerous—as you can see."

Someone gasped, and the voices started again.

"What will we do?"

"We've got to get out!"

"Is that why the lights went out?"

"We can't get out," Alastair said. "It's—done something to the exits. And it can't get out past the wards. So we're stuck in here together."

More gasps.

"What do you mean, we can't get out?"

"What happened to your back?"

"Oh my lord, and Mr. Desmond's away—"

"*Listen!*" Alastair hated to sound so harsh—he felt suddenly awkward, a fifteen-year-old boy giving orders to a group of full-grown adults—but there was no helping it. "I can get us to safety, but you've got to come with me now. Where's Kerrick?"

Muttering, they all looked at each other in confusion. "I think he went to find the fuse box," Esteban said. "He's been gone for a while now."

"Oh, no," Natasha moaned. "What if that—that *thing* got him, too?" Tears ran down her cheeks, and Marie put her arm around her.

Alastair did another check for the creature, making sure to look up as well as behind him, and thought hard. He didn't want to leave Kerrick to his own devices with the creature still on the loose, but he had to get this group back to safety. He couldn't leave them all here to be killed one after another while he went in search of one missing man. "Come on," he said. "Follow me. We've got to move fast."

"You poor boy," the head housekeeper, a motherly woman in her fifties, said. "Let me take a look at your back, so you—"

Alastair drove his frustration down. The slashes on his back burned, and his headache was growing steadily worse, but none of that mattered right now. "No *time*," he said. "Come on. Follow me, and stay together."

"Where are we going?" Marie asked. She still had her arm around the sobbing Natasha.

"Mr. Desmond's workroom." Alastair gripped the dagger and took another look around. "You'll be safe there—it's warded." *Assuming you can get in at all. But then, Selby did.*

"But—we're not permitted in there," Gretchen protested. "Mr. Desmond's orders."

"I don't think he'd rather you got killed, do you?" Alastair growled. "Come *on*. Let's go. I think I hurt that thing, but I'm sure it will be back."

Still, they didn't move. "Where's Selby?" Esteban asked, turning back toward the staff quarters hallway.

"And what about Samuels?" Max indicated the body. "We can't just leave him here."

Alastair made another effort to quell his compulsion to start grabbing them and shoving them bodily in the right direction. He supposed he should at least be grateful that they were all familiar with magic, so he didn't have to explain *that* to them. *They're scared,* he reminded himself. *Of course they are. I'm scared, and I know what's going on.* "Selby's safe," he said. "He's hurt, but he's already in the workroom. We need to *go*. Is anyone else in the house?"

"Samuels would know for sure," Esteban said, shaking his head in dismay.

"The others are out tonight," Natasha said. "It's just us...and Kerrick, somewhere."

"Good," Alastair said, relieved. So he'd only have to go in search of Kerrick, if he didn't return in the meantime.

"Grab Samuels's feet," Esteban ordered Max, bending down to pick up the dead steward under his arms. His gaze flicked up to Alastair. "We can't leave him here, sir. It wouldn't be right."

Alastair let his breath out. It would slow them down, and they'd never get him down the elevator shaft and through the hatchway, but the chef was right. At least they could move him closer to where they'd be. "Okay. Okay. Just—hurry up."

Esteban handed over his flashlight to Gretchen and hefted Samuels's upper body; after a moment, Max picked up the steward's feet.

"Stay close to the wall," Alastair said. "Gretchen, you go in front with the torch. Natasha, you in back with the other one. Stay in a tight group. I'll follow behind you and keep watch." He swallowed hard and swiped sweat off his forehead. The slashes on his back were getting hot, and he could still feel blood—or was it more sweat—running down. He swayed a little as a wave of vertigo gripped him, waiting until it passed before moving again. He wished he could put a shield up to cover them all, but he hadn't yet learned to extend any of his spells beyond himself. He'd just have to remain hyper-vigilant to ensure the creature didn't sneak up on them.

Normally, it would have taken less than a minute at a brisk walk to cross the great room and get down the hallway to the lift, but now, in the shadowy darkness broken only by the shifting beams of Gretchen's and Natasha's flashlights, it seemed more like a slow slog across some kind of murky no-man's-land. Alastair's magical sight revealed tension gripping everyone's auras, including his own, and the riot of shifting, agitated colors made it difficult for him to spot anything approaching. If the creature attacked them now, there was a very real chance it could take out one of the others, or even jump him, before he had a chance to react.

He hoped he'd hurt it sufficiently with the dagger slash that it would think twice about going after them again, but feared that wouldn't last long. And he still didn't know what the little shield thing did. Perhaps after he'd got this group safely downstairs, he'd have a moment to study it before he went in search of Kerrick.

By the time they reached the lift with its forced-open doors, Alastair's tense vigilance had reached a point where every muscle in his body felt strained and stiff. He paused, looking behind them again, as they gathered around the doors.

"What's wrong with the lift?" Natasha demanded.

"How will we get down *there?*" the housekeeper asked, casting a worried look down the dark shaft.

Alastair hadn't given that a lot of thought. The drop to the top of the lift cubicle wasn't a long one—perhaps twelve feet or so at most—but most of the staff weren't in the kind of physical shape to manage it without help. If they tried, he was sure at least one of them would lose their footing and plummet through the hatch, or fall and break an ankle. If he tried to levitate them all, though, even one at a time, he'd use up valuable magical energy—and he didn't have much to spare at this point. He still had to find Kerrick, and he was sure that thing was lurking out there somewhere waiting to catch him alone.

"We'll start lowering people down," Max said, indicating himself and Esteban. "Natasha, you first."

"Wait a minute," Gretchen said. "If it's stuck, how are we going to do this? We can't get down to the workroom if it isn't moving."

"It's at the bottom," Alastair said. "If you can get down there and get through the hatch, you can push the doors open and get out. But we've got to hurry!" Once more he snatched a glance over his shoulder. The hallway was still clear, but he couldn't help thinking that might be because the creature was off somewhere feasting on Kerrick to gain more energy before it came after them again.

Natasha looked dubious. "That looks like a long drop, even if you lower me down, Max."

"Wait," Alastair said. "Let me lower Esteban down first. He's tall. Then he can help grab people when Max lowers them from up here."

"How will you do that?" Esteban asked, clearly taking in Alastair's thin frame. "You don't look strong enough to—"

"Just hold still and don't panic. It makes it harder for me if you flail about." One more look down the hallway, then he focused on the chef. He'd never tried levitating anyone else before—only himself and inanimate objects. Desmond had never subjected himself to the indignity of potentially being on the wrong end of one of Alastair's concentration failures. "And get ready to catch yourself if I drop you."

He formed the pattern in his mind, ignoring the increased throbbing in his head, and lifted Esteban off his feet. *Do this fast...don't drop him...*

The others gasped. Apparently, despite the fact that they were familiar with magic, they didn't actually see a lot of it practiced. Alastair ignored them, carefully lifting Esteban, shifting him over, and lowering him down the shaft.

"I'm down!" the chef called up after a few long, agonizing moments. "Send the others!"

Alastair let his breath out in a rush and leaned against the hallway wall, gripping the dagger and the tiny shield-thing and letting the others manage the operation. Now that they had a plan, they seemed quite motivated to get everyone down there quickly, especially after Natasha and Gretchen together managed to pry the door open and announced that the wards hadn't stopped them. Finally, only Alastair and Max were left on the ground floor along with Samuels's body, laid as carefully and respectfully as they could against the wall with someone's jacket covering his face and torn throat.

Alastair regarded the burly Max and gathered his strength again. "I'll lower you down…"

Max shook his head. "I've got it, sir. You should come too, though."

"I can't. Kerrick's still out there somewhere. I've got to find him."

"Let me come with you, then."

"No—help take care of the others. Selby's down there, and he's hurt. It'll be harder on my magic if I have to look out for you too." He blinked sweat out of his eyes. His back was on fire now, and he was tasting blood again. If he didn't do this soon, he wouldn't be able to. "If you want to help, tell me where he might be. Somebody said he went to check the fuse boxes—where are they?"

"In the basement, sir. Best way to get there is through the door in the back of the kitchen. I'm sure there are other entrances, but I don't know where they are. The fuses are down there, not far from the kitchen."

Alastair took a deep breath and tried to slow his racing heart. The last thing he wanted, now that they were so close to the safety of the wards below, was to go back out there and face that thing again. Nobody would blame him if he didn't—if he chose to go to the workroom with the others and hide behind the wards until Desmond returned. But Kerrick had been his first friend and staunchest ally among the staff, and he was damned if he'd let the man get ripped to pieces without at least trying to help him. And if nobody told Desmond this thing was loose in his house, it might even attack him when he got home. Sure, the high and mighty William Desmond he could probably deal with it with one hand tied behind his back...but what if it caught him by surprise? What if he couldn't?

A sly, mocking voice spoke in his head: *So what if he can't? He wouldn't want you to use unauthorized magic, would he? That would be breaking his rules. So what if it means he could be killed over it? He didn't seem to care about what might have happened to Rosemary...he messed up your whole magical career over breaking one stupid rule for a good reason. Let him deal with some consequences for a change!*

But he quickly silenced the voice. He was better than that. Desmond might be a hidebound old fossil so set in his ways he couldn't budge to save his own skin, but Alastair wasn't.

"Okay," he said again, gripping Max's arm while hoping the groundskeeper didn't notice his hand shaking. "I'm off. Can I have your torch?"

Max handed it over. "Be careful, sir." He looked worried. "I don't feel right about this, letting you go off to—"

"Go," Alastair said, pointing down the shaft. "I don't want to leave until I know you're safe. Look after Selby. Kerrick and I will be back as soon as we can."

"Good luck, sir." He quickly lowered himself over the edge and a second later, Alastair heard his feet thump down on top of the lift box.

Right, then. Time to move.

He pushed himself off the wall and shined the flashlight down the hallway. Nothing moved, as far as he could see, but now that he'd gotten used to the dark, the light made him nervous. The shadow-thing's jagged red aura wouldn't be as easy to see in the harsh beam. Plus, he now had three things to carry, and he couldn't be caught trying to juggle them if the thing attacked again. He hated to shut off the light, but instinct told him magical sight would be more useful.

He reached the end of the hallway and switched it off, stuffing it in the waistband of his trousers. Then he peered around the great room using magical sight and still saw no movement. His heart pounded faster again.

Had he hurt it badly when he'd slashed it with the knife before? Was it off licking its wounds? Or was it already downstairs, stalking Kerrick as safer prey?

You won't know until you get on with it, he told himself angrily, trying to quiet his fast, nervous breathing. For a second, an image of his life back at Barrow flashed into his mind: this time of night, he'd either be in his room studying, or possibly down in the common room lounging on one of the threadbare old sofas, half-watching some mindless thing on the television. His biggest concerns would be the exam the next day, or whether he'd get permission to go into town on the upcoming weekend. Standing here now, fighting off pain, exhaustion, and panic, he thought it didn't sound like a bad alternative, all things considered.

You wanted this, the mocking little voice reminded him. *You wanted to learn magic three years early, like a big boy. So, are you an adult, or are you a scared kid who wants to run home to Daddy when things get nasty? Better decide soon. That thing's out there somewhere, and your sorry arse is Kerrick's only hope.*

"Yeah…" he growled softly. Once again, he tightened his grip on the dagger and strode out into the great room.

Nothing jumped out at him. The hall remained dark and, except for the far-off sound of the grandfather clock tolling the hour, silent.

Alastair quickened his pace, keeping his magical sight up and glancing occasionally behind him. He hurried through the dining room and down the back hall into the kitchen.

Here, the faint moonlight shining in through high windows mitigated the darkness a little. Damn, this place was eerie at night: all massive, looming appliances, dark granite surfaces, and wide-open floor space between them to allow a large number of chefs and their helpers to work around each other efficiently when preparing multi-course meals for dinner parties and other events. So many places for the shadow-thing to lurk while waiting for him.

He risked the flashlight for a moment, shining it around the room until he spotted the door near the back. That must be the one Max had referred to. He switched off the light and started across the kitchen.

"*I will have you…*" the sandpaper-on-rocks voice whispered.

Panicked, Alastair shifted back to magical sight and whirled around, dagger at the ready, but no jagged red aura was bearing down on him.

From the darkness, it chuckled. *"You can't hide forever...You will tire soon, and I will rip you to pieces and feast on your flesh..."*

"You get right on that!" Alastair called, his voice a shaky croak. He took off running, his feet skidding on the fine stone tile.

The creature's laughter echoed behind him as he reached the door and flung it open, then slipped inside and slammed it shut. He leaned against it, puffing. Could the thing get past the door? He was sure it could—in its flowing shadow form, it could probably get *under* the door. He didn't have time to waste waiting for it, though. He had to keep moving.

He switched on the flashlight again. Ahead yawned a sturdy staircase descending into blackness. He started down.

"Kerrick?" he called. It didn't come out very loud—unless Kerrick was at the foot of the stairs, there was no way he could have heard it. His breath rasped in his ears, and his hand on the dagger was slicked with sweat.

He reached the bottom. "Kerrick?" he called again, louder this time. "Are you down here?"

He thought he heard something, but couldn't be sure. It was off to his left. It could be the creature, toying with him, luring him away—but if he let it play with his head like that, he might as well go back to the workroom with the others. It might not be the right decision, but at least it was a decision. He set off to the left.

He'd made it only a few steps before his shins smashed against something, nearly knocking him over. The dagger slipped out of his hand and clattered to the floor as he bit back a cry of pain.

Damn it, he'd have to use the flashlight if he didn't want to break his neck down here! At least he couldn't miss the dagger, which showed up on magical sight. He snatched it back up, crouching to scan for the creature, then switched on the light.

He was standing in a wide, open space filled with orderly stacks of objects, many of them covered by heavy tarps. A stone wall, rough and stained, ran along the right side,. This part of the house had to be very old. Alastair wondered what kinds of ancient workings were down here—an old boiler, maybe, or an antique furnace? He wondered what workmen must think when they had to come down here to fix something.

"Kerrick?" he called. "Can you hear me? It's Alastair!"

The faint, far-off voice came again—but this time it wasn't as far off. "Sir?"

Relief so strong it almost staggered him surged through Alastair. "Kerrick!" he yelled. "Where are you? Can you come toward my voice?" Injuries and exhaustion momentarily forgotten in the rush of elation that Kerrick was still alive, he spurred himself to move faster, striding down the hall in the direction of the voice. "Can you see my torchlight?"

"Sir! I'm here!" Kerrick's voice was stronger now, but shook with fear.

Alastair rounded a corner and plunged through a doorway into a large room, shining the light ahead of him. If the creature attacked now he'd be vulnerable, but Kerrick was so close—he had to find him. "Kerrick!"

The beam fell on a huddled form pressed into a corner. It raised its hands, flinching against the harsh light.

"Kerrick!" Alastair shouted, hurrying over as he identified the tall, dirt-smudged form. He almost ran directly to him, but stopped halfway there to scan him with magical sight. To his relief, the familiar blue aura, a little shaky but strong, flared around the figure.

"Oh, dear God, sir, I'm so happy to see you." Kerrick's voice came out on a rush of air. "What's happened?" His gaze fell on Alastair. "Sir? Are you all right? You're pale as a ghost—and you're *bleeding*."

"No time," Alastair panted. "We need to get to safety."

"Safety? Where is the danger?" He looked around. "The lights went out, and I came down here to check the fuses, but then I tripped over something like a fool and my torch broke. I've been blundering around trying to find the door for—" Worry creased his features. "What's happened, sir? Why are you injured? And—aren't those from the dining room?" he added, nodding toward the dagger and the tiny shield.

Alastair swallowed, letting himself rest for a moment. "It's a long story. There's something loose in the house, and it's dangerous. It's already killed Samuels—"

Kerrick gasped. "Dear God…"

"We've got to get out of here. And contact Mr. Desmond. Do you know where he is?"

Kerrick appeared not to have recovered from the shock of the news about Samuels. "How—?"

Alastair wanted to tell him the whole story, but they didn't have time. "Selby. He summoned it—thought his brother was alive. It nearly killed him too. It wants Mr. Desmond." He cast a quick glance around, but still spotted no sign of the jagged red aura. "Do you know where he is?"

"Yes, sir." Kerrick visibly attempted to get himself under control. "He's—he's in London, attending a function." He glanced at his watch. "He should be back at the London house by now."

"Can you contact him there? Is there a phone down here somewhere?"

"The phones are out, sir. I tried to ring the power company to check on the outage before I came down here. They're dead."

Great. Should have expected it, though. "Okay. We need to get to safety, and then figure out a way to let him know he'll be walking into an ambush when he comes home."

"Safety, sir? Where are the others?"

"Downstairs in the workroom. They're all safe."

Kerrick stared at him. "And you...came down here to find me?" As Alastair turned to scan for the creature again, he gasped. "Your *back,* sir!"

"It's all right. It hurts, but I'm all right. We have to go. And I've got to figure out a way to contact Mr. Desmond without using the phone."

"Can't we...just all leave, sir? Will this thing, whatever it is, follow us?"

"We're stuck in here. It's done something to the doors and windows. We can't get out—and neither can it. The wards are holding it in."

"No..." Kerrick breathed. "So we're trapped in here with it."

"Yeah..." he muttered. "Need to have a word with Selby about that later..." He offered the flashlight to Kerrick. "Can you hold this? Keep your back to the corner here and shine it around. Look for anything that looks like a moving shadow, and yell if you spot it, okay?"

"A...moving shadow?" Kerrick's voice shook. "Yes, sir. What will you be doing?"

He held up the tiny shield. "I need to try to figure out what this is for. You don't know, do you?"

Kerrick shook his head. "No, sir. Mr. Desmond hasn't had that one very long, and he doesn't discuss his magical objects with me."

"All right. Just watch, and yell if you see *anything* moving that isn't us." Alastair crouched in front of Kerrick, shifting back to magical sight and focusing his concentration to use the magic-analysis spell Desmond had taught him. He hadn't had much practice with it and he wasn't very good with it yet, but anything he might be able to glean about the item would be helpful.

With its design, he suspected it had to be defensive in nature. Did it generate a shield? Augment one? Provide some other sort of protection? But against what? It hardly seemed large enough to act as a physical barrier for a full-sized person, so perhaps the effect was magical. He knew he didn't have much time to waste on it, but if it was something he could use, he needed to know it.

"Sir—" Kerrick's voice broke through his thoughts.

He went stiff. "Did you see it?"

"No, sir. But—shouldn't we be going? You've been staring at that thing for five minutes."

Had he? It hadn't seemed that long. He needed to be careful about getting lost in the magic. "Just a few moments longer. Keep watching."

It was easier to slip into the focus now that he'd had a look at the item. He fed a little power into it and examined the carefully ordered, bright blue lines that shimmered into being around its edges. A complicated design—he thought he was right that it had something to do with defense. Perhaps augmenting defense. Would it supplement a magical shield, if he could figure out how to activate it?

"*Sir, look out!*" Kerrick grabbed him roughly and threw him aside, diving after him. He got a quick impression of something black flitting past and then the creature was solid again, its claws tearing into the corner where they'd both been standing only an instant before.

CHAPTER TWENTY-EIGHT

ALASTAIR FELL HARD and nearly lost both the shield and the dagger. He rolled up quickly and spun just as the creature made a second pass. It seemed bigger now—taller than Kerrick, its long limbs and shifting edges making it difficult to get a clear look at it. As it dived at him, claws out, a fetid stench like burning, rotten meat filled the air.

Alastair barely got his personal shield up in time to block it, but it drove him back into the wall. He hit hard, his back flaring with pain, and couldn't suppress a cry.

"Over here, whatever you are!" Kerrick yelled.

Alastair looked past him and his whole body went cold with shock. "Kerrick, *no!*"

Kerrick had picked up a length of pipe from somewhere, and now brandished the flashlight in one hand and the pipe in the other, flailing both in a mad attempt to divert the creature's attention from Alastair. "Over here!"

The thing apparently didn't like the light. It ducked and weaved, trying to stay out of the beam, then made a sudden lunge toward Kerrick.

"No!" Alastair yelled again, dropping his shield and dashing forward with the dagger in front of him.

He expected Kerrick to dive out of the way again, but he didn't. Instead, he shifted sideways, wound up with the pipe, and swung for the fences.

If the blow had connected, it probably would have taken the creature's head off. But at the last second, the thing seemed to flow around the pipe, momentarily turning back to shadow and then reappearing behind Kerrick, claws slashing.

"*Kerrick!*" Alastair screamed, and did the only thing he could think of: he grabbed the man in a telekinetic grip and yanked him forward.

The creature's wicked claws sliced through the space where Kerrick had just been, missing him by bare inches as he crashed into Alastair, knocking him over and landing hard on top of him.

Pain flared again as Kerrick's weight knocked the wind out of Alastair. The dagger went flying in one direction, and the flashlight went in the other, rolling across the room and landing against the wall, its beam shining uselessly in the wrong direction.

The creature loomed over Alastair and Kerrick as they both struggled to disentangle themselves and get up. It radiated satisfaction along with the spoiled-meat smell, its strange, disorienting movements carrying it closer to them.

Kerrick, who'd managed to roll over on his back, stared at the thing, transfixed and terrified.

Alastair's thoughts raced. He had only a second to act, and his weapon was gone. In desperation, he poured energy into the tiny shield and concentrated hard on activating it, then summoned his own shield.

What happened next startled him so much he nearly lost his concentration. The shield sprang up as it always did, but much larger and brighter: a dome appeared over himself and Kerrick, lighting up the room with its glow. The creature slammed into it, screamed in frustration, and surged backward. A second later, it went shadowy again and flowed out of the room.

Alastair rolled to the side and snatched the dagger back up, still holding the shield. To his dismay, the tiny object didn't seem to make it any easier to maintain the shield—it still drained his rapidly-depleting reserves to do it—but it certainly seemed to make the barrier larger and tougher. Panting, he took a final glance around to make sure the creature had really departed, then let the shield drop. He didn't get up.

Kerrick was breathing hard, pale and sweating. "Sir...dear God...what *was* that thing?"

"Don't know exactly." Alastair's voice came out as an exhausted whisper. He sat up to take the pressure off his bleeding back, swallowed hard, and looked down at the tiny shield. It felt warm in his hand—not uncomfortably so, but the same way a machine might feel after being used for a while. He wondered if it was possible to burn it out from overuse.

Kerrick crawled over and grabbed the flashlight. "We should go...before it comes after us again."

Alastair nodded, but his mind wasn't on the man's words. "We can't let it get Mr. Desmond," he said.

"Sir?"

"It's going to ambush him. That's what it wants, and he won't be looking for it. I'll bet he doesn't even think it's *possible* for anything to get inside his house. If he doesn't see it coming, it will kill him before he can fight back."

Kerrick walked over to stand protectively over him, his back pressed against the wall. "I don't know what we can do, sir," he said gently. "He won't be back until tomorrow. Without the phones—"

"I know...I know..." Alastair bowed his head, studying the dagger and shield in his shaking hands. "And if we go to the workroom now and try to come back out in the morning to warn him, I'm sure that thing will be waiting for us. It won't let us spoil its plans." He sighed, shoulders slumping. Suddenly, it all seemed so overwhelming—he wasn't an action star or one of those superheroes from the comic books. He was a scared, exhausted fifteen-year-old boy, and he had no idea what to do next.

"Sir..." Kerrick leaned down and gently gripped his shoulder. "Come on. It will be all right. We'll figure something out. You've already done so much..." His voice trembled. "You saved the others...that was more than anyone had any right to expect of you. And then you risked your life to come down here to find me...you shouldn't have done that, sir. You shouldn't have..."

"I don't know what to do, Kerrick." Alastair bowed his head further, leaning it against his arms. His back hurt like fire, he was dizzy, and his head pounded harder than ever. He wasn't even sure he could make it back up to the workroom. If the creature attacked them again—which he was sure it would do—not only would he die, but so would Kerrick. And if the thing got Desmond tomorrow, eventually the others would have to venture out of the workroom—would it lie in wait for them as well, picking them off one by one? By the time anyone from the outside figured out something was wrong and found a way into the house, all they'd find was a massacre. "If only we had another way to contact Mr. Desmond...but it wouldn't matter. By the time he got back here from London, it would be too late even if we *could* reach him."

Kerrick was silent for a moment; when he spoke, his voice was contemplative. "No, sir...it wouldn't."

Alastair raised his head. "What do you mean?"

"You do know about the teleportation portals, don't you?"

"Yes...of course." Mages used a series of portals scattered around the world to travel quickly from one far-flung location to another. There was a private one—a rare thing, his father had told him—on the grounds of his own home back in Surrey. Without magical ability he couldn't use it on his own, and his father had never taken him through it, but he knew where it was. "But—"

"Mr. Desmond has one at the London house...and there's one here as well."

Alastair could hardly believe he'd heard correctly. The dizziness must be playing tricks on him. "A portal? Here? He never mentioned it..."

"No, sir. It's not common knowledge. But I assure you, they do exist. He used the one here to go to London earlier tonight."

A faint hope sprung up, but then immediately died. He slumped again. "That's brilliant—but it won't help if we can't contact him. I don't know how to use the portal, even if you showed me where it was. And I'm not sure I've got the strength left to get you to the workroom and come back down here and try."

Kerrick shook his head, sighing in frustration. "No, sir. You couldn't do it anyway. He's got special wards around it, as he does around all the other more private areas of the house. I doubt you'd be able to pass them."

"Then it's no use...Kerrick, I'm sorry...I tried, but I don't—"

He stopped, as a wild thought occurred to him. He raised his head again. "Kerrick..."

"Sir?"

"Those wards—the ones he has around the private areas of the house. What happens if someone tries to cross them?"

"Er—I believe it immobilizes them, sir, and..." A slow smile grew on his angular face. "...and it alerts Mr. Desmond to the intrusion." The smile faded. "But how will that help us? Surely the creature isn't foolish enough to—"

"No..." Alastair said. With renewed energy, he pulled himself to his feet. "No...but *we* are."

"What do you mean, sir? Are you suggesting one of us try to cross the wards?"

"You're sure it immobilizes only? It doesn't kill, or injure?"

"Yes, sir. I'm certain. Mr. Desmond feels quite confident he can deal with any threat to his house without resorting to murder or permanent injury. But I don't see—"

Alastair's mind was spinning out an idea faster than he could pin it down. It was probably a stupid idea. Definitely a desperate one. It would certainly require risk. But if it worked—

"Kerrick..." he said slowly, eyeing the man with a manic smile. "Let's set a trap, shall we?"

By the time he explained his insane idea, Kerrick was smiling too. It was more than a bit worried, but it was definitely a smile.

| CHAPTER TWENTY-NINE

FIVE MINUTES LATER, they were on the move, but slowly.

"Come on, sir...you can do it. Please...you've got to keep going."

Alastair staggered along next to Kerrick. His arm was slung around the taller man's shoulders, and Kerrick was half-supporting, half-carrying him along. He still clutched the tiny shield in one hand, but the dagger was now stuck through his belt. Kerrick held the flashlight, shining it ahead of him. Alastair could feel him trembling, almost as much as he himself was.

"I've...got to rest...please, Kerrick, let's stop a moment." His voice came out as barely a whisper.

They'd made it back to the stairway leading up to the ground floor. The door at the top was still open, just as Alastair had left it when he'd come down. He slumped in Kerrick's grip, sagging against the wall as if he might faint.

"Sir—" Kerrick cast a frightened glance up toward the stairway. "If you can just make it a bit further—"

"I can't...please...just—" He shifted to magical sight, glancing around without raising his head. He'd have to time this with absolute precision, but if he'd sold it well enough, it shouldn't be long now—

A shadowy form flowed down along the wall, resolving itself into a jagged red aura with frightening speed and leaping at Alastair's slumped figure.

Now!

Alastair, moving with far more speed than he'd seemed capable of a moment earlier, flung himself forward into the opposite wall, gripping the shield in his sweat-slicked hand. Everything would come down to this moment. If he messed this up, he wouldn't have another chance.

He blocked out everything: the pain, the exhaustion, the fear of failure, the worry about what would happen to Desmond, Kerrick, and the others if he failed. None of those mattered now. The only thing that mattered was what he'd do in the next two seconds.

The familiar barrier sprang into being, augmented by the power of the tiny shield item Alastair still carried. But this time, it didn't flare around Alastair himself, or around Kerrick.

Instead, it rose up around the creature, pinning it against the wall—the outer wall of the house. The wall protected by Desmond's powerful ward, that it couldn't pass through.

"Go!" Alastair croaked, gripping the stair rail and struggling to keep the barrier going. Assuming the creature couldn't break through the shield, he was sure he wouldn't have more than a minute or two before his mental strength failed and it came down.

Kerrick was already running. "Hold on, sir!" he yelled, and then he was gone around the corner, dashing off in the direction of Desmond's portal room as they'd discussed.

Alastair, alone now with the shadow-creature, gripped the rail tighter and focused on nothing but his concentration. Sweat ran down his face and into his eyes, but he didn't break his trembling grip to wipe it away.

Hurry up, Kerrick, he begged, along with offering a desperate prayer to whatever gods looked after underage mages that Desmond *was* actually at the London house. If he'd decided to stay late at his function, or went out to a late dinner and drinks with friends, everything would be lost.

Each second ticked by like torture. Inside the barrier, the long-limbed creature raged and screamed, tearing at the inside of its prison with its claws, every swipe sending painful spikes of feedback into Alastair's head. It wasn't as bad as if he were powering the shield without the help of the object, but it still felt as if someone were poking knives in and out of his brain. In his hand, the little shield-thing grew warmer and began a faint thrumming. He gripped it more tightly, narrowed his eyes, and glared hard at the barrier as if doing that might somehow make it stronger.

Where was Kerrick? He'd told Alastair where the portal room was—it should have taken him less than a minute to get there at a run. All he had to do was try to cross the wards and get himself immobilized so Desmond would be alerted.

Maybe he already had. Maybe Desmond *had* gotten the message, but had to get to the portal in London—

Or get back to the London house, because he wasn't there. Alastair refused to let himself think about that. If that were true, he was lost and there was nothing he could do about it.

Focus...

The little shield-thing was getting hotter, the thrumming becoming full-fledged shaking. It rattled like a door handle somebody was trying to force open, and his hand grew uncomfortably warm. Would it burn him if he kept holding it?

It doesn't matter. Keep holding it. No matter what.

His whole body was shaking now, and he was sure the shield was beginning to waver. That wasn't just his own faulty perceptions, was it? No, it was definitely losing coherence, like a TV picture shifting out of phase. Desperately, Alastair tried pumping more power into it, but he didn't have any more to give. He winced and gritted his teeth, sobbing with pain as the little metal shield grew hotter still, burning his palm.

Desmond wasn't coming to save him. His plan had failed. In a few more seconds, he'd be dead. When Desmond arrived, he'd find the bloody body of his former apprentice at the foot of the stairs, and maybe Kerrick's as well.

I tried...

The creature, sensing its imminent release, tore at the shield with renewed fervor, its claws flashing and its strange shadowy edges slipping in and out of reality. The shield grew brighter as the creature's efforts began to overload it.

With a tiny *pop* that might only have been in Alastair's head, the little shield object broke apart in his hand, going white-hot for a second and then crashing to the ground in three pieces, lifeless and cracked.

Alastair screamed as the object's augmentation abruptly faded, leaving nothing but his own will holding the shield up. "*NO! You* won't—"

Perhaps two more seconds passed before his flagging willpower gave out and with it the last of the shield.

The creature, its fang-filled mouth stretched in a triumphant, impossibly wide grin, lunged at him as he slumped to the stairs, barely conscious, still gripping the railing like a lifeboat in a storm. His other hand scrabbled at his belt, trying to reach the dagger, but fell back as he didn't even have the strength to lift it.

The creature loomed over him. He stiffened, waiting for the fangs to close around his throat—

Behind him, a bright light, so bright Alastair had to flinch away from it, appeared.

A voice—booming, stentorian, brimming with confident authority—thundered a series of commands in some arcane language.

Alastair sagged against the stairs and blinked as the creature shrieked and fell back, whirling to face the new threat. As it did, he got a look at it himself.

William Desmond, clad in his formal suit, his face full of wrath like some kind of vengeful god, had both hands raised and pointed at the creature. Arcane light flowered around them, crackling with enough energy to put Alastair's hair on end. The small, dim and dusty room was suddenly alight with magical power.

Desmond roared another command, and released the energy. With a loud *crack* it surged at the creature.

The thing shrieked again and tried to shrink back toward Alastair, but barely moved before the energy tore into it, flowing around and through it, burning away its edges and its claws and its mouthful of fangs. It writhed, twisting, trying with desperate strength to pull free, but the energy tightened and gathered until at last it took the creature to pieces. Its death-scream pierced the air and burrowed into Alastair's brain until he thought it would never stop.

And then, abruptly, it was over.

The creature was gone as if it had never been, leaving behind an electric stench of burned meat and ozone. The room was dark again, except for a glowing ball of light hovering around Desmond's hand.

Desmond stood there a moment, taking in the scene, and his gaze fell on Alastair. He hurried over, gripping his shoulder. "Mr. Stone!"

Alastair had no more strength. He fell back against the stairs, unable to even pull himself to a seated position. As he felt his consciousness fade, he looked up at his former master. "Sorry..." he whispered, hand fluttering toward the ruined pieces on the floor. "I broke your...shield thing..."

And then the lights went out.

| CHAPTER THIRTY

"SIR?"

The voice was gentle, poking at the edges of Alastair's awareness like an insistent kitten. Something warm closed around his shoulder.

He didn't want to wake up. Wherever he was, it was soft and comfortable and he didn't hurt anymore. He drifted along on a pleasant wave of apathy, and knew if he let himself wake up, he'd have to care again.

"Sir?" The voice was more persistent this time, still gentle but a bit louder. The warm pressure on his shoulder increased, just a bit.

"Mm?" he mumbled without opening his eyes. He brought a hand up and rubbed at his forehead, then let it flop back down again.

"Sir, please. I hate to disturb you, but you need to eat something."

Alastair cracked open his eyes just enough to identify the blurry form of Kerrick leaning over the bed.

Kerrick was alive?

His eyes flew open the rest of the way and he tried to jerk up. "Kerrick!"

"Shh…shh, sir." Kerrick pushed him back down into the soft pillows. "You're not ready for that yet. You've been through quite a lot."

The memories surged back. The creature, Kerrick, the shield—

He pushed himself up again, fighting a wave of light-headedness. "Where is everyone? The creature—"

"They're fine. Everything's fine now, sir. It's gone."

He remembered Desmond standing there with his hands raised, magical energy crackling around them, his voice booming words of power. "It worked…" he breathed. "Our plan…"

"*Your* plan, sir. And yes. It did. That…*thing* is gone." Kerrick reached around to a cart behind him and placed a tray across Alastair's lap. "You need to eat, sir. Get your strength back."

It occurred to Alastair once again that nothing hurt. That was weird—things *should* hurt. The slashes on his back, his burned hand where he'd held the shield, his head—"How long has it been, since—?"

"You've been sleeping for nearly a full day, sir," Kerrick said. "The doctor—the healer—has been by and seen to you. Your back and your hand are good as new, but she said you might feel some lingering weakness for a few days. That's normal."

Alastair looked around the room. It wasn't the cell-like chamber he'd been occupying for the past three weeks, but a larger and more sumptuously appointed space. The heavy drapes were open to reveal the sun filtering in through a layer of overcast. "Where is this? Am I still at Caventhorne?"

"Yes, sir." Kerrick pulled up a chair and sat down next to the bed. "Please—you must eat. Esteban and Gretchen have prepared some of your favorites."

Alastair wanted answers, not food. But as soon as the tantalizing aromas began to register on him, he realized he was starving. He pulled the cover off a bowl of soup and took a tentative taste, then picked up speed. In between spoonfuls, he cast a worried glance at Kerrick. "You said everyone was fine. They got out? Selby—?"

"Selby is being take care of, sir. He was severely injured and the healer won't be able to set him completely right, but I assure you, he's alive and will be well in due time."

Alastair nodded, glad to hear it in spite of the fact that Selby had been responsible for this whole mess. "Everyone got out, then?"

"Yes, sir. Mr. Desmond found me in the portal room, and I explained the situation to him as best I could. He'll want to talk to you, of course."

"Of course..." Alastair bowed his head. He wasn't sure he wanted to talk to Desmond. As soon as he was strong enough, all he wanted was to get out of here. "What about my father? Has he been told?"

"I don't know, sir. You'll have to discuss that with Mr. Desmond." He stood. "You finish up there. We can talk again later. You'll need a lot of rest to regain your strength." His expression changed, and for a moment he seemed to be debating whether to say something. Finally, he put his hand back on Alastair's shoulder. "Whatever happens, I want to thank you. I'm sure the rest of the staff will want to as well. If you hadn't done what you did—"

"Not everyone," Alastair mumbled, staring down into his soup as a sudden bitter memory struck. "Samuels is dead."

"Yes, sir. He is. It's a terrible thing, of course. But it could have been so much worse." He gripped Alastair's shoulder more tightly, then pulled back. "Rest, sir. I'll come back for the dishes later."

He hurried out of the room, leaving Alastair once again alone.

He leaned back against the pillows with a sigh, picking at the rest of the food on his tray. The hearty soup had taken the ravenous edge off his appetite, and despite his best efforts, the fog of fatigue was creeping in again. He tried to fight it for a while, but it did no good. He nodded off still clutching a half-eaten piece of toast.

The next time he awoke, it was dark. He lay in the same bed, though the tray (and the toast) were gone. A lamp on the nightstand provided a pool of cozy light.

"I was wondering when you might rejoin us, Mr. Stone."

Alastair started at the familiar but unexpected voice. William Desmond himself sat next to the bed, an old book he'd obviously been reading in his hand. For the first time, he was out of his formal, old-fashioned suit; instead, he wore a simple white shirt and dark trousers.

Alastair frowned. What was Desmond doing here? How *long* had he been here, watching him as he slept? "Sir—?"

"How do you feel?"

He considered that. Most of the light-headedness was gone along with the pain, though he still felt hungry. "All right, I guess."

Desmond nodded. He closed the book and put it down on the nightstand. "Kerrick tells me you've been quite busy around here while I was gone."

Alastair stiffened. Was Desmond going to punish him? "Sir, I—" he began, and he was sure his indignation came through in his aura.

Desmond raised a hand to quell him. "Mr. Stone, please. I have not come to chastise you—though what you did was dangerous, rash, and I would not have faulted you in the slightest if you had chosen not to do it."

"Sir—"

Again he raised his hand. "Dangerous, rash—and one of the most courageous and resourceful things I have ever seen any mage—including those far older and more skilled than you are—do. You saved not only yourself, but most of my staff—and possibly me, if I'd been caught unawares upon returning home—from severe injury or even death. How can I do anything but thank you for that, Mr. Stone?"

Alastair didn't look at him. He spoke into his lap, unable to keep the bitterness out of his tone. "I broke your rules. I can't even count how many times I used unauthorized magic. I even broke your shield thing. And now, I'll still be packed off home as soon as I'm well enough to go, won't I?"

"You did break my rules." He took a deep breath. "As for being packed off home...I have been doing some thinking, Mr. Stone, over the last day while you've been asleep."

Alastair dragged his gaze up. "Have you?"

Desmond nodded. "As you might have discerned, perhaps I was a bit...overzealous in my insistence that my apprentices refrain from magical improvisation. Gareth Selby's death was not easy on me, and I vowed from that day forward that I would not lose another apprentice due to my own negligence—if I should ever be persuaded to take one again, that is."

"Kerrick told me you took Gareth's death hard," Alastair said. He didn't think at this point Kerrick would mind him sharing that confidence. "But I'm not Gareth."

"No, Mr. Stone," Desmond said. "You are not Gareth. Nor, does it appear, are you Roderick."

"What will happen to him?" Alastair adjusted his position so he could sit up and get a better view of Desmond. "After he's well, I mean."

"He has been relieved of his position, of course."

That didn't surprise him. "He didn't mean it, you know. He thought his brother was alive. You never told him what happened—just that he died. That...thing showed him Gareth, so he thought you must have been wrong."

Desmond inclined his head for several moments. "That was another error on my part. Yes, I do make them, Mr. Stone—and I do admit to them when I do."

Alastair blinked. Was it possible that the lofty William Desmond was looking *uncomfortable*?

"Mr. Stone...what I mean to say is that I have made a mistake with you. I agreed to give you a trial despite your youth—because I thought I could more easily control you and keep you safe—but I also expected less of you *because* of your age. You performed far more impressively than I expected you to, and even your minor transgressions were just that—minor. The sorts of things I had no right not to expect from someone so young."

Alastair could hardly dare to hope. He let his breath out slowly. "Sir...are you saying that...you're not kicking me out after all?"

"I am saying," Desmond said, "that I made a mistake. And if you still wish to study with me, then...I am formally offering you a full apprenticeship. And a revised set of expectations regarding your behavior and performance." His expression grew stern. "But be assured, Mr. Stone, that I shall not be lenient on you if you accept. You will work every bit as hard as I expected you to before—possibly harder, because I see your potential and will push it as far as it will go. But I will also look more understandingly on your...innovations. With the exception of summoning, of course." He stood. "You needn't give me your answer now. Rest, and think about it. I will be available when you wish to respond." He turned and walked toward the door.

Alastair sat up a little more. "I don't need to think about it, sir."

Desmond stopped and turned back, his face its usual unreadable mask, and waited.

"I want to come back, sir. I want you to teach me. And I'll work hard—you know that." He smiled, just a bit. "But you *should* probably expect a few...innovations."

Desmond didn't smile. Alastair really *was* beginning to think he wasn't capable of it. But his eyebrow went up, and the corners of his eyes crinkled, just a bit. "I shall look forward to seeing what you come up with, Mr. Stone."

Alastair waited until he made it almost to the door. "Mr. Desmond?"

"Yes, Mr. Stone?"

"What made you change your mind? I...didn't think you did that very often."

"I do not. But aside from your recent actions—which would have been enough in and of themselves to convince me, I might add—Kerrick stopped by my study to have a few...rather pointed words with me yesterday."

That hadn't been at all what Alastair expected to hear. "Kerrick, sir?"

"Yes, Mr. Stone. He felt that I had severely underestimated you, and urged me in most adamant terms to reconsider my decision." He paused and reached for the doorknob. "He also threatened to leave my employ if I failed to do so."

Alastair stared at him, stunned. "He threatened to quit if you didn't change your mind?"

"It appears you have a valuable friend here, Mr. Stone." Desmond opened the door. "See to it that you do not let us—either of us—down. I expect to see you downstairs first thing tomorrow morning, ready to work. Do you understand?"

Alastair grinned. "Yes, sir. I understand."

He settled back on his pillows and let his breath out, still tired but satisfied.

Perhaps, if Desmond gave him a break sometime in the next month, he might even see about borrowing Max's Vespa to go into town for some fish and chips.

| CHAPTER THIRTY-ONE

THE CROWDS IN THE MEXICAN RESTAURANT were almost all gone now, and a couple of busboys had come out with brooms and rags to begin cleaning the place in preparation for closing. The chip basket was long since empty.

"We should go," Stone said. "They're trying not so subtly to kick us out." He stood and tossed a twenty on the table to supplement the tip he'd already left on the check. "Sorry," he called to the busboys. "We're leaving."

Verity followed him out. She'd sat through the entire tale, munching tortilla chips and downing glasses of water, without a word. She didn't speak until they'd gotten outside and were walking down the mostly-deserted street toward where they'd parked.

"Wow," she said at last. "That's...some story." She grinned. "Somehow I can't picture teenage you getting handsy with a girl in the back row of a crappy movie theater."

"*That's* what you took away from all that?" Stone asked in mock indignation.

She shrugged. "It's a lot to take in. I see what you mean, though—you had to help that girl Rosemary, even if it meant using magic you weren't supposed to. That's how I feel, too—what was I supposed to do, let him kill Jason?"

"Of course not," Stone said gently. "Magic is a tool. Mr. Desmond discouraged innovation, because he feared what might happen if an untrained mage took on more than he could handle. I perhaps encouraged a bit too much of it in my last apprentice by taking more of a hands-off approach. With you, I tried to find a midpoint. I'm not sure how well I succeeded, but I think you're doing all right."

Her expression sobered. "Doc...you lost an apprentice too, didn't you? I remember you said something about it just before you agreed to take me on, but you never talked about it again."

Stone didn't answer right away. "It's...not something I like to discuss," he said eventually. "Not right now, at least."

"That's fine," she said. "Sorry."

"Don't be. I'll tell you about Ethan sometime. Just not now."

They walked in silence for another block. "Is Mr. Desmond still alive?" Verity asked abruptly.

"Of course."

"He must be pretty old by now."

"I've no idea. I never asked him how old he is—but as you know, mages tend to live a long time. He could be over a hundred for all I know."

"Do you ever see him? Or did you lose touch after you finished your apprenticeship?"

Stone chuckled. "Oh, no. I still see him periodically. Not as much as I used to when I lived in England, but we worked together on several projects in the years following my apprenticeship. Hell, I almost married his daughter."

Verity stopped and stared at him. "You what?"

"That's a story for another time, I think. Look, here's the car."

She took his arm. "Doc, you can't just drop that one on me without any details."

"I promise—I'll tell you. You should meet Desmond anyway, so I can prove to him that I made something useful of myself." He hit the button on the BMW's fob to unlock the doors. "Come on—you can stay in my guest room tonight. I warn you, though—Raider snores."

She didn't get in the car. Instead, she moved closer to him. When he didn't back up, she pulled him into a hard hug. "Thanks, Doc," she mumbled into his coat.

"For what?"

"For—everything. But right now, for that story. I'm still gonna have nightmares about what happened, but at least I think I have some perspective now. And I know I'm not the only one who had to make a decision like that."

He held her close. "I can almost guarantee it won't be the last time you'll have to make that kind of decision, Verity. But you're a damned good mage already, and your head's on straight—a hell of a lot straighter than mine is, that's certain. You'll be fine."

She pulled back, stood on tiptoe, and planted a gentle kiss on his cheek. "You're okay, Doc. And I'm gonna hold you to that meeting with Mr. Desmond. Anybody who intimidates you, I want to meet. And anybody who almost married you, too. Oh, hey," she added. "Whatever happened to Madeleine? Did you two ever end up—"

He shook his head. "We got together one more time after Mr. Desmond took me on—for dinner at the chip shop. Then she dumped me for a football forward from her school a week later."

She grinned as she got in the car. "Someday, Doc, you're gonna find the right woman. You'll see."

"Suppose you worry more about your magical training, and less about my love life, apprentice. How would that be?"

"I'll think about it." She slammed the door shut before he could answer, but he didn't miss the merry, mischievous sparkle in her eyes before she did.

Yes, she was going to turn out fine.

And maybe, if he was lucky, he would as well.

Alastair Stone will return in

NECESSARY SACRIFICES

Book 12 of the Alastair Stone Chronicles

Coming in Fall 2017

ACKNOWLEDGEMENTS

Thanks to Jaqulyn Viehmann, from the *Alastair Stone Chronicles Fans* Facebook group, for suggesting the name of Caventhorne Hall.

If you enjoyed this book, please consider leaving a review at Amazon, Goodreads, or your favorite book retailer. Reviews mean a lot to independent authors, and help us stay visible so we can keep bringing you more stories. Thanks!

If you'd like to get more information about upcoming Stone Chronicles books, contests, and other goodies, you can join the Inner Circle mailing list at **rlkingwriting.com**. You'll get a free e-novella, *Shadows and Stone,* that's not available anywhere else.

ABOUT THE AUTHOR

R. L. King is an award-winning author and game freelancer for Catalyst Game Labs, publisher of the popular roleplaying game *Shadowrun*. She has contributed fiction and game material to numerous sourcebooks, as well as one full-length adventure, "On the Run," included as part of the 2012 Origins-Award-winning "Runners' Toolkit." Her first novel in the *Shadowrun* universe, *Borrowed Time*, was published in Spring 2015, and her second will be published in early 2018.

When not doing her best to make life difficult for her characters, King enjoys hanging out with her very understanding spouse and her small herd of cats, watching way too much *Doctor Who*, and attending conventions when she can. She is an Active member of the Horror Writers' Association and the Science Fiction and Fantasy Writers of America, and a member of the International Association of Media Tie-In Writers. You can find her at *rlkingwriting.com* and *magespacepress.com*, on Facebook at www.facebook.com/AlastairStoneChronicles, and on Twitter at *@Dragonwriter11*.

Made in the USA
San Bernardino, CA
09 October 2017